To the ██████ Public Library

██████

CC.

4/26/15

NUCLEAR FARM

CHARLES C. ANDERSON

outskirtspress
DENVER, COLORADO

SuSP/
#2

Nuclear Farm
All Rights Reserved.
Copyright © 2014 Charles C. Anderson
v2.0

Outskirts Press, Inc.
http://www.outskirtspress.com

Paperback ISBN: 978-1-4787-2207-6
Hardback ISBN: 978-1-4787-2211-3

Outskirts Press and the "OP" logo are trademarks belonging to Outskirts Press, Inc.

PRINTED IN THE UNITED STATES OF AMERICA

1.

Nadia Popov sat in the living room in her husband's easy chair in Farmville, Virginia. The LED kitchen clock glowed 3:15 AM. A Browning twelve gauge semi-automatic shotgun lay across her lap. With the porch light on, and every light inside the apartment turned off, her husband would be a silhouette target. She usually didn't drink alcohol, but tonight she was sipping her second vodka, straight up. She knew where Demetrius was.

It was a routine for him, almost every weekday for the past month. He would finish work at C and L Welding at 5:30 in the afternoon. Instead of coming home to her, he would drive past their walk-up apartment on the corner of Oak and West Third Streets and spend the entire evening getting sloshed at R.J.'s, a sleazy night club just across the Appomattox River in Cumberland County, Virginia.

Eventually he would hook up with Cindy Blaney, that slut from behind the bar who sneaked him extra beer. When the bar closed at 2:00 AM, they would go to her apartment, located upstairs from R.J.'s. After another hour, she would send him home.

Nadia didn't think she would need but one shell of 00 buck, but she loaded four more in the shotgun, just in case. He would stagger up the steps, reeking of beer, machine oil, cheap perfume, and vaginal discharge. But Demetrius would not lie down next to her again.

Nadia hated her job in the God-forsaken town of Farmville. Aleksi Ivanov, her grandfather, had assigned her and Demetrius to document the movements of Dr. Andy Carlson from the couple's apartment directly across from the emergency department where the doctor worked. Six months of hell. Six months of watching her husband screw American bitches while the price of gold steadily climbed to

5,540 dollars per ounce. Aleksi claimed that Dr. Carlson had hundreds of millions of dollars in Confederate gold hidden in the limestone caves under his farm. Her Uncle Boris had supposedly seen it. Since America's financial collapse, Aleksi could think of nothing but the gold. He called once a week to ask where Dr. Carlson was and what he was doing.

She planned a terrible tragedy, a case of mistaken identity. Demetrius would be a prowler breaking in. He would be fumbling with his keys. He would be blown backwards off the porch into the yard.

Aleksi should have given her a larger allowance for this job. She was tired of taking money out of her Wal-Mart paycheck for the monthly premium on her husband's $250,000 life insurance policy, while he spent his free time and money on crystal meth and other women.

She counted his footsteps as he ascended the steps to the small porch. The muzzle of the shotgun was resting against the bottom glass pane in the door when he attempted to insert his key.

Demetrius peered through the glass. His eyes bulged. She smiled back, pointing the muzzle at his groin. Weighing the satisfaction of seeing Demetrius without any genitalia against the dissatisfaction of seeing him survive, she adjusted the barrel to his abdomen and pulled the trigger.

Demetrius dropped to the porch and writhed in the fetal position. Nadia opened the deadbolt, stepped outside, and broke the glass next to the deadbolt with the stock of the shotgun. While he moaned at her feet, she reached up with her gloved hand and unscrewed the light bulb on the porch, replacing it with a burned-out bulb from the pocket of her robe. She kicked Demetrius' keys off the porch into the grass. She returned to his easy chair and considered what she might have forgotten. Satisfied, she dialed 911.

Most of the time a close range 00 buck wound to the belly kills quickly. But tonight Nadia would experience a bewilderment shared by every specialist in trauma medicine: Self-destructive people, drug and alcohol abusers, street thugs, and idiots are more likely to survive their wounds than ordinary folk injured just as severely through no fault of their own.

In this case, Nadia's aim was still too low, resulting in several of the 00 buck pellets striking Demetrius' brass Harley Davidson belt buckle, which resembled a tarantula. Demetrius had lost twenty pounds due to his meth habit. He had doubled his belt back through his pants loops to take up the slack. Almost half the lead pellets had to penetrate two layers of leather instead of one.

Also in Demetrius' favor, his Oak Street apartment was located directly across the street from the Emergency Department at Farmville Community Hospital. One of the finest trauma specialists in Virginia was on duty.

Ryan Butler and his EMS partner had just finished cleaning out their Prince Edward County Rescue Squad ambulance and were headed toward the exit of the hospital parking lot when their radio directed them to an accidental shooting on the corner of Oak Street and Main Street.

"That's right over there," Ryan said.

"I think there's somebody waving on that porch," Tim said. "But there's no light."

Ryan stomped on the accelerator and whipped the wheel to his right. He jumped the curb and sidewalk twice on Oak Street and stopped in the grassy front yard of the apartment building.

"It was an accident," a lady screamed from the second floor porch. "I thought he was breaking in. He's my husband. Is he going to be all right?"

Ryan touched every third step on his way to the porch. The wooden deck was already slippery. He pulled his flashlight off his belt and shined it on the victim. Demetrius was lying on his right side with his knees drawn up, his face obscured by stringy black hair. Ryan squatted, pointed the flashlight at the man's abdomen, and pulled down on his bony knees to get a better look.

"Som bitch," the victim grunted.

The emaciated man appeared to be about thirty years old. He held both hands over the bloody lower third of a greasy blue shirt, tucked into baggy jeans. "Demetrius" was stenciled above the cigarettes in his pocket. Blood seeped around his fingers from the holes in the shirt. Ryan followed the blood with the beam of light, past his own boots, pooling on the deck before dripping to the first step. The man was calling for Nadia.

"Tim, we're going to load and go," Ryan called down to his partner. "Put the stretcher at the bottom of the stairs."

The Farmville Police pulled up on Oak Street. Two officers left the doors of their blue light special open and ran toward the steps.

Estimating that Demetrius could not weigh much more than 115 pounds, Ryan snapped his flashlight back on his belt, picked the patient up in his arms, and carried him down the steps to the stretcher. Ryan and Tim slid the stretcher into the back of the ambulance. The wheels of the stretcher locked in place. Tim jumped in beside the stretcher.

"What happened?" asked the policeman, who was wheezing from his fifteen-yard sprint from the cruiser.

Ryan recognized the voice. "Jimmy, this guy has a belly full of buckshot. Talk to the lady upstairs." He closed the back doors of the ambulance. "She said she thought he was breaking in. It's her husband."

Tim sat down in the captain's chair in the back of the ambulance, at Demetrius' head. He applied an oxygen mask to the patient's face and turned the regulator to six liters per minute. Ryan jumped the curbs on Oak Street again. The tires screeched in front of the ambulance entrance.

Ryan didn't have time to call the emergency department, but he knew that Dr. Carlson could hone in on the voice of the night shift 911 dispatcher over the din of a full ED. Even if Dr. Carlson was caught flat-footed, he wouldn't act flat-footed.

When Demetrius rolled through the door, Andy already had several trauma packs open in Trauma One, the first room on the left from the ambulance entrance. In his short-sleeve surgical scrubs, he looked more like a professional linebacker with a surgical mask and gloves than a forty year old doctor.

Andy was a favorite of the ED staff and the only member of his six-man physician group who volunteered to work all night shifts. Most ED physicians hate twelve-hour night shifts. The level of responsibility is greater. The medical patients are sicker. The trauma patients are more challenging and more numerous than on the day shift. The number of staff throughout the hospital after midnight is half that of the daytime and evening shifts. Andy usually worked four or five twelve-hour night shifts, and then took four days off. He had a two-week vacation coming up.

Andy joked with his two night shift nurses to keep them loose. When events turned dicey, he was the U-boat captain who could make orders for avoiding a depth charge sound like conversation. He was as feared and respected by the staff as a captain must be on a warship. Compared to his previous career as a Navy SEAL, the action in the ED in Farmville was several steps down in intensity, something Andy regretted.

He had only worked a few night shifts with Sasha, a new nurse from Texas. Since he hadn't seen her performance under any real pressure, he was undecided about her level of talent. Lots of efficient day shift nurses collapsed when they were required to function independently on a frantic night shift. Sasha was attractive, blonde, maybe even seductive. He guessed five feet ten. Some men would be attracted by her figure.

Sasha spiked two plastic bags of Normal Saline and hung them over the stretcher in Trauma One. She ran the electrolyte solution in each bag to the tips of five foot lengths of intravenous tubing.

"Gunshot wound to the abdomen," Ryan said to Andy. "Buckshot."

Andy picked up the patient from the EMS stretcher and placed him onto the ED trauma stretcher. Two nurses pounced on Demetrius, cutting his shirt off and removing his shoes and pants. Sasha wrapped an automatic blood pressure cuff around his left upper arm.

"Alina, go for two large bore IVs in the arms," Andy said.

Alina was Andy's most dependable night nurse. He admired her determination to succeed. Her parents were Cuban immigrants. She worked for six years in an International House of Pancakes to save money for nursing school. If a drunk spit in her face, she would smile and ask, "Could I get a paper cup to help you with your oral secretions?" Alina had recently married a Farmville detective and sported the radiance of a new bride.

Ryan attached the oxygen mask to the flow meter on the wall at the head of the ED stretcher in Trauma One. He stepped on a pack of Marlboros and a clear baggy of white powder, which had fallen out of the remains of the patient's shirt in the floor. These personal items were placed in a wire rack underneath the stretcher.

Andy inspected the lower abdominal wounds. Sasha attached the EKG leads, pulse oximeter finger probe, and automatic blood pressure cuff to the monitors over the patient's left shoulder and turned them on.

"The belt and buckle caught half the load," Andy said, gently palpating the abdomen. The patient winced each time Andy touched his belly. "I see six entrance wounds above belt level."

Sasha felt the radial pulse and looked up at the monitors. The blood pressure was 80 over 60, heart rate of 122. Pulse oximeter 98%.

"She missed big red and big blue," Sasha said. "She missed the spinal cord and the chest."

Andy glanced at her. Most small town ED nurses didn't see enough gunshot wounds to make an accurate physical assessment so rapidly. Sasha was correct that Demetrius would likely be dead already if either the aorta or vena cava, the largest artery and the largest vein in the body, had been hit. The patient's blood pressure and pulses would be gone within a couple of minutes after such an injury. Sasha had noted that the patient was moving his legs, a clear sign that his spinal cord was intact. The most interesting word that Sasha used was "she." How did she know that a woman had shot the patient?

Alina inserted an eighteen gauge IV into a vein in Demetrius' left forearm, but was unable to tape it in or attach an infusion line due to the patient's kicking and flailing his arms. Andy sat down on the patient's chest and pinned Demetrius' left forearm to the stretcher with both his hands. Alina taped in the IV and opened up the infusion of Normal Saline.

"He's going to fight everything we do," Sasha said. "Can we put him down?"

It was another good observation, and a good recommendation.

"Etomidate sixteen milligrams IV to anesthetize him, followed by eighty milligrams of succinylcholine to paralyze him," Andy said. "I'll get my laryngoscope and endotracheal tube ready. Hold the drugs until I give the signal."

Sasha went to the PIXUS machine to get the drugs. Alina protected the IV.

Andy assembled the laryngoscope, an eight millimeter endotracheal tube, and a stylet to make the tube rigid. He bent the end of the tube to the shape of a hockey stick to make it easier to insert. He attached a ten milliliter syringe to the slender tube that ran along the side of the endotracheal tube to the air cuff just above its tip. By inflating this balloon inside the patient's airway just below the vocal cords, air could be forced into both the patient's lungs with a self-inflating bag of oxygen. The light on the laryngoscope was bright. He was ready.

Sasha returned with the Etomidate and succinylcholine.

"As soon as these drugs are in, draw trauma labs," Andy said. "Type and cross-match this patient for six units of blood. Send me two units of type-specific blood as soon as they're available. I need a portable chest X-ray, a flat plate abdomen, and a cross-table lateral of the abdomen. Ready, Sasha?"

"Yes, sir."

"Give the Etomidate first, then the succinylcholine," Andy said, looking up at the clock overhead.

Sasha delivered both drugs as fast as she could push them and then followed the drugs with a syringe of saline to flush them into Demetrius' bloodstream. It was the work of an experienced trauma nurse. The patient was asleep and paralyzed within twenty-five seconds.

Andy stood behind the patient's head. After thirty seconds of ventilating Demetrius with a mask and 100% oxygen, Andy opened the patient's mouth with his right thumb and index finger while holding the endotracheal tube between his right index and middle fingers, like a cigarette. He held the laryngoscope in his left hand.

While paralyzed, Demetrius could not breathe for himself. Consequently, an airway had to be secured quickly, before damage was done to his brain due to lack of oxygenated blood. Ventilating the patient with 100% oxygen prior to placing the endotracheal tube gave Andy sixty seconds to insert the tube safely.

A young woman in a robe burst into Trauma One and draped herself across the patient's chest and face. She was crying. Andy backed up a step.

"Could someone kindly remove this person?" he asked. "And call the respiratory therapy tech."

"I can't leave him," she cried. "He needs me."

Alina and Sasha could not budge the woman, who put her arms around the patient's head and locked her hands. Ryan was filling out his run sheet in a chair across from Trauma One.

"Ryan, would you deal with this lady?" Andy asked, pulling the sterile laryngoscope and endotracheal tube away from the woman's hair.

Ryan grasped the woman's forearms and jerked her hands apart just long enough to encircle her chest and upper arms from behind and pull her off the patient and out of Trauma One. The lady attempted to scratch Ryan's face and kick him. Being an experienced EMS provider, he lowered her body so that her feet dragged the floor. By pinning her upper arms against her chest he prevented her from reaching his face.

"You better not let my husband die," she screamed at Andy.

Andy re-opened the patient's mouth with his right thumb and forefinger, as if the interruption had not occurred and the clock was not running down on Demetrius' brain.

"This guy's teeth are almost all eroded away," he said. "Meth-mouth."

He inserted the laryngoscope with his left hand, guiding the blade along the right side of the patient's tongue. Lifting up, he searched for airway landmarks in the blood welling up from Demetrius' stomach. He inserted the blade a bit deeper.

"Crike pressure," he said.

Sasha pressed on the cricothyroid cartilage in the neck, just below Demetrius' Adam's apple. The epiglottis popped into view. Lifting just a little more with the laryngoscope blade, Andy saw the vocal cords. He inserted the tube between the vocal cords with his right hand, and backed the laryngoscope out with his left hand. He placed the laryngoscope next to Demetrius' left ear.

"I'm at twenty-three centimeters on the tube at the corner of the mouth," Andy said, inflating the cuff of the endotracheal tube with ten ccs of air. He attached the self-inflating bag of 100% oxygen to the proximal end of the endotracheal tube. Squeezing gently, he emptied half the bag with each squeeze of his right hand. He nodded to Alina, who held her stethoscope to the right side of Demetrius' chest for several squeezes of the bag, and then listened to the left side for several squeezes.

"Breath sounds are normal and equal," Alina said. "Chest wall movement is symmetrical."

Andy looked at Sasha. "Start another wide open IV in the opposite arm after you draw his trauma labs. He needs a nasogastric tube and a Foley catheter. Let's get it done before he wakes up."

Andy taped the endotracheal tube in place and discussed the ventilator settings with the respiratory tech. They stood and watched the pulse oximeter, the heart rate, and blood pressure on the monitors as the ventilator took over Demetrius' breathing.

"Looks good," the respiratory tech said.

Andy walked to the unit coordinator's desk. "Call the surgeon and anesthesiologist on-call and the nursing supervisor. And we'll need an OR nurse crew."

Once an uncooperative trauma patient is on a ventilator, unconscious and paralyzed, the ED physician and nurse can do their jobs without interference. There are two general rules, second nature to Andy: cut off every stitch of clothing and stick a tube or a gloved finger into every natural orifice of the patient's body, looking for blood in all the right places. After these intrusions in the supine position, the patient is log rolled onto each side.

While Sasha held Demetrius securely, Andy inspected the entire back and flanks for entrance and exit wounds. He found none. He walked down the spine with his fingers and searched for bulges and bruises. He palpated every square inch of exposed skin for subcutaneous foreign bodies. Bullet wounds often hid in the armpits or in rolls of fat. No tattoo or body piercing would go unnoticed, nor would it escape documentation. No hole would go un-probed. Andy thought that if the average person knew what happened to his naked body in a trauma resuscitation, he would be more careful in his daily life.

But Demetrius wasn't the average person. He would not recall any of the unpleasant parts of Andy's evaluation and treatment. He would not recall Andy. He would be narcotized throughout his hospital stay. He would learn nothing from his experience and would make no changes in his lifestyle. This is the rule among trauma patients, not the exception. Andy suspected he would see Demetrius again.

Some trauma patients are incredibly tolerant of pain and emergency procedures. Andy had treated many wounded soldiers in this category. Cooperative patients recognize that their lives are at stake. They discern that the professionals gathered around their body are trying to save their lives. They endure the tubes and lines and fingers without a fight. In Andy's experience, cooperative patients presented on the day shift.

Patients like Demetrius did their best to interfere with every life-saving procedure. They were invariably intoxicated or stoned on something. A trained eye could spot them among a train wreck of multiple trauma patients. Unfortunately, an IV must be inserted to administer the drugs that sedate and paralyze uncooperative patients. In practice, the first few minutes of a major trauma resuscitation could be a greased pig fight, blood serving as the grease.

You would think that a man slashed across his abdomen with a knife would be happy to receive care. Not if he were high. Andy had seen a trauma patient bolt off the stretcher, carrying his ragged loops of small bowel in one hand while ripping out his only IV with the other hand. Sometimes Andy's brute strength and combat skills were required to restrain a trauma patient long enough to save his life.

Andy walked back to Trauma One and looked up at the heart rate and blood pressure. He extended his right hand toward Sasha without taking his eyes off the monitors. She handed him a fresh pair of surgical gloves. He sat down on a stool at Demetrius' neck. She opened a central line kit and changed her gloves. When Andy needed something from this kit, he opened his hand. Sasha didn't just slap the instruments on his palm. She oriented every item from the tray to its functional position, pointed toward the patient.

The safest way to insert a large diameter resuscitation catheter into a patient's neck is to use an ultrasound probe to find the target vein, the internal jugular vein. This procedure usually requires a nurse who knows something about ultrasound probes, since the doctor needs both hands in the sterile field. Andy asked Sasha to tilt the stretcher to a head-down position. This filled the veins in Demetrius' neck and made them larger targets.

Sasha moved the flat ultrasound probe back and forth across the patient's neck while Andy identified the structures underneath the skin on the ultrasound monitor.

"Hold it right there," Andy said. He watched his skinny needle travel from the skin in Demetrius' neck to the lumen of the internal jugular vein on the ultrasound monitor, avoiding structures that pulsated. After unscrewing the needle from the hub of the syringe, Andy inserted a flexible guide wire into the hub of the needle and advanced the wire ten centimeters toward the patient's heart. The skinny needle was then withdrawn and a large intravenous line advanced over the wire. The wire was then removed. Slam dunk.

Within seconds, Demetrius had a pencil-sized internal jugular trauma line. Sasha attached a bag of Normal Saline to this line while Andy sutured it to the skin of the patient's neck.

One liter of resuscitation fluid could now be delivered within an inch of Demetrius' heart every sixty seconds. Bleeding patients die when the heart doesn't have enough fluid in it to pump to organs. When the heart is empty, CPR does nothing but break ribs. Andy infused two units of type-specific blood and four liters of Normal Saline into Demetrius through this line in the ED.

The radiology tech took a portable chest X-ray to confirm good position of the endotracheal tube and to look for shotgun pellets in the chest, free blood in the chest, and air in the wrong place in the chest.

Andy checked the monitors again. Blood pressure 100/70, heart rate 120. Oxygen saturation 100%. About 150 cc of blood had been suctioned from the nasogastric tube, confirming injury to the stomach. He looked down at the Foley bag. About 200 milliliters of urine. Absence of blood in the urine probably meant no injury to the kidneys, the ureters, or the bladder. "Lucky guy," Andy said. He sat down at a long desk opposite the unit coordinator and began writing on the patient's chart.

"Alina," he called, "nuke some blankets in the microwave so he won't get hypothermic, and hang a Propofol drip for ongoing sedation. Better start some antibiotics to make the surgeon happy--Zosyn 3.375 grams IV."

The nursing supervisor arrived at the foot of the bed. She stared at Demetrius' abdomen for a moment before punching numbers into her cell phone and leaving the department.

Andy got up and walked over to the PAX machine, a huge computer screen used to view X-rays, CT scans, and ultrasounds.

He clicked the mouse on "Recent ED films."

Demetrius' chest X-ray and abdominal films showed nothing unexpected. Six 00 pellets had entered his colon, stomach, and small intestine but appeared to have missed the lungs, liver, and kidneys. The pellets were too far from the midline or not deep enough to hit the spine, the aorta, or the vena cava. There were smaller arteries and veins all over the abdomen, and the six 00 pellets had found some of them. Andy's job was to keep the bucket full of resuscitation fluid and blood, even though there were six holes in the bottom of the bucket. It would be up to the surgeon on-call to deal with the bleeding and fecal contamination inside Demetrius' abdomen.

Sasha sat down next to Andy at the PAX machine. "Looks like he'll live."

"You did a great job on this patient, you and Alina," Andy said. "You obviously have trauma experience."

"And so do you, Andy."

She had never called him by his first name before, although she had invited him to breakfast once after their night shift was over. He didn't take the bait.

"Since you're new to our community," Andy said, "my wife and I would love to have you visit our farm for dinner. Every nurse in the ED has been our guest."

"That would be nice," Sasha said. "I'm trying to fix up an old house outside of town."

"I'm a good fixer," Andy said. "Perhaps I could help. Lindsey likes to meet everyone I work with. Why not tomorrow night for dinner?"

"That would be great."

He drew Sasha a map to his farm on his prescription pad, tore it off, and handed it to her. "How about six o'clock?"

Sasha smiled and moved away as the surgeon walked through the ambulance entrance.

Dr. Harold Jones strode directly to Trauma One. Andy walked in behind him, put his hand on the surgeon's shoulder, and apologized for getting him out of bed. Dr. Jones did not turn around. He didn't acknowledge the apology or the gesture of friendship. He listened to Andy's account of the physical exam and resuscitation with his head down. After the report, the surgeon on-call left Trauma One to scrub for Demetrius' surgery.

Andy didn't take the surgeon's behavior personally. He wasn't seeking an "atta boy." Most surgeons are assholes after midnight. Both of them knew that Demetrius would ruin the surgeon's entire day. Dr. Jones would be forced to reschedule his elective surgeries. These patients and their families would be upset. He would be late to see office patients, who would also be pissed at him. He would be exhausted all day, and his office staff would be disappointed that he wasn't smiling. GSW patients rarely have medical insurance. In fact, about all that Dr. Jones could look forward to after four grueling hours on this feet in the operating room was the opportunity to be sued.

Unlike Dr. Jones, Andy didn't care about being paid. He wasn't upset if his patients failed to say "thank you." He practiced emergency medicine because he needed to stand at the crossroads of life and death. He had run toward danger all his life, even before he became a SEAL. Although he didn't wish ill on anyone, he drove to work hoping that awful things, if they were going to happen, would happen on his watch. He would not say this out loud, but since he broke into a smile and ran the stairs when the hospital operator announced "Code Orange," a life-threatening in-hospital emergency, or "Code Blue," a patient in cardiac arrest, Andy's yearning for action was no hospital secret. Hospital employees and staff physicians loved to have Andy on duty, but they had no idea what made him tick.

"I need to speak to a relative or friend," Andy said. "What about that woman?"

"She's in the conference room with two detectives," Alina said.

Andy picked up the chart, glanced at the name of the patient, and knocked on the door. The two detectives and the woman looked up.

"I'm Dr. Carlson, the emergency physician," he said, extending his hand to the woman.

Her hand was sweaty.

"I believe that Demetrius is going to survive," Andy said. "The surgeon is here. The patient will shortly be on his way to the operating room. We've stabilized his vital signs."

The detectives nodded toward him. Andy studied the woman's face.

She clinched her teeth and closed her eyes. When her eyes opened, she stared past him. There were no tears or smiles. After a moment she said, "Thank God."

Andy was anxious to tell his wife about the talented new trauma nurse named Sasha, whom he had already invited to dinner.

2.

Driving home from his night shift at 7:15 that Friday morning following the gunshot wound to Demetrius Popov, Andy noted that someone had moved into the old house on the corner of South Airport Road and Plank Road. This house had been vacant for more than a year. Nobody seemed to stay there very long, and it wasn't hard to see why. The structure was at least eighty years old, one story, white composite shingles, and tin roof. The outstanding feature of the yard was a propane tank, now rusted and almost covered by weeds.

The owner was a black lady whose maiden name was Carter. Her father had built the house and lived in it until he was in his nineties. As a boy, Andy had helped Mr. Carter get up his hay. The daughter now lived in New Jersey and rarely visited the property. She couldn't bear to part with the house, but she didn't have the time or resources to keep it in rental condition.

Unfortunately, most of the previous occupants of the house were in the category of undesirables in the neighborhood. Lots of loud noises, drugs, alcohol, and motorcycles. New curtains hung in the two rooms facing Plank Road. Could this be the old house Sasha referred to?

Since the Battle of Carlson farm almost a decade before, Andy and Lindsey's precocious twins, Jack and Ava, had not just grown up. They had taken over. They were born during this battle. Jack now considered himself Andy's understudy in all matters. Ava considered herself equal to any boy except Jack. Both parents had prepared themselves for an orderly progression of childhood landmarks, like walking by age one and talking in short sentences by age two.

The children had maintained a high degree of alertness as infants.

This was their parents' first clue to what was in store for them. Both children had unusually long attention spans as infants and toddlers. At age six months they rocked in mechanical swings and watched television programs intended for two year olds.

At ten months they listened attentively for an hour at a time as Lindsey read from books for three year olds. Andy knew that a ten month old, who couldn't walk, wasn't supposed to have a vocabulary of fifty to one hundred words. Lindsey had looked forward to several months of *Ma-ma* and *Da-da*, but every day seemed to bring new words about ever more subjects. At fourteen months the toddlers walked into Lindsey's kitchen and announced, "We think Big Bird is stupid."

At age eighteen months, Jack and Ava, still in diapers, clung to the coffee table, side by side, and mimicked the TV exercise routine of Richard Simmons from the waist down.

"I don't want them to learn even half of Richard Simmons," Andy said.

"I think it's the music, Andy," Lindsey said. "They're not bouncing their butts to imitate Richard Simmons." She looked at the flat screen TV. "At least I hope not."

The twins sang their ABCs and counted to 100 at eighteen months. At age two, Lindsey gave them a video called "Elmo's Potty Time." The children watched this video several times with great interest and then announced, "We're potty trained." They backed up their claim within a week.

By age three Jack and Ava read *Curious George* to each other. Soon they graduated to *Little House on the Prairie* and *The Lion, The Witch, and The Wardrobe*.

The twins were introduced to the woods on the farm as toddlers. They could recognize each animal on the farm by age three and had been taught by their dad to stalk animals at age five. It was Andy's philosophy that the worst thing a father could say to his child was "You're too young to do that."

Instead, he thought the parent should be saying, "That's such an important subject that I'd like to teach you about it myself, so that you won't make the same mistakes I did."

As he explained to Lindsey, "If you want your son to love carpentry like you do, never relegate him to fetching tools and watching. Teach him that it's okay to hit the nail twelve times to drive it in. Let him hit his thumb. The parent should be the one handing tools to the child."

Another of Andy's favorite theories about parenting had to do with enthusiasm. "Kids learn enthusiasm from their parents," he said. "If your child sees that you're not excited about doing something, he won't develop enthusiasm for that activity, either. The world is full of kids with no enthusiasm for anything except watching TV, playing video games, and texting on their smart phones. You can't learn anything about self-defense or survival outdoors on Facebook."

Not surprisingly, both twins were enthusiastic about the same things that Andy enjoyed. Lindsey watched her seven year olds paint their faces with camouflage makeup at 4:30 in the morning before walking out in the dark with their bows and arrows. It was easy to see why they enjoyed doing things together. Andy loved to teach. The twins really wanted to learn everything. They wanted to be like their daddy. She couldn't tell who was having the most fun.

Andy taught the twins to observe the behavior of animals. He taught them each animal's strengths and weaknesses. One of his favorite teaching games was to stalk a deer on the ground and pat the deer on the rump before it bolted.

They would start the game by sitting in a camouflage tent with their dad just inside the wood line of an alfalfa field. Ava might say, "It's my turn. I'll bet you can't walk up to that big doe next to the pine tree, the one with the twin fawns."

Before leaving the blind, Andy would review the wind direction, the types of cover available, the possible interference from every other deer in the field, and the best use of the terrain and cover in and around the field. Then he would paint his own face and sneak out the back of the blind while the twins watched his progress with their binoculars.

Sometimes Andy would stand or sit for fifteen minutes without moving. "Deer are great at picking up movement," he explained, "but they can't see your human outline if you wear camouflage on your body and paint your face. If you approach slowly from downwind and never make eye contact, the deer thinks you're a natural part of his environment."

When Andy patted a doe on the rump, he always said, "Hello darlin'." Ava would giggle. Jack Andrew Carlson longed to be that stealthy.

In military terms, having two gifted children was a force multiplier. The children drove the dynamics of the family, jolting Mom and Dad's expectations of learning, complicating relationships with other children and adults and, at times, straining Andy's relationship with Lindsey.

Lindsey struggled to keep up with the development of the children, who demanded much more entertainment and education than other children. When they were not given enough stimulation in the form of challenging games or activities, they became bored and acted out.

Jack lasted three days in kindergarten at age five. The teacher said, "He asked me why I was so fat and why we didn't have any computers."

Ava intimidated the class by bringing three musical instruments to school and playing all of them well. She was sent home at the end of the first week when the teacher observed her demonstrating a martial arts choke hold for her classmates. When asked how she had learned this technique, she replied, "I watch Bruce Lee on DirecTV when Mom and Dad are locked in the bedroom."

It soon became painfully obvious that it was a waste of everybody's time to put the twins on a county school bus. Home schooling was the only answer. Stopping the calls from the teachers was nice, too.

Ava and Jack had good reasons to be unusual children. Lindsey had a nursing degree, a summa cum laude degree in physics, and a Ph.D. in nuclear physics from Stanford. She spoke fluent Russian, Arabic, and French. She played the piano by ear. She was employed by the CIA as a nuclear threats analyst when her path crossed Andy's.

Andy had been a three-sport standout in high school and college, a U.S. Navy SEAL, and a summa cum laude graduate of Emory University Medical School in Atlanta. He was board certified in emergency medicine and had completed a fellowship in critical care and trauma medicine. He was practicing as an emergency physician when he met Lindsey. Because his parents had been missionaries, Andy discovered early in life that he had a gift for learning foreign languages.

Almost ten years old, Jack and Ava looked no different than any other child their age. Their passions were Andy's passions--building, camping, exploring the secrets of the farm, stalking animals, and hunting with primitive weapons. Each could routinely hit a three-inch spot out to twenty-five yards with a stick bow and a three-inch spot out to 150 yards with a twenty-two caliber rifle. Andy taught them to respect life, to take it seriously when they killed an animal, and to live within the harmony of the pecking order of nature. Animals were only killed if they were varmints or predators or if you intended to eat them. It was nice to kill a buck with a giant set of antlers, but you still ate the meat.

Andy had reviewed the previous battles on the farm with his children and walked them play by play through Carlson movements and tactics to fend off Indian attacks, the British, the Yankees, Russian arms dealers, and rogue CIA agents. The Carlsons had bought their 4000 acre plantation from King George II in 1743. It had been affectionately referred to as "the farm" since 1865. After the Civil War it was not fashionable to own a plantation.

Andy's best friend was a black man with whom he shared a last name. Ben Carlson owned 300 acres of the farm. His ancestors had worked on the Carlson plantation for over 200 years, before and after the Civil War. No other family had ever lived on the property.

Andy indoctrinated his children with his own beliefs, which included skeptical views of the federal government, the current president, and his motives. Since the country's financial collapse over the last two years, Andy had stepped up their education in economics and self-sufficiency on the farm.

By age seven, Jack and Ava had killed deer, turkey, groundhogs, bobcats, coyotes, and bears with their stick bows. They were capable of hunting alone, traveling above ground in the dark, or moving about in the limestone caves and tunnel system underneath the farm.

The last decade had been the happiest years of Andy's life. He had a devoted wife and two precious but challenging children. The twins' unpredictability and their need for constant stimulation ameliorated Andy's own needs for excitement. Although he had been a binge drinker as a SEAL, he had been sober since he met Lindsey.

Ava's natural talents frightened her parents. Her combination of brains and ability to manipulate adults was unnerving. She had recently bet Jack that she could sell Girl Scout cookies to fifty consecutive houses. The stakes were high: one month of washing the supper dishes. Ava always left a house with a smile on her face and an order for cookies in her hand. She wouldn't reveal her sales secrets.

Lindsey complained to Andy that she had difficulty knowing how to talk to Jack on any given day. Andy thought he would never suffer such anguish. His approach would be simple. He would answer each question honestly, no matter how embarrassing. It was his view that if he lied to his son, or sugar-coated the truth, Jack wouldn't trust him.

Andy learned that complete honesty with precocious children came with a price. "They miss nothing that I say," he grumbled to Lindsey. "And just when you least expect it, they will recite your chapter and verse."

Andy thought that two photographic memories in the family were too many, especially if neither belonged to the parents. "I was a bachelor too long," he told Lindsey. "I became accustomed to saying exactly what I thought. Now I can't protect myself."

By age seven, conversations between Jack and Ava were no longer viewed as comical entertainment, but as potentially embarrassing reflections of Mom and Dad.

"I know yours is different from mine," Jack said to Ava one evening while toweling off after his shower, "but Dad says one day you'll rule the world with what's between your legs."

"How will I do that?" Ava asked.

Lindsey leaned forward from her seat in the great room of the farmhouse.

"I don't know yet," Jack said.

"Honey, I'm going to take out the trash," Andy called.

3.

When Sasha drove over the covered bridge on Saturday afternoon, she thought that it was one of the most impressive pieces of wooden architecture she had ever seen. She stopped in the center of the bridge and looked out of the windows on either side at the creek. The branches of the trees overhanging the gravel road up the hill from the bridge formed an attractive tunnel.

She continued up this hill, passing a five-acre alfalfa field on her left before reaching a "T" intersection. She glanced at her map and then turned right. A collection of buildings appeared among the mature white oaks on either side of another gravel road. Within a short distance she saw the long ranch house with two chimneys in front on her left. The horizontal cedar siding on this house matched the color of the trees around it so well that it would be easy to drive right past it. A large barn appeared on her right, opposite the farmhouse. She stopped in the road, unsure where to park. As she rolled down her window, she detected movement in the woods next to the barn.

The barn had an unusual yard. There were seven different animals in the yard, animals that usually didn't tolerate each other. At least they looked like animals. None of these animals were moving. After staring a few moments, she decided that the animals must be three dimensional targets, the kind used by bow hunters for practice. They were cleverly scattered among trees, bushes, and a couple of boulders.

Sasha turned off her Nissan and stepped out onto the side of the road. She heard Andy's voice. "Firing positions." She dropped to her knees behind the open door of her car and scanned the terrain around her.

Two American Indian children, both towheads, appeared from the woods on the opposite side of the yard from the barn. A nine or ten year old boy stood up behind a boulder. He held a simple stick bow in his hands with an arrow on the string. The other Indian child, the one with a ponytail, appeared to be a girl, about the same age, but slightly shorter. She had her back against a tree, facing away from the animal targets. Both children had camouflage makeup on their faces, bandanas around their foreheads, and a single feather in the back of their heads. Both wore camo shorts and moccasins. The boy wore no shirt on his tanned chest. The girl was not wearing a shirt either, but she had painted a nice bra on her bare chest with camo makeup.

Andy barked, "Bobcat."

The boy stood up from behind the boulder and drew back his stick bow. A wooden arrow made a thumping sound as it entered the center of the chest of the bobcat target, some thirty yards away. At the same time the girl pivoted around the tree to face the target with a musical instrument in her hands.

"Mine got there first," the Indian girl said.

Sasha walked toward the target to confirm what her eyes were telling her. The Indian girl had put a dart into the bobcat, approximately one half inch from the arrow. She was holding a clarinet. At least it looked like a clarinet.

"Jack," Andy called as he walked out of the door of the barn. "When I say 'firing position', I want you to start to draw your bow before you show yourself. Ava, only your head should appear from behind a tree. The idea is to expose yourself for the minimum amount of time to fire your weapon. Let me show you."

He reached out for the boy's stick bow. The Indian boy handed him an arrow. Dr. Carlson crouched on his knees behind the rock. After calling "Firing position," he brought the bow to full draw without raising his head. The arrow was pointed ninety degrees from the bobcat. In one motion he rose, turned his bow toward the target, and released the arrow. There was a crunching noise.

"Aw Dad, you ruined another one of my arrows," the boy moaned.

"I'm sorry, Jack. I'll make you another one. Come over here. I want you to meet somebody nice."

The three walked toward her. "This is Jack, and this is Ava." Andy said, pointing and smiling.

"Pleased to meet you, ma'am." Jack offered his hand.

"Same here," said Ava, extending her hand.

Sasha shook both hands. "I'm so happy to meet you both. I work with your dad at the hospital."

"We know. He told us," Ava said. "You're not his type. He likes petite women with auburn hair and small breasts, like Mom."

Andy clenched his eyes.

"You want to see us work?" Ava asked.

"Work?"

"Show her, Dad," Jack said.

"Firing positions," Andy called.

The kids ran for cover. They reloaded their weapons.

"Buck," Andy called.

Each child emerged from behind something, fired accurately at the three dimensional buck target, and then moved to another point of cover in the yard and reloaded.

"Firing positions. Bear."

The bear got whacked by both kids, who ran to new firing positions and reloaded.

"Groundhog."

Whacked by two kids.

"Coyote."

Whacked by two kids.

"Doe."

Whacked by two kids.

"Turkey."

Whacked by two kids.

"Cease fire," Andy called.

The dynamic duo rejoined Andy and Sasha on the gravel road.

"You two are fantastic," Sasha said.

"We're pretty good," Jack said, "but you haven't seen Dad shoot anything."

Sasha said, "I saw him shoot your bow. It looked like an amazing shot."

"Show her the apple trick, Dad," Ava said.

Jack went to the barn to get his dad's wooden recurve bow and quiver of practice arrows.

Ava ran to the coyote target and placed a red rubber ball on its head.

Sasha asked, "You're not going to try to shoot that little ball from here, Andy?"

"Nope. That would be too easy," he said. "I'm going to step over here to our right and back up, where we can't see the coyote's head or the ball."

Sasha stood behind Andy. "The buck is in front of the coyote. How do you shoot the ball if you can't see it?"

"An arrow has a trajectory," Ava said. "It arches over things. Dad can hit the ball without seeing it."

"At fifty yards?"

"An arrow shot at a target fifty yards away will arc much higher than an arrow shot at a target twenty yards away," Ava said.

"And he can see the coyote's legs between the deer's legs," Jack said, pointing.

"I see the legs," Sasha said. "But what good does that do?"

Andy had already released his arrow, which sent the red rubber ball flopping, skewered like a piece of steak on a shish-ka-bob. The coyote did not move.

"The coyote's head is always in the same place, Sasha," Ava said. "We're not as fast as Dad, but we can make shots like that, too."

"Andy, you're teaching your kids to be warriors," Sasha said.

"Yep," he said. "Our country is going to need good soldiers."

"They're too young to be shooting guns," Sasha said.

"She doesn't get it, Dad," Ava said.

"I've been shooting guns for years," Jack said. "but I don't prefer them. They're bulky and heavy. I don't need a gun to kill anything here on the farm."

"Guns give away your position," Ava said. "They're greasy. They can damage your ears so you can't hear your iPod."

"We practice on human targets," Jack said.

"Why would you do that?" Sasha asked.

"Human beings are the greatest predators on the planet," Ava said. "Let me ask you a question."

"Go ahead."

"What are you prepared to do when somebody points a gun at a member of your family or at you?"

"I never thought of it like that," Sasha said.

Jack said, "It would be nice if the world was a safe place where everybody showed respect for each other. But the fact is that the world is full of people who would gladly kill you and your family if you had something they wanted."

Ava said, "Our dad told us that he had seen hundreds of dead children in the streets of countries in the Middle East. These children didn't know how to protect themselves from IEDs, or rocket-fire, or shells. They didn't know how to fight back."

"Do you read newspapers?" Jack asked.

"Yes, I do," Sasha said.

"Then you should have some idea who our enemies are in this world," Jack said. "Our own country tells Muslim fundamentalists to 'come on down.' These people are responsible for most of the terrorism in the world. Then there's the mentally ill that shoot up schools. Children in America are very much at risk today. We're not training to be casualties."

"Andy, supper's ready," Lindsey called from the steps of the farmhouse.

Ava walked next to Sasha and took her hand. "You're going to be a little shocked when we go inside," she said. "So get yourself prepared for all the animals on the wall and the furniture."

Lindsey noticed that Sasha was tall and had a nice, full figure. Over dinner, she said, "Andy can't stop talking about what a great nurse you are, Sasha."

"Don't worry. I can be a klutz sometimes."

"You couldn't prove it by me," Andy said. "It's a pleasure working with someone with your level of experience. Most nurses with your talent want to live in metropolitan areas."

"I worked in a trauma center in Houston for a while," she said, "but driving to work was such a hassle, and this guy I had been dating for a long time wouldn't leave me alone."

"If you'll tell me what he looks like," Ava said, "I'll take care of him if he shows up here."

"Thank you, Ava, but I don't think he could find Farmville."

"Tell us what we can do to help with that old house," Lindsey said. "Andy loves to fix things."

"You don't need to do anything for me," Sasha said. "I can take care of myself."

"Dad said he wanted to bush hog your yard," Jack said.

"You'll never get all of those weeds out of there with a lawn mower or a weed whacker," Ava said.

"The first thing I need to do is figure out a way to haul all of the junk out of that place," Sasha said. "Nobody ever threw anything away, except into the yard."

"Andy has a dump truck," Lindsey said.

"I'll drive over with one of the tractors and cut your grass," Andy said. "Jack can drive the dump truck over and leave it. You can fill it up over a few days. I'll help you pick up the big stuff. No problem."

"That's so kind of all of you."

"Sasha," said Lindsey, "let me take you over to the Cow Palace one day next week. It's Andy's personal Home Depot. He's been collecting building materials all his life. There are sinks and toilets and counter tops and all kinds of stuff, still in their original boxes. When a big outfit like Lowe's comes to town, the mom and pop stores go out of business. Andy buys their inventory."

"Could I ask a few questions about your interest in weapons?" Sasha asked.

"Sure," Ava said.

"My grandfather was a weapons expert and I grew up around guns," Sasha said. "Andy can obviously hit targets that he can't see. I would think he needed to know the exact distance to each target to make shots like that. Arrows drop pretty fast after about thirty yards, don't they?"

"There are no sight pins on my bow," Andy said. "I don't waste time making calculations about distance or matching specific sight pins to targets. The key is to have a clear mental image of the trajectory of *your* arrow from *your* bow. I make my own arrows, and I've been shooting the same bow with the same broad head for more than twenty years. When I see a target I know how far above the animal's chest to aim. The same mental image allows me to hit moving targets, like flying turkeys and running deer."

"You can shoot turkeys out of the air?"

"Turkeys are slow," Jack said. "Dad shot three in the air on Thanksgiving Day with three arrows."

"The breast is the only part of a wild turkey that really tastes good," Ava said.

"It's a shame that nobody fights with bows and arrows anymore," Sasha said. "All that knowledge about trajectory doesn't have much application to modern weapons."

Jack and Ava held their stomachs in mock laughter.

"Did I say something wrong?" Sasha asked.

"I apologize for their behavior," Lindsey said, focusing her stare at Jack and Ava. "There aren't many people who understand the advantages of quiet weapons that can be accurate, even in the dark."

"Can somebody tell me what an arrow that travels thirty to fifty yards has in common with a .308 sniper rifle that can hit an apple at 1000 meters or a Barrett .50 caliber that can take your head off at 3000 meters?"

Andy's eyebrows twitched.

"Long before there were proximity fuses and radar-guided anti-aircraft guns," Jack said, "military gunnery instructors noticed that some people had a mental image of the flight of their artillery shells. They instinctively knew where the path of the shell they were firing intercepted the course of an airplane."

Sasha nodded her head.

"This kind of spatial visualization can be improved with practice," Ava said, "but most people just don't have it. Without modern laser sights, computers and guided missiles, the average soldier couldn't hit a barn with a bass fiddle."

"That may be overstating a bit," Andy said. "The point is that every projectile, even a shoulder-fired rocket, has a predictable path unless it's guided by computers or wires."

"That's fascinating," Sasha said, "but how can you practice with a shoulder-fired rocket if each shell costs a few thousand dollars?"

"Dad and I wanted to be proficient with the AT4 recoilless rifle," Jack said, "so we bought tracer rounds and added yellow chalk. Our tracer rounds fly exactly like the high explosive anti-tank (HEAT) round. They leave a trail that you can see, and the point of impact is not an explosion. You see a puff of yellow smoke. We practice on the power line that cuts across our farm. It has a 150 foot right of way for almost two miles."

Ava said, "The CS version deploys water from the rear of the tube when it's fired, and this spray captures the back blast, making the recoilless rifle safe in confined spaces."

"It sounds like you're reading off the specs," Sasha said.

"She is," Jack said. "We help Mom and Dad remember stuff."

"My grandfather would love this conversation," Sasha said. "Were you in the military, Andy?"

"He's not supposed to talk about it," Ava said.

"Maybe you could come out some time and shoot with us," Jack said.

"That would be great. Did your dad teach you to shoot, Jack?"

"He taught us to shoot most everything while we listened to rock 'n' roll music. The earphones protect your ears, and the music makes it difficult to depend on calculations and judging distances."

"You guys are something else," Sasha said.

The family was delighted to find a new friend who lived close by, especially someone who shared their interest in weapons. The Carlsons shared their interest in weapons with few people. They shared their secret of Confederate gold with no one.

Who would have guessed that Confederate gold would end up in the cave system underneath the Carlson plantation, thirty miles from Appomattox, Virginia? Historians do not dispute that wagonloads of gold bars disappeared from the Confederate treasury in March 1865, reportedly to fund a second Civil War after the South recovered. The Carlsons had no incentive to explain to misinformed Yankees exactly why the Confederacy held so much gold at the end of the war. It was best to remain quiet when old rebels speculated about which Confederate general's grave guarded the gold bars from the Confederate treasury.

If Jefferson Davis had so much gold, the Yankees said, then why didn't he spend it on General R. E. Lee's ravaged Army of Northern Virginia? If your family included two Confederate generals, you knew the answer. After the fall of Vicksburg, the effective blockage of all Southern ports, the destruction of the "breadbasket of the Confederacy" in the Shenandoah Valley, and Sherman's scorching march from Atlanta to South Carolina, *there was nothing left in the South to buy for the Army of Northern Virginia.* The South was an agrarian society, dependent upon Northern manufacturing and imported raw materials and finished goods. The Confederacy did not lose the Civil War due to a lack of funds.

4.

Andy was asleep Sunday morning at 7:00 when Lindsey gently shook his shoulder. "Honey, it's me. I'm sorry. Something terrible has happened and I can't watch it by myself."

"Watch what?" Andy blinked his eyes and sat up. Lindsey's eyes were red. He put his arms around her.

"It's started, Andy."

"What's started?"

"The first nuclear war in the twenty-first century."

She led him into the great room, where CNN spit a continuous visual and verbal stream of horrific news. A nuclear blast had destroyed the Saudi port of Ras Tanura in the Persian Gulf. Andy sat down on the couch with Lindsey. Jack and Ava were already riveted to the TV.

"For those of you just joining us," the reporter said, "there has been a catastrophic explosion at the Saudi port of Ras Tanura. There is no doubt that this was a nuclear terrorist attack. We have no comment yet from the royal family of Saudi Arabia. What you are seeing now are bits of video shot from a helicopter after the detonation."

The reporter continued, "Ras Tanura was one of the largest oil export terminals in the Persian Gulf. It had two giant piers and eighteen berths, including storage tanks with the capacity of fifty million barrels. Multiple pipelines terminated at the facility, which handled fully ten per cent of the entire world's supply of oil."

"That's a mushroom cloud," Jack said, pointing at the television screen.

"The Ras Tanura terminal in Saudi Arabia has come under attack once before, by Al Qaeda," the reporter said. "Because of the vulnerability of this port in the Persian Gulf and the vulnerability of the Strait of Hormuz, the Saudis have constructed pipelines to the western coast of their country. While still able to pump oil to Juaymah in the Persian Gulf and at Yanbu on the Red Sea, nearly half of Saudi Arabia's export business has been shattered. Oil futures have rocketed to 400 dollars per barrel. The economies of the world were already straining to accommodate oil at 200 dollars per barrel. This blow will be felt around the world and its long-term effects will be especially hazardous to European and Western countries that are large importers of oil. As yet, no one has claimed responsibility for this terrorist act."

"Are we at war yet?" Jack asked.

"Ras Tanura is not a population target, and it's not in America," Andy said, "It *is* an Achilles' heel for Europe and the West. Our ignorant president insists that environmentalism is more important than self-sufficiency in oil."

Andy spent an hour listing things he would like to do before the United States became involved in another war. Then he went back to bed. After a series of night shifts, he required at least one day to reset his biological clock. At one o'clock in the afternoon, he was again awakened, this time by Ava, who handed him the phone.

"It's that ignorant president," she said.

Andy looked at the caller ID and groaned. The digital screen said, "POTUS."

"Hello," Andy said.

"Dr. Carlson, this is President Umar. Could I have a moment of your time?"

"Certainly, sir."

Andy sat up in bed and punched on the speaker phone. Lindsey and the twins sat on the bed. Andy put his finger over his lips and made eye contact with Jack and Ava.

"No doubt you've been watching the events of this morning on the television," the president said. "I regret that I've not met you personally, but I've read many good things about you."

"Exaggerations, sir."

"Don't be modest, Dr. Carlson. We have a fat file on your many good qualities, as well as those of your wife. I have very disturbing news that I can't share with you over this telephone."

"Why should I be involved, sir?"

"The bombing at Ras Tanura has great implications for King Fahd of Saudi Arabia," the president said. "We know that you and your wife are good friends of his; in fact, you are better friends with him than anyone else in the United States. For this reason I need for you to take a personal message to the king, and I need that message to travel as fast as possible. It's not something I can send any other way."

"Mr. President, my wife and I have a family now and we don't consider ourselves ambassadors. In fact, sir, with all due respect, I didn't vote for you and I oppose almost everything you've done in office. The king communicates with me by encrypted email. I can relay him any message from you. I intend to send my condolences and offer my help. It's a lot to ask a man to leave his family and fly to a country that has just been attacked with a nuclear weapon. There are probably no airlines flying."

"Dr. Carlson, if you love your country, you will put your political differences with me aside. We are in grave danger. My message cannot travel by email. Please go to Farmville Municipal Airport, where a jet will be arriving in thirty minutes to pick you up and bring you to Washington. I'm sorry to be leaning on you like this, but time is short. You can do something for your country that nobody else can."

Andy looked at Lindsey, who indicated her vote with a thumb down gesture.

"Yes, sir," Andy said.

The president hung up.

"Andy, you're smart enough to recognize a button pusher," Lindsey said.

"Sweetheart, he's not giving me any choice here. I took an oath to support the president, even if I didn't vote for him."

"I don't like this either," Ava said. "You've done your duty for this country already."

"Lindsey, would you help me pack my bag?" Andy asked. "I'll need my real passport and some cash. I'm going to Washington and then to Riyadh. Please set out a pocket recording device with my suit, so that I can tape the president's lies."

"Why do you say that?" Jack asked.

"You don't get that job unless you're a professional liar. It's part of the job description."

"You're going to be gone at least three days, aren't you?" Lindsey asked.

"Afraid so," Andy said. "I need to take a shower. I'll call you from the plane. I can leave the S-10 at the airport."

Before leaving, Andy advised Lindsey to take Jack and Ava to the Confederate cave, lock down the farm, turn on all the monitors and motion detectors, and avoid contact with the outside world.

5.

Andy was shown into the Oval Office. The president rose to greet him. He picked up a piece of paper from his desk.

The president was a thin, dapper, middle-aged black man in a dark suit and tie. He appeared physically fit but had a fine tremor in his hands. His hair was short and speckled with grey.

"Sit down, Dr. Carlson, while I fill you in on some important developments. You should start by reading this letter I received two days ago."

Andy sat down and read the letter:

10 May 2015
Mustafa Rashid Umar
President of the United States
The White House
1600 Pennsylvania Avenue
Washington, D.C.

Dear President Umar:

Within a few days there will be a nuclear explosion in the Middle East. You are receiving this advance warning in order that you might better comprehend what is in store for you if you interfere in the coming Middle East war.

For hundreds of years European and Western countries have divided up Arab lands and drawn borders. These

countries made us their colonies, stole our resources, installed and supported dictators and monarchs, and gave our property to the Jews. You have forced us to use your dollar to buy commodities while you steadily destroyed the value of your currency. You impoverished us so that you could live a king's life on borrowed and printed money.

Islamic countries have waited patiently for your economy to collapse. We are glad that you are bankrupt. Now that we have cast off the yoke of your dollar you cannot manipulate us so easily. You truly deserve the depression and hyperinflation that you have heaped on most of the world through your greed.

Since the United States and Great Britain have been the chief criminals in the Middle East for many decades, it is appropriate for you, Mr. President, and you, Mr. Prime Minister, to make the decision we put before you today.

At this time we have two nuclear warheads already in the United States, much larger than the one that you will hear about in a few days. Such weapons are also in place in Britain. These warheads can annihilate any city. They do not need to arrive by missiles. They are already manned by martyrs.

We are going to give you a choice. We intend to restore to its rightful owners the land that you took from us and gave to the Jews. Either you will hold your military back while we do this, or we will destroy American and British cities.

It is a simple choice, but few people must know about it. If you notify the Israelis of our intentions, we will detonate our warheads immediately. If you move troops, or ships, or airplanes to the Middle East, we will detonate the warheads in your country immediately. If you inform your Congress or Parliament, or make this communication public, we will detonate all warheads.

If you count the cost, you will see that protecting Israel is not worth the destruction of your cities. If you hold back your military, we will not harm America or Britain.

We are not one country. We represent Islam in all countries. You do not need to answer in words. We will know your answer by what you do. And then we will know what we must do.

The letter was signed **Islamic Jihad**.

Andy nodded and acknowledged the anguish in the president's face. He rose from his chair and placed the letter on the president's desk.

"Although he doesn't trust you," Andy said, "King Fahd has many reasons to fear disruption in the oil trade. A Middle Eastern war would threaten his kingdom."

"Do you understand what we need from King Fahd?" Umar asked.

"We need any insight he might have into who is the instigator of this blackmail. Whoever destroyed Ras Tanura is responsible for the nuclear threats to our country. We need Saudi oil more than ever."

"You have analyzed the situation succinctly, Dr. Carlson."

"What are you willing to do for the king in return for his information and oil, Mr. President?" Andy asked. "In the Middle East, favors do not come to you without favors given."

"You know the king better than I do, Dr. Carlson. What do you suggest?"

"The king is interested in the security of his regime and his business, which is selling oil. I can point out that the explosion of a nuclear device in the United States would result in blame being spread over the entire Arab world, including Saudi Arabia. But this would not be enough to get his complete cooperation. He's not naïve. The United States has already tried to steal Saudi oil and blame the royal family for a terrorist event."

"I'm aware of that unfortunate circumstance, Dr. Carlson."

"The United States needs for Saudi Arabia to stay out of the coming Middle Eastern war," Andy said. "That means no money for terrorists. We need for the king to publicly denounce an Arab-Israeli war when it starts. I would suggest that we promise to guarantee the rule of the House of Saud in return for the information and oil we seek. This also serves our best interests."

"I believe that my national security advisors will see your logic, Dr. Carlson."

"Have you informed the Israelis?" Andy asked.

"I don't see how we can do something that we've already been told will precipitate a nuclear attack on U.S. soil," Umar said. "I can't discuss Islamic Jihad with the Congress. I can talk to a couple of leaders. Congress is probably the greatest collection of blabbermouths from fifty states. There are so many unanswered questions. Nobody has been able to give me a satisfactory explanation as to how foreign nuclear weapons could get into this country in 2015."

"I don't think they just arrived," Andy said. "These two warheads have likely been in our country for thirty-five years."

Umar leaned back in his chair. "Go on, Dr. Carlson."

"During the Cold War the Soviet Union wanted the U.S. to think that their ICBMs were extremely accurate. Their own data showed that Soviet missiles commonly missed their long range targets by fifty miles.

Their missile detection satellites were even more pathetic, often identifying non-existent missile launches in the U.S. Then Ronald Reagan came up with his Star Wars Initiative. If your ICBMs were unreliable, and your early warning system was unreliable, what could be more threatening than the U.S. shooting down the missiles that you launched?"

"Where are you going with this?"

"Don't you recall Mikhail Gorbachev's frantic efforts to get President Reagan to cancel his Strategic Defense Initiative?"

"I was a teenager," Umar said.

"So was I," Andy said. "Get the CIA to give you their files on Soviet tactical nuclear warheads transported across the Canadian border in the 1980s. These were small warheads by today's standards, ten to fifty kilotons. Hiding portable warheads in America solved Soviet issues of ICBM inaccuracy and unreliable satellite detection of U.S. missile launches. Warheads already on the ground couldn't be shot down by Reagan's SDI. Our northern border was wide open at that time, a lot like our southern border is now."

"How do you know this?"

"My wife and I were involved in defusing some of these warheads. I bought several from ex-KGB agents at the direction of the CIA. We thought that the ex-KGB agents who were marketing these old warheads were all killed in a battle on my farm ten years ago."

"You believe there are Soviet Cold War nuclear weapons in the U.S.?"

"Since my wife and I disarmed several of these in Virginia, their existence is not theoretical. Please confirm this with Mr. Hamilton at the CIA. I can't say we got all the warheads. I can't tell you who might be currently buying or selling warheads. The Russians have never acknowledged sending any warheads to America."

Umar leaned forward and placed his elbows on his desk. He folded his hands together and rested his chin on them. "If the CIA is considering your hypothesis, they haven't discussed it with me."

"The origin of the warhead at Ras Tanura can be determined by doing soil analysis," Andy said. "If it was an old Soviet warhead, my wife could tell you exactly where it was manufactured. She disarmed thousands of Soviet warheads when we had a disarmament treaty with Russia. Each manufacturing site has its own nuclear signature. If tests show that the Ras Tanura explosion was from a Soviet source, then any warheads in American and British cities are likely old Soviet weapons. The same Jihad is responsible."

"I'm hoping that the king of Saudi Arabia has some insight into the Islamic Jihad, and that he will share the results of any studies done at Ras Tanura."

"I will ask about tests, but there are other issues you must consider."

Umar rocked back in his chair again. "Please go on."

"It would be important to find out if the Ras Tanura warhead had a forty year old tritium reservoir or a recently manufactured tritium reservoir. Any new reservoirs would mean current Russian cooperation. The destruction from a warhead with a new reservoir, packed with neutrons, would be far more devastating than the detonation of a warhead with an old tritium reservoir."

"And this could also be determined by tests?"

"The International Atomic Energy Agency will be analyzing data from Ras Tanura, but I doubt if they can compete with my wife's lab. She has developed software for her multi-channel analyzer that allows her to rapidly identify the nuclear signature of every known source of enriched uranium and plutonium, as well as determine if a warhead has a new tritium source."

"That's encouraging. Perhaps you can get her some samples."

"There is one other way we can answer almost all of our questions," Andy said.

"You seem to have a good handle on this subject. What are you suggesting?"

"If the CIA can find either of the two warheads mentioned in the

Jihad letter before they are detonated, almost all questions could be answered."

"You have any ideas?"

"Not at this time. Let me talk to the king and get some soil samples. You should be aware, however, that the U.S. is not one of King Fahd's favorite countries."

"Are you referring to something specific?"

"Since Saudi Arabia dropped the dollar as the reserve currency for trading oil," Andy said, "our state department has not made much of an effort to cultivate friendship with the royal family."

"And that is why I think you are the right messenger, Dr. Carlson, and not the state department."

"Do I have the authority to offer the royal family our complete support in consideration for the information and oil we seek?"

"You do. Please leave for Riyadh immediately. I will arrange transportation."

"I need a copy of this letter you received, Mr. President," Andy said. "The king will want to read it himself. He may see a clue that we've missed."

"You must guard this letter with your life, Dr. Carlson," Umar said, walking around his desk and handing Andy the copy he had already read.

Andy tucked the letter in his briefcase and stood.

"Dr. Carlson, I have something I want you to take with you."

He reached behind him on the desk and handed Andy what appeared to be a military field telephone. "This is a secure encrypted satellite phone," the president said. "When you need to talk with me, just press number one. No one else can understand our conversation."

"Thank you, Mr. President."

After Andy left the Oval Office, President Umar called Mr. John

Hamilton, the Director of the CIA. "Hamilton, you didn't give me all the files on the Carlsons. I want every file you've got on Dr. and Mrs. Andrew Carlson. And I want every file you've got on Soviet nuclear weapons brought into this country during the Cold War. I expect these files within an hour."

6.

U sually Andy stopped at Dulles airport for a security and customs check when he flew from Farmville to Riyadh. But this time the limousine from the White House took him to Andrews Air Force base. The jet on the tarmac had no markings. The flight across eight time zones gave Andy plenty of time to think. He accessed his encrypted email account through the Saudi Embassy on his laptop and began to type.

Dear King Fahd,

I am en route to Riyadh to discuss matters of grave importance to Saudi Arabia, related to the destruction of Ras Tanura. I have new information regarding this attack. I will be arriving in Riyadh at 2:00 Tuesday afternoon. Suggest that we discuss this matter in the most private of locations.

Your friend,
Andy Carlson

During the flight to Riyadh, Andy used the small tool kit in his briefcase to disassemble the satellite phone given to him by the president. As he expected, the phone had a GPS chip and a recording device. He left these in place.

As the hours dragged on, Andy reviewed how his relationship with King Fahd had developed. Perhaps there was a clue to Islamic Jihad in his friendship with the king.

Andy's rapport with King Fahd resulted from his insertion into Saudi Arabia as a SEAL sniper, supposedly to eliminate terrorists and donors to terrorists. Their relationship matured as Andy learned how often the U.S. government lied to the king. Eventually Andy's conscience, nourished by his missionary parents, forced him to be honest with the king. The CIA was manipulating both of them. The CIA had no conscience.

Almost ten years before, Andy had prevented a United States invasion of Saudi Arabia by exposing a plot to blame the Saudi royal family for a faked nuclear terrorist attack on the port of Hampton Roads. The feeling of good will and trust between Andy and the king had graduated far beyond the exchange of gifts. Andy's wife was the only foreign woman the king had ever had a personal conversation with in Arabic. The king knew that a man who valued integrity over orders coming from his own country was a worthy friend.

Once Lindsey visited Saudi Arabia, she recognized a great business opportunity. Saudi Arabia was a tough place to be female. Not only were women prohibited from going outdoors without their husbands, they had to wear black total body cover in the form of a voluminous cloak called an abaya, plus a scarf covering their hair, and a veil over their face. Aside from her father and brothers, and a few close relatives, a young female had no exposure to a young male in Saudi Arabia. However, in the king's palaces, where women were allowed to remove their abayas, Lindsey noted that Saudi women enjoyed fashionable dresses, even Western clothing. They loved bright colors and lavish material. They were fond of jewelry.

Borrowing an abaya and scarf from the king's palace, Lindsey ventured out with Andy to see the sites in Riyadh. There were hundreds of gorgeous shops to choose from, many handsomely built with marble and carved stone. Lindsey noticed something peculiar to all the shops, something overlooked by her husband. All owner-operators were men. Although there were many shops filled with items that only women would want to buy, the transactions had to occur with an adult male.

A veiled female monitor sat in a chair to observe transactions, apparently to protect the virtue of the shopkeeper, but she did not advise customers nor demonstrate the wares in the stores. Thus, women were forced to visit shops selling negligees, bras, panties, makeup, and other "female" items and make all purchases from a strange man, while accompanied by a male relative.

There was no such thing as girlfriends or wives getting together and shopping in Saudi Arabia. The religious police, the Wahhabis, had the authority of the government. A woman could be arrested in Saudi Arabia for breaking the rules of dress. Lindsey noticed that transactions were all made in cash. Women could not order goods online because they had neither credit cards nor access to computers without their husband's permission. Even then, they might be arrested for looking at the wrong website. Women were not allowed to drive. They could not travel in a car unless escorted by a male family member. In Saudi Arabia a woman could not sit in a restaurant, even with her own husband. There were no casual conversations with anyone of the opposite sex outside the home.

It was not Lindsey's intent to alter the culture of Saudi Arabia, but to provide a service that would help both the king and his forty wives. Technically, he could only have four at a time on the active roster, but there was a high turnover. The royal line must continue expanding in order to cement its control. If an American male didn't want his wife tagging along every time he went to town, and he hated those lists she gave him at the door, imagine the pressure on the king from forty wives who needed something at the mall.

Lindsey proposed to the king, through Andy, that she make a catalog of items that the royal wives would find helpful in their shopping. Each catalog would have its own tape measure so that the wives could order the correct size of personal items. She pointed out that the king would not need to force the princes in the family to accompany their sisters everywhere they wanted to shop. The king could maintain control over what they ordered. He could even make discreet selections for his wives.

The idea was a spectacular success. Orders poured in. Suggestions were made about new lines of products. The king realized that he could discreetly order things for himself through Lindsey's business. The shipping containers were delivered directly from the farm to the king's palaces.

When these containers were shipped back to Farmville, Andy could load up on hard-to-find items through the king. Lindsey's business began with one shipping crate per month. Andy bought a forty-foot international shipping container and a tractor trailer rig. The trailer was backed through the roll-back door opening of the garage. An electric hoist over the mechanic's pit allowed Andy to pick up the container using hooks on the four corners of the container's top. The flatbed trailer could drive out from under the container. Once trade with King Fahd flourished, Andy bought more containers, several flatbed trailers and another diesel rig. Within a year, Andy had five shipping containers and Lindsey had developed three different types of catalogs.

The king would deposit payment into one of four Swiss accounts, which were not opened in Andy or Lindsey's names. Looking at the big picture of international trade, the volume of goods exchanged between the king and Lindsey was insignificant to the U.S. Because Andy knew how the U.S. government used the IRS to punish its own citizens, he was careful to avoid taxes legally.

Lindsey had asked the king to buy her a complex multi-channel radioisotope analyzer to evaluate soil samples, uranium samples, and plutonium samples in her private underground physics lab. Buying such equipment in her own name would have drawn unwanted attention, even for a nuclear physicist.

Amazing things changed hands. The king ordered 200 black negligees and Andy ordered one half ounce of the sweat of a Golden Poison Frog from Nicaragua called Phyllobates terribilis. Andy concentrated on stocking the Confederate cave with the modern weapons he felt would be necessary as America slid further toward anarchy.

As the word spread among the wives of the royal family, Lindsey realized that the king not only had many wives, he also had hundreds of princesses, hundreds of wealthy mothers-in-law, and thousands of female relatives.

The Saudis had unlimited funds to spend. Lindsey's personal profit from this trade rocketed to $10 million within two years. Much of this money was invested in foreign currencies and commodities, but not under Andy's name. In Andy's view, the U.S. dollar was doomed. Both Lindsey and the king were enormously satisfied with their relationship.

Andy had a special ally in the Saudi Arabian Embassy in Washington. Sahar, a young Saudi woman whom Andy had rescued in the desert more than a decade before, had married a Saudi diplomat. She traveled frequently to Saudi Arabia and also enjoyed the confidence of the king, primarily because of her friendship with Dr. Carlson. Sahar had been recruited as a partner in Lindsey's business. She gave Lindsey insight into what Saudi women wanted. She also managed the Carlsons' financial assets in overseas accounts and provided Andy with a secure encrypted email system through the Saudi Embassy.

It was clear to Andy that the U.S. government could never repay its debts or balance its budget. Heeding his great-great grandfather's advice, which he had found in a letter on a stack of Confederate gold bars in his cave, he prepared for the day when Americans would overthrow their oppressive government. The price of oil had taken the civility out of many Americans already. Every car required a locked gas cap. The only thing preventing riots in most American cities was the power grid. Whenever power was lost, for even an hour, massive looting and violence broke out. The federal government was clearly out of control and unable to govern. Flashpoints of anarchy at home cast a poor light on the priorities of green energy and global warming, constantly shoved down the throats of Americans by the government. America could not protect itself with green energy, yet its government refused to develop its own oil resources. Muslim fundamentalists had brought war to America already, but it was politically incorrect to say this or to exclude them from traveling freely in the U.S.

Andy and Ben chose weapons for the Confederate cave that could be carried by hand and had been proven effective against a heavily armed enemy in guerilla wars. Gradually, fifty to 100 at a time, they bought American-manufactured FIM-92 Stinger shoulder-fired surface to air missiles, Russian-made RPG-7 shoulder-mounted anti-tank rocket propelled grenades, Chinese-made AK-47 assault weapons, British 60-80 mm mortars, American-made AT4 CS recoilless rifles, American-made grenades, American M-16 rifles, and hundreds of containers full of ammunition.

Blessed with an almost endless amount of underground storage space, Andy could keep these weapons in their original packing cases, still coated with grease. Andy was doing exactly what his ancestors had done. The cave system had weapons dating back to the 1600s. According to John Andrew Carlson's notes in the family Bible, the Carlsons had continuously maintained an arsenal from 1750 until the Civil War ended.

After twenty-two hours of snoozing and reflection, Andy felt the CIA jet slow and begin its descent into Saudi airspace.

7.

Andy was greeted in Riyadh with a limousine and a rapid ride to one of the king's palaces. Security officers stood at every corner. Saudi Arabia was on a wartime footing.

The king greeted Andy with a warm handshake. They retired to a private chamber and sat in Western chairs. Andy knew that the king did not like Western furniture. It was a measure of the king's good will toward him. King Fahd wore his sixty years well. His white robe was trimmed with crimson and extended over his head, revealing only his face. Andy could see the strain around his friend's eyes.

"King Fahd, let me extend my family's deepest condolences for your loss and pledge my help." Andy spoke in Arabic. He knew that the king spoke English. Which language was used was up to the king.

The king nodded and smiled. The smile meant that the king appreciated his omission of the usual bullshit greeting from a representative of Umar.

The king raised his left hand and a servant appeared with two drinks. Andy took a sip of Dr. Pepper. The king never forget personal details. He knew all of the birthdays in Andy's family. He knew to avoid conversations with Ava.

Andy continued in Arabic, "You know, my friend, that I hold you in the highest respect and that I would not intrude upon you at this time of trouble were it not a matter of vital importance. I am here as your friend first, and as a representative of the United States second."

The king switched to English. "Thank you, Andy."

Andy pulled the letter out of his suit pocket. "Please read this, and then we'll talk further. This letter was received by President Umar two days before the bombing at Ras Tanura."

The king reached for his spectacles on a table next to his chair. He studied the letter. As he read, his brow betrayed him. When he completed reading, he closed his eyes and bowed his head. For a few moments, he guarded his reaction to more bad news.

When he lifted his head, the king spoke without emotion. "We don't know for certain who is responsible for the destruction of Ras Tanura. The United States should know that I do not want a Middle East war. Our oil business depends on some measure of stability in the Middle East."

"I believe you, King Fahd, but I fear the reaction of Americans toward your kingdom if nuclear weapons are exploded on American soil. I know that you can't control all the extremists in your country, any more than we can control all of the extremists in our country. Some Saudis would love to see a war with Israel. Some are large contributors to organizations that the United States classifies as terrorists."

"America has used terrorism on many groups of people, both in its own country and abroad. I am sick of the Americans pointing their fingers at the Middle East and using that word. Was burning down the teepees of the American Indians and killing their women and children not terrorism? Was the fire-bombing of every large city in Japan not terrorism? Until a few days ago, the U.S. was the only nation ever to use nuclear weapons on another country. America is the world's biggest hypocrite and the world's greatest terrorist."

The smile that greeted Andy had vanished.

"I agree that the United States has used terrorism to advance its own agendas," Andy said. "I cannot defend my country in that regard. However, our countries now have common enemies. Let us work from there."

"A war with Israel would have catastrophic consequences," said the king. "Once all of the hatred of Arabs for the Jews is let out of the bottle, it will not be easy to force it back in. The war would be bloody and solve nothing. Even if the last Jew were killed, the Shiites and Sunnis would fight over the same land. The oil trade would be a casualty of this war, and the world economy would suffer greatly."

"My sentiments exactly," Andy said. "Let us move on to an issue of great importance to you. The United States is prepared to protect Saudi Arabia and your oilfields and pipelines in exchange for information and greater access to Saudi oil."

The king stood and walked around the luxurious room. When the king did this, he wanted everyone else in the room to remain seated.

"What information?" he asked.

"Umar needs help identifying who is responsible for the Islamic Jihad."

The king returned to his chair. "We are interested in such an offer."

"King Fahd, if war breaks out, Umar would expect you to publicly denounce it and prohibit members of the royal family from contributing to the war. Regardless of what some members of the royal family may think of America, they should appreciate that the U.S. has the ability to protect your ports and oilfields."

"Does Umar want to put boots on Saudi ground?" the king asked.

"Only if you specifically requested them," Andy said. "We can protect you with our warships and surveillance resources. Most importantly, sir, our loyalty would be to the House of Saud, and to no other faction in Saudi Arabia."

"You are making great promises, Dr. Carlson. Will your president abide by this understanding?"

"You have my word. That is the best that I can do."

"Your word has always been enough for me. I will arrange more access for American tankers in our Red Sea ports."

"Thank you, King Fahd. What is your own assessment of the Islamic Jihad?"

"The worshipers of violence in our region are legion," the king said. "We do not lack for ruthless, power-hungry people who hide behind religious zeal. Hamas stepped up its rocket attacks on Israel when President Umar began supporting the Muslim Brotherhood. Hezbollah owns southern Lebanon and already threatens Israel with shoulder rockets paid for by Iran, who also supports Syrian warmongers. By themselves, neither Hamas nor Hezbollah could pull off such an operation as this. Neither could a weakened Al Qaeda. There is only one country in the Middle East with the money and the insanity-in-charge to start such a war."

Andy said, "I trust your judgment."

"President Ahmadinejad of Iran was a long-time thorn in our side. Although he has been pushed aside by the ruling ayatollahs, the fundamentalist nature of the regime is unchanged. They still want nuclear weapons. These fundamentalists see themselves in a continuous religious war, not a political war. America refuses to recognize this fact. Your president projects weakness while wrapping himself in the cloak of Islam. To an Islamic fundamentalist, anyone who is not a follower of Islam is an infidel. In their minds, all infidels must be killed eventually. The chief infidels are Israel, the United States, and Great Britain, although Jihadists are active in hundreds of other countries. Every Muslim does not believe as the fundamentalists, but every German didn't believe the Nazi fundamentalists. America's chief enemy, as well as my own, is Iran. Iran seeks the domination of the Arab world by Shiites and the worldwide destruction of infidels. When you have madmen as your neighbors, you never feel safe. Some of those organizations that your country calls terrorist are necessary to balance the power of Iran. We are never quite certain whether Iran is more interested in nuclear weapons to use against Israel or to use against Sunnis."

"Our president has been reluctant to give up on his sanctions against Iran," Andy said. "He won't act against an Islamic country without concrete evidence. If Iran is the instigator of this Middle East War and Islamic Jihad, we must find objective evidence for it."

"I did not expect that Iran was capable of producing and delivering several nuclear warheads to the U.S. and Great Britain," the king said.

"I told Umar that I believe the Islamic Jihad warheads have been in America since the Cold War. They are old Soviet tactical nuclear weapons. I may be able to identify the person who sold them to the Iranians."

"I'm happy that you are the person who brings this information to me," the king said. "I know you, Andy. You already have a plan to find this person."

"My priority is to find the warheads in the U.S. If the warheads in America and Britain can be found before a Middle East war begins, the Iranian blackmail would unravel."

"I agree," the king said, "but this is a tall order, even for a man as resourceful as you."

"King Fahd, have you heard anything about a successor to Boris, the late ex-KGB arms dealer--someone who could still be selling old Soviet Cold War warheads?"

"No, I haven't."

"Would you use your resources to search for him in the Middle East?" Andy asked. "I think that he does exist, and he goes by the name of Aleksi. I do not know his last name."

"I will be happy to do this. If he spends any time in this part of the world, I can probably find him."

"I suspect that he lives in the United States, but travels here," Andy said. "I'm certain that he's the source of the warheads that now threaten the U.S. and Britain, as well as the source of the warhead used at Ras Tanura."

"How can you be so sure?" the king asked.

"I killed Boris on my farm ten years ago," Andy said. "Boris and Aleksi were in business together. I was trying to buy as many warheads as possible to keep them out of the hands of people like Ahmadinejad. Although my friend Ben and I killed every person on site who knew about the Confederate gold, Aleksi did not come to the battle."

"Have you told your president about this man?"

"The president doesn't know anything of Aleksi," Andy said. "If he did, he would surely bungle any effort to use him to find the location of the warheads before they're detonated."

"What do you mean by 'bungle'?" asked the king. "My English is good, but I'm not familiar with this term."

"President Kennedy bungled the Bay of Pigs. President Carter bungled the Iranian hostage crisis. President Johnson bungled the Viet Nam War. Nixon bungled a simple burglary. President Clinton bungled his chance to kill Osama bin Laden. President George W. Bush bungled us into an unnecessary Iraqi War. Our Islamic president has bungled us into the vulnerable military situation we are now in. And Ronald Reagan is dead."

"Mr. Reagan also bungled a few things," said the king, "but he had leadership skills which I have not seen in an American president since he left office. I like the word bungle. We have bunglers here, in my own family. Tell me why this man you call Aleksi should come to you."

"Aleksi knows about the gold that I have," Andy said. "Boris wouldn't go to war on my farm without telling his partner what was at stake. They both worked for the KGB at one time. They may even have been related. They apparently needed each other to do business. Aleksi has been dreaming of Confederate gold for almost a decade, waiting for an opportunity to go after it, watching the gold price move higher and higher. What was worth a few dollars an ounce in 1865 is worth 5,600 dollars an ounce today."

"Do you think he has spies in Farmville?'

"I do," Andy said. "Aleksi has already been to my farm once, to sell me warheads. This is why I'm reluctant to leave town except to see a friend like you. There is a fair-sized community of Russian immigrants in the Farmville area. A spy could easily fit in."

Andy had learned to read the king's eyes, a valuable asset in Arab countries, where eyes might be the only part of another person visible, male or female.

The king recognized the plan. "You want to invite Aleksi to your farm."

"That's exactly what I would like to do."

"I've heard stories about people going to your farm and not coming back. I'm sure that these were all evil people."

"Of course, King Fahd. I've taught my family that anyone who comes to our farm to kill or to steal should be killed. This has been the policy of my family since 1743. 4000 acres is a lot of room for graves."

"That's an enlightened policy, Dr. Carlson, one that I believe myself."

"If you could announce in three days that my entire family will be your guest at one of your palaces, Aleksi would likely see this as his last opportunity to get the gold."

"His last opportunity?"

"If he's involved in the pending destruction of American cities with Russian warheads," Andy said, "he will likely be preparing to relocate. The International Atomic Energy Agency will determine the origin of these warheads. The CIA will be looking at all Russian-born citizens and travelers. It seems likely that he has made arrangements to leave the country before the warheads are detonated. He would have difficulty resisting an opportunity to leave America with nearly 400 bars of gold."

"What if you capture him? What incentive does he have to tell you about Iranians?"

"Aleksi will know where the warheads in the United States cities are because he is the source of them. He will tell me what I want to know on one condition."

"That you will kill him if he doesn't talk?"

"No, he will tell me because he plans to shoot me as soon as he sees the gold."

"Why shouldn't he lie?"

"I will make him prove that he's not lying," Andy said. "I won't show him the gold until he tells me what I need to know. Shooting me before he sees the gold would do him no good. He knows that the gold is underground and that he isn't likely to access it without my help."

"What days do you wish to say that you are my guest?"

"How about Friday, Saturday, and Sunday, three days away? You could give an announcement tomorrow and say that you have called me to discuss the tensions in the Middle East, the destruction of Ras Tanura, the price of oil, etc., and give the exact time of my visit. While I'm supposed to be here, you could make further announcements about our discussions."

"I understand, and it will be done," the king said.

"King Fahd, the International Atomic Energy Agency is already studying soil samples from Ras Tanura. As you know, Lindsey is a nuclear physicist. Testing soil from sources of radiation is one of her specialties. You have helped her buy equipment for her lab. Why not give her some soil samples, so that you can better interpret the results announced by the IAEA?"

"There is no one I would trust more," the king said. "There are several Russians here already with the IAEA, probably to guide the results. I will have soil samples packaged for you to take back to Farmville."

"Thank you. Please forgive me, but I have one further request. I must fly home in the president's jet, but once I'm back in the U.S. I don't want the president or anyone else to track me. Could you lend me a personal jet and a pilot?"

"I'm so glad you asked," the king said. "I just purchased a new jet, a Cessna Citation X. This plane travels 700 MPH. I can get you into almost any country with it, using diplomatic credentials. The pilot speaks English and Arabic. He is trustworthy."

"What kind of markings are on this plane?"

"I had it registered to a leasing company in the United States, so that it would be difficult for anyone to know who was on board. I don't like my subjects to know when I'm out of my kingdom, either."

"That sounds like what I need," Andy said. "Ask the pilot to follow the president's CIA jet back home and to call me when he lands at Farmville's airport."

"Should you need doors opened, I can do this for you. You would be surprised at what countries will do for oil these days."

8.

On the flight home Andy reviewed the security measures on the farm. Inviting Aleksi to visit was risky, but he could see no other way to establish contact with the man who had already provided nuclear weapons to terrorists.

Since the twins were born, Andy had made several key changes in the cave system. A new underground tunnel connected the gun closet in the basement of the farmhouse with I-95, the north-south section of the cave system running underneath the farm. Through this tunnel, the family could move from the farmhouse north to the Grand Chamber of the Confederate Cave or south to the 1743 plantation house without being seen.

Ben Carlson lived on the edge of the Carlson farm with his wife Precious and their three kids. Ben ran much of the day-to-day business of the farm, including the procurement of weapons and the tending of alfalfa fields. A tunnel connected Ben's barn with the I-40 East tunnel, making it possible for Ben and Andy to cover each other's backs.

The farm now had a continuous renewable electric source. In the early 1800s slaves had dug a canal on the Carlson plantation that spanned a quarter-mile neck in the Appomattox River. The canal was used to divert part of the water in the Appomattox River to a grist mill, which was powered by a waterwheel. Andy rebuilt this waterwheel and created his own power station.

The water wheel in the canal was an undershot type, as opposed to the overshot wheel in the grist mill next to Andy's farmhouse. Water flowing under the bottom half of the steel wheel turned the wheel backwards. Using a combination of gears, the water power was harnessed by a generator, which charged huge batteries. Inverters converted the direct current from the batteries into alternating current required by common appliances. When the batteries were fully charged, the generator shut off automatically. This entire operation could be monitored from the Grand Chamber or the farmhouse.

Ben and Andy worked on the electrification of the cave system for two years. Every tunnel and chamber now had electricity and lighting. The system was quiet, the transmission lines were all underground in three and a half miles of conduit, and the source of power was far more reliable than the local electric cooperative. No matter what was going on in the deteriorating world above ground, the Confederate cave offered reliable power, a modest hospital, weapons, an independent water source, secure communications, and huge storerooms for supplies and food.

Andy installed outdoor cameras throughout the farm. These cameras could be monitored in the farmhouse or the Grand Chamber. Every foot of his perimeter, except that protected by the Appomattox River, had eight-foot chain link fences topped with two strands of electrified wire. The fences had motion detectors. On the south side of the river opposite the farm were two prisons, a tri-county facility and an immigration facility. These prisons were surrounded by tall electric fences that extended to the river and along its south bank. An intruder from the south would have to break into one of the prisons or float down the river underneath the lights of the perimeter fences of the two prisons.

Gun tragedies and crime related to blackouts had been used by the government to solidify its monopoly on weapons. The removal of weapons from the populace was sold as a means of suppressing violence. It seemed so natural and logical to the naïve. Take away the guns and nobody can get killed. Many gladly gave up their personal liberties and the right to self defense, thinking the world would be safer.

Since Umar's re-election, the pendulum in America had swung decidedly against gun control. As city government's ability to constrain crime deteriorated, Americans demanded their guns back. The government restricted the lawful purchase of guns and ammunition by expanding its permit process and squeezing gun makers with the IRS. Criminals never gave up their guns.

Andy worried most about his daughter Ava, who had not yet hit her growth spurt. While her brains and manipulative skills were formidable, she did not have an inconspicuous personal weapon, like the knife Jack always carried in his boot. After careful research, Andy decided on a weapon for Ava that would have both offensive and defensive capabilities.

The box had arrived by UPS.

"This is the weapon that you will use to protect yourself and your family," Andy said.

Ava watched her dad cut open the box on the coffee table in the great room of the farmhouse. He handed her a hollow wooden tube, eighteen inches long, three quarters of an inch in diameter. "This is a blowgun, but I'm not through with it."

"It's not ready to use?" she asked.

"I'm going to disguise this blow gun as a clarinet. I'll cut your clarinet lengthwise and insert the blowgun. You will have a front and rear sight."

Ava turned the blowgun over in her hands.

"This is a deadly weapon," Andy said, "even for someone with your small lung capacity."

"What do you mean, deadly?"

"I want you to start out with plain darts, which have tiny points on one end and a fluff of cotton on the other. This cotton fluff stabilizes the dart in flight. Because it fits snugly inside the gun, none of your breath is wasted when you blow into it."

"What can little points do?" she asked.

"That depends on what's on the tip of the points," Andy said. "I have two drugs that I can put on the tip of your darts. We'll make a little reservoir for each drug and a magazine for extra darts. You would stick the dart tip into the rubber cover of the drug reservoirs. The blowgun would be loaded by removing the mouthpiece of the clarinet. The first drug will temporarily paralyze any animal or human being for four to five minutes. The other drug will put the animal or human being to sleep, but they won't wake up."

"Does that mean I don't necessarily have to kill something to protect myself?" she asked.

"That's exactly what it means," he said. "You should avoid the second drug unless I specifically tell you to use it. This second drug comes from the sweat of a Golden Poison frog from Nicaragua called Phyllobates terribilis. The first drug is a muscle relaxant. It will allow you to practice on small varmints, like groundhogs."

"Then groundhogs better get off the farm," Ava said. "I'm tired of stepping in their holes."

"You can put a sling on this clarinet and take it anywhere because nobody else will know how to use it."

"How far can it shoot?" she asked.

"That's up to you, Ava. I believe that you'll soon be able to hit an apple every time at thirty yards. That should be your first goal. I'll teach you how to load it safely. I want you to be able to protect yourself as well as support the other members of your family."

"Do you think we'll get attacked again here on the farm?" she asked.

"Absolutely," Andy said. "There is one other feature that I like about your weapon."

"What's that?"

"You can shoot it through the vertical firing slots in our magic stumps," he said. "That gives you a safe firing position. No one can hear your weapon and no one will know where the dart came from. You will be a sneaky little girl."

"Wow," she said, turning the blowgun over in her hands.

"Dad, was Mom a sneaky girl?"

"The sneakiest I ever met, Ava, but you don't have to tell her that. Let's go try it a few times before we make a clarinet out of it."

On the way outside, Andy calculated that it would take about one hour for the information to go from Ava to Jack to Lindsey, who would want a detailed explanation as to why she was considered sneaky years ago.

Andy concluded that the twins were ready.

He was smiling when the CIA jet made its descent to Andrews Air Force Base.

9.

A limousine escorted Andy to the White House. Andy relayed the king's assessment that Iran was likely behind the destruction of Ras Tanura, as well as the nuclear threats to American and British cities. The king had agreed to refrain from involvement in an Arab-Israeli war. He had promised to find objective evidence for Iran's involvement in the Islamic Jihad. More oil would be coming to the U.S. from Saudi ports on the Red Sea.

"Has the IAEA examined soil from Ras Tanura?" the president asked.

"No conclusions yet. I brought some soil samples back for my wife."

"Since you left we've had communication with the Israelis," the president said. "They're convinced that it's time for a first strike against Natanz, Iran's chief nuclear weapons facility. Israel has a history of first strikes against an Iraqi nuclear facility and a reported nuclear facility in Syria. It's going to be difficult to restrain them in this instance."

"The king has many sources of information," Andy said. "He feels that a breakthrough is imminent. He promised to give me daily updates. Perhaps you can convince the Israelis not to act unilaterally. I fear the consequences of an Israeli attack on Iran at this time."

"Take this card, Dr. Carlson." The president fished a card out of his jacket pocket. "If you don't have the satellite phone with you, use any of these numbers. I'll respond twenty-four hours a day."

"Thank you, sir," Andy said, reaching for the card. "What's the CIA doing?"

"CIA activities are classified, Dr. Carlson."

"I'll let you know when I hear from King Fahd," Andy said.

"Let me know about the soil samples, too."

Andy pulled in front of the farmhouse in his S-10 Chevy truck, which he had left at the Farmville Municipal Airport. He anticipated a warm greeting. Lindsey was standing on the brick walkway in front of the farmhouse. She wasn't smiling. He surmised that she had heard him drive over the heavy planks in the covered bridge. Something was definitely wrong.

Andy opened the door of his truck and attempted a smile.

"Andy Carlson, was it truly necessary for you to tell your son before you left that he was probably going to have lots of brothers and sisters because his mom was hot?"

Andy could think of no good answer to this question, but he was an agile man.

"Honey, that was a terrible choice of words," he said. "You know how inquisitive he is. He keeps asking questions until you say something that's over his head. It's no excuse. You're right. I'm sorry."

"You're sorry. And you think that's all it takes to smooth this over, don't you?"

"No, Lindsey. I made a big mistake. I should have come up with another explanation of family size."

He dropped his briefcase and held out his arms.

She lunged toward him, wrapped her arms around his chest, and soaked up her tears with his shirt. Her distress seemed out of proportion to his offense, but Andy thought he should tread lightly.

He dug his handkerchief out of pocket and offered it to her. She grabbed it. The sobbing died down as he led her to the bench in the front yard. They sat down.

"Your comment was poor timing, Andy," she said, blowing her nose. "It's not all your fault. Well, it's mostly your fault. I was catching up on all the stuff in my lab. I got the new curtains up in the great room. You finally agreed to move two of your animal heads out of the house and into the Cow Palace."

Andy wondered where this was going. Two short figures were standing in the doorway, behind the storm door. They were watching, keeping a safe distance.

"Andy, I'm pregnant again," she said. "Eight weeks." She looked away.

He tried not to flinch, but he did anyway. After a moment of indecision, he got down on his knees and wiggled his chest between her legs. His hands found hers. He forced their fingers together, palm to palm.

"Lindsey, I know that this is not what we planned."

"I just got busy and missed a few pills."

"Nevertheless, a child is a gift," Andy said. "You are a wonderful mother. We have two children who could pass for Jurassic Park creations. They are very demanding. You bear the majority of the responsibility for raising them. I'm negligent that I don't tell you every day how much I admire you for what you do to make this family work."

She straightened up. Their eyes locked.

"I love you so much," he said. "And that love has brought us another blessing. Let's approach this positively. I promise that I will help more. Let's recruit the twins to help us. They're smarter than we are. We should make sure they understand your having another child is going to require some responsibility on their part."

"Okay," she said, handing the handkerchief back.

Andy stood up and took her hand. They walked toward the front door of the farmhouse. Ava and Jack hadn't moved from their position behind the storm door.

As Lindsey approached the front steps, Jack opened the door. "Mom, are you feeling better?"

"Yes, I'm feeling better."

"And Dad fixed her," Ava said.

"Your father is a good ass-kisser," Lindsey said.

"What does that mean?" Ava asked.

The family exchanged hugs underneath the watchful eyes of fifteen Pope and Young record book animal heads in the great room, mostly antlered animals. Andy had reassured Lindsey that other people decorated their houses this way, especially if all the animals in the house were taken with a bow and arrow. Lindsey did believe in blessings from God, like the child she was carrying. In her eyes, it was a blessing that Andy only invited the ED staff to his house of animal heads. How many people could know about his limitations?

"Your father has volunteered to answer all of your questions for the next few weeks," Lindsey said. "I will make colorful and provocative comments from time to time, about anything and everything, and your father has agreed to explain what you don't understand. So remember, all explanations come from Dad, beginning right now."

Solomon himself could not have come up with a wiser verdict, Andy concluded. He would accept his punishment.

"You didn't say what an ass-kisser was, Mom," Ava said.

Lindsey smiled and opened her hand, gesturing toward Andy.

"Ava," Andy said, "a good ass-kisser is someone who can admit his mistakes and is willing to do just about anything to make up for them, including kiss your mom right here." Andy put his hand on his right buttock.

"Do other people kiss Mom like that?" Ava asked.

"Oh no, it's a special treat just to keep me humble."

"What mistake did you make?" Jack asked.

"I was insensitive regarding your mother's desirability as a woman. It was a crude comment."

"That sounds serious," Jack said, stroking an imaginary beard. "Could this have been your comment about Mom being h..."

"That's the one," Andy interrupted. "And it's the kind of comment a husband shouldn't make about his wife, especially in front of her children. It's also the kind of comment that a man's son should have had the good sense to keep to himself."

Jack lowered his head.

Ava turned toward Jack, nodding and frowning.

"Whatever it means, it didn't go over well," Ava said.

"After supper, I'll explain everything," Andy said.

"I certainly hope this isn't going to be a monologue," Jack said.

"Nope. It's going to be better than that. In fact, let's hold all of your questions until we eat. Then I will offer both of you all the wisdom that I have."

"Sometimes men are so full of it," Ava said.

After grace was said and everybody had at least taken a mouthful of food, Andy waded into the swift current. "One night about eight weeks ago I felt a special kind of love toward your mother."

"You mean that you wanted to have sex with her?" Jack asked.

"Yes, I did. And it was wonderful. It was so wonderful that God made a baby that night. And this baby will be your brother or sister in about seven months."

Jack and Ava looked at each other.

"Can we choose?" Ava asked.

"No, we just take what God gives us. But your mom will have a test in about six weeks that will tell us whether it's a boy or a girl."

"You breezed over the sex part," Ava said. "Exactly why was it so wonderful and how did you and God and Mom make this baby?"

Andy said, "About a year ago I bought a book just for this occasion. It's called *When Your Child Asks About Sex*. It's loaded with pictures and explanations that are far more informative than I could be. Let me find it for you when we've finished eating."

"I smell a cop-out," Ava said.

"You're right," Andy said. "It is a cop-out. But it's the best I can do after twenty-three hours on a jet. If I had known I would be greeted with this news, I would have prepared a much better explanation. Please forgive me."

"Okay," Ava said, "you're forgiven."

Jack nodded his forgiveness.

"The important thing for you to recognize now is that having a baby growing inside you can make you tired, and sick to your stomach, and overwhelmed," Andy said. "Each one of us must give up some of the selfish things that we do and be more supportive of your mother. She needs our help. Remember, she'll have to continue home schooling even though she has all of the extra stress of being pregnant."

"Why did you and Mom wait almost ten years to get together with God again?" Ava asked. "I'd like to know why we don't have any brothers or sisters already."

"A very good question," Andy said, raising his index finger. "One that deserves a detailed answer. After you've read the book, I'll try to answer it."

Andy glanced at Lindsey. Her smile was way too enthusiastic.

"What can we do to help?" Jack asked.

"Tomorrow we're going to Wal-Mart and buy a chalkboard," Andy said. "I intend to attach this chalkboard to the back of the kitchen door. Each of you will have a list of assignments that Mom will write on the chalkboard. It will be your responsibility to complete the jobs that you're assigned and then draw a line through them."

"I think Dad should have his name on the chalkboard, too," Ava said.

Lindsey finally opened her mouth. "I think that we should vote on whether Dad should have a list on the chalkboard."

Three hands shot up.

"I'm a victim of democracy," Andy said. "Lindsey, I brought you some soil samples from Ras Tanura. They're in a lead footlocker in the truck."

"Then I take back all the things I told the kids about you while you were gone."

10.

T wo dark figures waded along the south bank of the Appomattox River. They wore black wetsuits and dark running shoes. The wetsuits covered everything but their faces, which were darkened with face paint. Each wore an empty shoulder holster underneath the left arm and a dark fanny pack. Each held a .45 caliber semi-automatic pistol with a silencer over his head. They located a natural crossing point upstream from the prisons by following deer tracks in the sand. Two sandbars opposite each other left only twenty yards of water to wade. The deepest water at this point was four feet.

The current was not overpowering. By a half moon and starlight, they walked slowly toward the deer tracks on the sandbar on the north bank of the river. They followed the north bank, holding onto roots that jutted into the river, sometimes in two feet of water, sometimes on sand and rocks. The taller of the two led the way. When they reached the prison fences, they slid back into the water and duck-walked until they found the landmark they were looking for.

Logs, rocks, and stumps choked the river just below Dr. Carlson's farmhouse. They tried to climb the muddy north bank at this obstruction in the river, but there was nothing firm enough to grasp. They holstered their pistols. The mud felt like axle grease in their hands. The smaller of the two slipped and fell backward into the water.

The tall figure moved closer to the pile of debris at the choke point. He found a large root from an oak tree. Eventually the water would uproot this tree completely and it would fall into the river. He climbed the root to level ground and rolled onto his back above the mud. The shorter figure climbed the same root, and then reached for an outstretched arm. They sat on the bank and checked their gear. Each pulled a fanny pack around and unzipped it.

"My phone was in a zip-lock bag," a woman's voice said, "but it's wet. It may not work. I think I fell on it."

"Mine looks okay," a man's voice said. "Use your towel to clean your pistol."

She wiped the pistol carefully and then pulled the slide back, ejecting a round. "It's fine."

"This trip may turn out to be useless," said the man, "but it's worth a try for 900 million dollars in gold. Dr. Carlson thinks he's set a trap for us. It's too much of a coincidence for him to advertise his family's absence so shortly after Ras Tanura. I think our odds of getting the gold are much higher with the Carlsons at home than if they're gone."

"I wish we had time to discuss this before you arrived," she said.

"The best way to get this gold is not to search for it," the man said. "We must take a hostage. We know that the family is hiding together. No one can rescue them. They're expecting us to break in and expose ourselves. Instead, we will sit quietly and wait for one of them to make a mistake."

"I'm certain Dr. Carlson and his family are here this weekend," she said. "I've been sitting in that house on the corner of Plank Road and South Airport Road watching the two of them come and go every day. The Richmond paper said they left Friday morning, but no jets have landed or taken off from the airport in three days. I know their vehicles. None of them has passed my house to go to another airport."

"It's clear they're expecting us," he said. "Dr. Carlson knows that I'm the only person who could sell Soviet weapons in the United States. He knows that Boris would tell me about his Confederate gold. What he doesn't know is that Boris was a fox hunter in the Old Country. He taught me even a fox can be fooled."

"I don't think that Dr. Carlson expects visitors who swim the river," she said, "probably because of the prison fences on the south bank.

He should have continued his fence along his side of the riverbank, like we have at our farm."

"If we can capture any member of his family," the man said, "we can get the gold. A man like Dr. Carlson would not allow his family to be shot for gold."

"I agree. He's a Boy Scout."

"I would even be willing to give him details of the warheads already sold in exchange for the gold," he said.

"Why would you do that?"

"Because preventing nuclear explosions is also more important to Carlson than gold," he said. "The Americans are fond of saying dead men tell no tales."

"Aleksi, I've played in the back yard with those children. I know where the motion sensors and cameras are, but you must not underestimate these kids. They're intelligent and they can use weapons. Either one of them is capable of killing, especially that little raptor named Jack."

"I will keep this in mind, Sasha. If we can't take a hostage tonight, we'll just wait for another night. Carlson probably thinks I'm leaving the country. This fox does not know that he is the prey."

11.

The Carlson family was nestled in the cave for the weekend, planning to watch the monitors and motion detectors for any sign of intruders on the farm. The only scheduled excitement was the twins' tenth birthday on Saturday.

On Friday night, Andy had reviewed the plans for the weekend with the family.

"There will probably be some intruders on the farm this weekend," he said. "They think that we're out of town and they want to steal the gold."

"But we're not going to let them," Jack said.

"No sir, young man. And I'm depending on both you and your sister to follow orders. During a battle it's not permissible to argue about an order. This isn't like your mom asking you to take out the trash. You may be able to delay taking out the trash by asking your mom if you can finish what you're working on first. But in a battle, everyone must do exactly as he or she is told, or we could all get killed."

"I'd like to paralyze somebody," Ava said.

"You may have such an opportunity, Ava, so be ready. We have important advantages on the farm with all of the secret passages and tunnels, but we can't squander these advantages by doing something stupid. If I want you to use your clarinet, I'll tell you exactly what your firing position will be and what your target will be. I will hand you the clarinet if the dart has been dipped in the sweat of the terrible frog from Nicaragua."

"That's the drug I haven't gotten to use yet," she said.

"Yes. I pray that you won't be forced to use your weapon on a human being, but if that human being threatens any one of us, I might order you to shoot that person. If I'm not there to give that order, you must make the decision to shoot on your own."

"I understand."

"You know your firing positions--the magic stump next to the garage, the overhead limbs of the willow oak on the right side of the path near the garage, and the magic stump in the front of the farmhouse."

"I will show them no mercy," she said.

"Where did you hear that?" Lindsey asked.

"Jack taught me," Ava said. "He said that if these people were our friends, they wouldn't be sneaking in here. If they bring weapons here, we should defend ourselves and this farm to the last man ...or woman."

"That's what I said," Jack said.

Andy turned toward his son. "Jack, there are two weapons that you will be responsible for this weekend. The first is your bow and hunting arrows. Make sure that they're ready to go. When I give you an order, you must obey it immediately, especially if it is an order to kill. This is a hard lesson. Both of you have killed deer and bear. Unlike the game we hunt for food, the people coming here this weekend are not noble animals. They would shoot children to get what they want. You must understand beforehand that the only way to stop such people is to kill them. There is nothing noble about dying just because you are a child. You must appreciate that people who have not seen hundreds of dead children cannot understand the need for children to protect themselves. Let your arrows do your talking. We owe them nothing more than we gave the Yankees who invaded this farm 150 years ago."

The kids nodded toward each other and to their dad.

"Jack, the other weapon you'll be responsible for is the AT4 Anti-Armor rifle. You've fired a bunch of tracer rounds on the power line. Two HEAT rounds are under the bush hog with two tubes."

Jack said, "I like the night vision scope."

"Those little toys cost 2500 dollars each from Mr. Pollard in

Buckingham," Andy said, "and another 3500 dollars for each night scope. If someone plans to haul gold off the farm this weekend, they'll have a truck parked somewhere nearby. If we get the opportunity, that truck will be your target."

Jack began smiling and humming a tune. Lindsey closed her eyes and concentrated on the melody. It wasn't really a melody. He hummed the same five notes, over and over. She must be mistaken. She had personally locked out all access to Quentin Tarantino movies. There was no way for Jack to know her password. She changed it once a month. And Jack would never go snooping where she hid passwords.

"Lindsey is second in command," Andy said. "Should something happen to me, or you can't locate me, then she'll tell you what to do. Keep your cell phones on vibrate."

"Nothing is going to happen to you, Dad," Ava said, "as long as I have a dart dipped in the sweat of the terrible frog from Nicaragua."

"I appreciate that."

Ava began to hum Jack's repetitious five notes.

Lindsey looked at Andy, who shrugged his shoulders. He was tone deaf. Her only daughter, who would be ten years old tomorrow, was humming a tune popularized by a female Japanese rock and roll band in a Tarentino movie, *Kill Bill*. While the band played, Uma Thurman had sliced up eighty-eight sword fighters with a Hattori Hanzo sword.

"For now, we're all staying in the cave and watching the monitors," Lindsey said. "If you don't mind, kids, would you not sing that song?"

Friday night passed uneventfully. By Saturday evening the kids were restless.

"Dad, can we go for a walk in the tunnel?" Jack asked.

"I need some exercise," Ava said.

"We need to stay together this weekend, as we planned," Andy said. "If you go for a walk, something important could happen while you're gone. Who would I have to give orders to?"

This explanation seemed to make sense to the kids, who returned to their computers.

After supper, Lindsey finished the icing on the birthday cake and reached for the candles. A wave of disappointment crashed over her. The birthday candles were on the shelf in the kitchen of the farm-house, not on the shelf in the kitchen of the Confederate cave.

12.

Lindsey slipped out the tunnel from the Grand Chamber of the Confederate Cave onto I-95 south, toward the farmhouse. She turned on the tunnel lights. In ten minutes she was at the door inside the gun closet in the basement. After listening for five minutes, she punched in the security code, opened the steel door and closed it behind her.

The light from the half moon pointed the way up the basement stairs to the kitchen.

My twins are ten years old today. They'll have a playmate soon. My husband is a rock, a man without equal. He loves me. I am so blessed. But he's so paranoid. If I asked him, he wouldn't let me leave the cave for birthday candles. Men don't understand how important a tenth birthday is. Jack and Ava will remember this day for the rest of their lives. There's nothing on the monitors anywhere on the farm. I'll be back before anyone even knows I'm gone.

She tiptoed toward the kitchen cabinet to the left of the stove.

A strong forearm around her neck choked her until her knees buckled. She recognized the hard object in her back.

"Welcome home, Mrs. Carlson."

"Hello, Lindsey."

They were familiar voices.

The woman held her in the choke hold and shoved her toward the great room with the pistol in her back.

"It's nothing personal, Lindsey, just keep your mouth shut," Sasha said.

Aleksi turned on the table lamp next to the couch.

"Put her on the couch, face down," Aleksi said. "Tie her feet together. Tie her hands together."

"Lie down, Mrs. Carlson," he said, "or should I call you Lindsey?"

Aleksi tossed rope from his fanny pack to Sasha and sat down in Andy's leather chair. He scanned the room.

"I've never been inside this room," he said. "When I was here before, we conducted our business in the front yard. You were pregnant at the time. I didn't realize that your husband was such a hunter. So many animals on the wall. You didn't say what I should call you."

"You can call me Lindsey. And my husband is good at many things."

"So I've heard," he said. "If you see him again, tell him that home decorating is not his greatest achievement. I see only one picture in this room."

"That's General Robert E. Lee's portrait on the mantelpiece," Lindsey said. "It's a one-of-a-kind oil painting, a family heirloom."

"Sasha says you have twins. They don't deserve pictures?"

"We have lots of pictures of the children in our bedrooms," Lindsey said.

"Are your bedrooms also full of animal heads?"

"Not that many."

"I'm going to take your word for that, Lindsey," he said. "I've waited a long time for this opportunity."

Lindsey stared up at Sasha. She had pulled the head cap of her diver's suit back, exposing her blonde hair.

"Did you think that I have been living in that shack on the corner of Plank Road and South Airport Road just because I liked the neighborhood?"

"But I thought that you were our friend. What have we ever done to you?"

"I'd rather have 900 million dollars in gold than another friend," Sasha said. "Since you're going to die anyway, you may as well die with a happy thought in your head. I invited your husband to visit my bedroom on his way home, several times. He wasn't interested in having any women in his life except you and Ava."

"Thank you for telling me that, but I knew it already. Andy doesn't just say that he loves me. He shows me every day. He would die for me."

"He's going to get that opportunity," she said.

"I hate to interrupt," Aleksi said, "but we have a phone call to make to your husband. If you would give us the number, you can hear his voice one more time."

He held the receiver to her ear.

The phone rang in the Grand Chamber. Andy picked up the receiver.

"Andy, I'm sorry," Lindsey said. "Two people were in the farmhouse."

Aleksi pulled the phone away. "Dr. Carlson?"

"Yes." Andy recognized the voice.

"It's good to hear you again," Aleksi said. "You must know why we're here. I have a simple proposition for you. Either you hand over the gold or I'll kill your wife. My colleague has finished tying her up on your couch. You must tell me where you are."

"I'm at the garage," Andy said, "about 300 yards north of you, at the end of the gravel path. The gold is locked under the garage. I'll turn the light on and stand outside without a weapon. You'll see me in the light."

"Dr. Carlson, if I don't come back with some gold, my colleague will shoot your wife, probably after he has had his way with her. If he hears anything unusual, like a gunshot, he will shoot your wife and ask questions later. Do you understand?"

"I understand. You don't have to hurt my wife. I will help you load the gold."

"Be sure to stand outside where I can see you."

"I'll do that."

Andy hung up.

"ATTENTION," Andy called.

Jack and Ava ran to him.

"Your mother has been captured at the farmhouse. She's tied up on the couch. There is one person in the house who plans to shoot her within a few minutes. Another person is walking down the path to the garage to meet me. Here are your orders:

"Jack, take your hunting arrows and your stick bow and run as fast as you can through the tunnel to the farmhouse. Your target will have a gun. I want you to climb the stairs to the great room and shoot that person. Don't delay your shot for any reason. It doesn't matter who this person is. After you shoot, untie your mother. Both of you should return to the cave through the tunnel in the basement. Good luck, son."

Jack raced for his bow and quiver.

Andy picked Ava up and placed her on the coffee table facing the couch. He sat down in front of her and searched her eyes. "Ava, today you will become a warrior."

"Yes sir," she said.

Andy dipped the tip of one dart into the clarinet's reservoir of sweat from the terrible frog from Nicaragua. He inserted the dart in the clarinet and handed it to Ava.

"Take up a firing position in the magic stump in front of the garage," he said. "Climb up the steps and stay inside the stump. The light outside the garage will be on. You'll be able to see well through the vertical firing hole. A man will come to the garage and we will talk. This man will only give me information because he intends to kill me as soon as he sees the gold. He must live long enough to give me something useful."

He paused, leaned over, and kissed her on the forehead.

"How will I know when to shoot?" Ava asked.

"Just listen to me. I will use the word *clarinet*. The man you shoot with the terrible frog from Nicaragua will stagger and fall down. This will save my life. I will be so proud of you."

She grabbed the clarinet and ran toward a closet on the east side of the Grand Chamber. Inside this closet was a two-foot wide, thirty-foot long vertical steel culvert with welded steps that led to a magic stump at the entrance of the garage.

"Remember," Andy called after her, "it's not brave if you aren't scared. Good hunting, darlin'."

13.

Jack sprinted from the Grand Chamber to the farmhouse, a tunnel he knew well. He could move faster than his mom because he could run with his head ducked. She had left the lights on. Five minutes later he entered the security code and slipped into the gun closet. He listened. There was no light coming from underneath the door to the basement. Opening the door, he stepped into the room and looked up the stairwell toward the kitchen. He could hear his mom talking.

"Sasha, Andy admired you so much."

"I know what you're trying to do," Sasha said, looking out the window in front of the farmhouse.

Aleksi was walking back toward the farmhouse with Dr. Carlson. She watched them go to the shed and get in the orange RTV. They drove past the farmhouse toward the garage. Dr. Carlson was driving. Aleksi was standing in the back of the bed holding onto the roll bar with one hand and his gun with the other. He would use the RTV to haul the gold. She smiled and walked toward Lindsey. She sat down on the coffee table, facing away from her.

"Have you shot many people who were tied up?" Lindsey asked. "And pregnant?"

"That was information I didn't need."

"Perhaps hearing about new life is exactly what you need."

Sasha stood and walked back to the window.

"Do you need money so badly that you kill your friends for it?" Lindsey asked.

"Yes, I do," she said. "Farmville is not my cup of tea."

Sasha checked the silencer on her pistol and then turned it toward the couch. Lindsey closed her eyes. Sasha's cell phone rang. She placed the Glock on the coffee table and pulled her fanny pack around front. Looking down, she unzipped the pack and found her phone. She saw the caller ID.

Lindsey watched her turn toward the front window and lift the phone to her ear. Was this her execution order?

When the cell phone touched her ear, a wooden arrow appeared, like a magician's trick. It protruded six and a half inches from her left breast and wetsuit. Sasha looked down at the arrow. It was tipped with a bloody one and one quarter inch wide three-blade deer hunting broad head. She dropped the phone. Below her chin, a second bloody broad head and wooden arrow shaft protruded from her right breast.

She grunted, "Jack" and fell forward onto her face.

The fletching from both arrows seemed to rise as her chest settled to the floor below the antlers of Andy's seven by seven Colorado bull elk.

"Jack," Lindsey cried, "you did it."

Jack ran to his mom and hugged her head, then looked over his shoulder at the body on the floor.

"You did the right thing, Jack. Thank you."

"Aw, Mom. Dad told me what to do."

Jack cut away the rope on her hands and ankles with his knife.

"Dad said for us to get back to the cave," he said.

They looked at the woman lying prone on the great room floor.

Jack examined the bright yellow fletching on the end of the arrows extending vertically from the back of the body. "The fletching didn't get messed up," he said. "I can use these again. The rubber wetsuit slowed down my arrows."

"You did good, son. She was a bitch."

"I've never heard you use that term."

"She tried to seduce my husband."

"But she was going to kill you, Mom."

"Another good reason to shoot her."

14.

Aleksi could see Dr. Carlson standing in the light of the garage. Andy raised his hands over his head and began walking toward him. Aleksi held a flashlight in his left hand and his pistol in his right hand.

Andy called out, "Aleksi, I expected to see you this weekend."

"And I expected that you would be here on your farm, Dr. Carlson, and not where the papers said you would be. I'm glad to see that you love your wife enough to spare her life for a precious metal."

Aleksi had gained weight since Andy last saw him. His hair had turned to silver, with only sprinkles of brown left. He wore a black diving suit with the head cap pulled back, and running shoes.

"You'll need my RTV to load all the gold," Andy said. "We can drive down a concrete ramp into the basement of my garage, where the gold is locked up."

Aleksi looked behind him. "And where is this RTV?"

"It's in the shed. Over there," Andy said, pointing. "I'll drive and you can hold your gun on me."

Aleksi motioned with his pistol for Andy to point the way to the Kubota RTV.

At the shed, Andy got in and backed the RTV out into the light from a lamp on a pole nearby.

"Hop in the back," Andy said.

"It would be foolish for you to try to throw me off this vehicle, doctor."

"I agree. I'll drive slowly and you can stand up and hold on to the roll bar behind me."

Andy drove past the farmhouse until the garage was in sight.

"Is this the place where you keep the gold?"

"Yes."

They pulled up to the building.

"Aleksi, if you'll allow me to turn this vehicle around, I'll back up to the door. We have to back down a ramp. There's no room to turn around in the cave. All that gold will take several trips."

Aleksi jumped out of the bed and pointed the gun at Andy while he maneuvered the RTV into position. "I appreciate your helpfulness."

Andy stepped out of the RTV. "You know me well, Aleksi. I would give you all of the gold that I have to spare my wife's life, but fortunately I don't have to make that choice at this time."

"And why is that, doctor?"

"My son was in the house when you broke in. He has killed your partner by now."

Aleksi laughed. "This is the son that your wife was carrying the last time I was on this farm?"

"That's correct."

"Then he could be no more than ten years old, hardly a threat to me or my partner. I wouldn't bet my wife's life on the fighting skills of a boy. He probably couldn't control the muzzle of a pistol. I haven't heard any shots."

"My son isn't hunting with a gun tonight. Jack is a very special boy, mature for his age. Why don't you call this partner and ask if he has met my son?"

"If you insist. My partner was concerned about your children."

Aleksi flipped out his cell phone and pressed a speed dial number. The number rang several times. It stopped ringing. There was a strange noise. No one answered.

"The reason that your partner is not answering is because my son shot him through the heart with an arrow."

"Her cell phone got wet crossing the river," Aleksi said. "I didn't think it would work. It doesn't matter. You must give me the gold or I'll shoot you right here and now."

"But if you shoot me, you will have wasted your trip to this farm, and you will never get the gold. It's in a vault. There's no amount of conventional explosive that will open the door of this vault. Do you mind if I sit down? I believe we can work this out."

Aleksi rolled his tongue around in his mouth. He motioned with his gun.

Andy sat down and leaned against the garage door. He drew his knees up and circled them with his hands.

"Dr. Carlson, you know what I want, but I don't know what you want."

"I'll give you all of the gold under one condition."

Aleksi's face brightened. "And what is that condition?"

"I need to know where the nuclear warheads are in this country, the warheads that you recently armed and sold."

"You wish to keep these bombs from exploding?"

"Yes, I do. I will trade my gold for your information."

"Perhaps we can do business. I don't really care if these warheads explode or not. I've already been paid for them. This is not my country."

"Then where are they?"

"One is in a container at the Port of Long Beach."

"Why Long Beach?"

"Dr. Carlson, part of your Constitution is a Bill of Rights. This Bill of Rights includes the Right to Be Stupid. Your country exercises that right every day."

"We agree on something, Aleksi, but what exactly are you referring to?"

"No country needs to send spies to America," he said, "because America publishes all of its weaknesses on the Internet. A child could look up the most vulnerable ports in America. He can read exactly what security precautions are taken at each port. The Americans don't know how to keep their mouths shut, and they know nothing about security."

Andy nodded.

"There are several scientific papers on the Internet that identify the Long Beach port as the most vulnerable of all ports in America," Aleksi said. "Long Beach and Los Angeles are the two busiest ports. These papers say exactly how large a warhead would put both ports out of business, how to get the warhead into Long Beach, how many people would be killed, how many square kilometers would be contaminated by fallout, how many refineries would be shut down, and so on."

"Who did you sell this weapon to, Aleksi?"

"You ask too many questions."

"Each of my gold bars is worth over two million dollars, and I have 400 bars."

"But you've been very good at holding onto your gold. Boris told me about this gold, but he never returned from this farm."

"Boris got into a shootout with the CIA," Andy said. "He was loading forty bars of gold into a helicopter when he was shot. I promised him forty bars and I gave him forty bars. All I am asking from you is some information. It seems so little for 900 million dollars in gold."

"What information do you want?"

"I need to know which container the warhead is in at the Port of Long Beach."

"That information will do you no good."

"Why?"

"There are two men inside that container with the warhead," Aleksi said. "This container is air-conditioned. It's more like an apartment. They don't have to come out, but they have the ability to unplug holes in the sides of the container. They have a cell phone to communicate with their friends, and they have a manual detonator switch. Should anyone come near that container, they will detonate the warhead."

"How do you know this?"

"Because I drove these gentlemen in the container to Long Beach myself."

"Then we should be able to resolve this minor difficulty easily and you can leave with your gold. You must have a copy of the bill of lading for that container."

"You can't expect me to walk around with such a document on me."

"But surely you can pull up a copy of it using my laptop." Andy pointed toward the bench outside the garage. "Every shipping company has a website, Aleksi. You must know this. Every business that uses containers has an account with a shipping company and an account number. The bill of lading would have the GTIN, the Global Transportation Item Number, and the container number. Using your account number and your password, you should be able to find all of the information that I need. I don't need to look over your shoulder. I don't need to see your account number or your password."

"Is this why you have your laptop with you, Dr. Carlson?"

"It is. If you can prove to me where this warhead is, you can have 900 million dollars in gold. You don't have to worry about what happens when someone comes too close to the container. That's not your responsibility. Give me the information I need and I will give you the gold. It's that simple. I do need to know who bought the weapon."

Aleksi studied Andy's face and looked toward the laptop on the bench. "I sold this weapon to two Iranians for 250 million dollars."

"Then you have made a good deal already," Andy said. "It would be even better if you had 900 million dollars in gold and drove away with it alive. If you give me the information that I need, I won't come looking for you."

"I'm not worried about your looking for me. Your government has been looking for me for almost forty years and they have never come close."

"Then we should conclude our business and both walk away."

"Let me see your computer," Aleksi said. "Remain seated. You would be surprised at how quickly I could put a bullet through your head."

"I'm sure that won't be necessary."

Aleksi sat on the bench and typed. He stared at the monitor screen a moment and then raised his eyebrows. He stood up and left the laptop on the bench.

"Dr. Carlson, this is the container you want. There is even a picture of it."

He backed away and held the gun on Andy. Andy crawled on his knees to the bench and looked at the laptop screen.

"The contents are labeled Disaster Relief for Guatemala," Andy said. "What disaster is that?"

"There is a disaster in Guatemala once a month," Aleksi said. "They have mudslides, hurricanes, earthquakes, floods, forest fires, drought, and famine. Who can keep up with all these disasters?"

"The container is labeled RECU6570382 and carries the name of Ready Cargo Shipping. It's a refrigerated container, requiring a 440 volt power line," Andy read from the bill of lading.

"The power comes from the port while the container is being stored," Aleksi said. "Onboard the container ship, the ship provides the power. The trucks that carry them have generators. Many construction companies use these containers for on-site offices."

"Who is Arco Genetics, Aleksi?"

"They are a company that I use to ship certain items."

"According to this, the container will not be picked up for another six days."

"If you want something to lie around a port for weeks, then label it

Disaster Relief. The shipping company donates the cost of transportation, but the container is last in line."

"How did you get the bomb into this container?"

"So many questions. You are trying my patience."

"We are very close to a bargain. How do I know that this is not just a container that you picked out to show me?"

"As you pointed out, I could only pull up this picture and this information if I had a business account and a password."

"All right. So this is your container. That doesn't mean it has a nuclear warhead in it with two Iranians who wish to visit Allah."

"Dr. Carlson, use the ZOOM feature on that web page and look at the side of the container in the picture. You will notice that a four foot by four foot section of the side has been removed with a torch and then welded back in place. The weld has been ground down, and the container has been repainted, but you can still see the section if you look closely. This was necessary to avoid breaking the security lock on the back of the container."

"I see the section. What type of weapon is it?"

"A twenty kiloton."

"And when was the tritium reservoir replaced?"

"Four months ago."

"And you drove this container into the Port of Long Beach yourself?"

"I did."

"Where is it parked?"

"The union members handle all the containers. They picked it up from the flatbed truck with a crane and I drove away. There is no way for me to know where it's stacked now, but that information would be available at the port."

"I'm curious," Andy said. "Why was this weapon not picked up by radiation detectors?"

"In American ports, only containers leaving the terminal by truck are scanned by radiation detectors. There is no screening of containers on trucks arriving at the port for export. No one is concerned about the United States exporting nuclear weapons. They are only concerned about imported weapons."

"I thought this was true," Andy said. "My wife and I ship crates from Hampton Roads."

"The security at American ports is pathetic," Aleksi said. "One thing for certain, the very last container to be inspected will be a container shipped from a legitimate business and stamped *Disaster Relief for Guatemala*. None of this matters. That container is never leaving the Port of Long Beach. It is the Port of Long Beach that is leaving."

"Then we only have one more item to discuss."

"But I thought we were close to a bargain."

"There is still at least one more weapon."

"You will have trouble finding it."

"Why is that?"

"The Iranians picked it up themselves. I don't know where they were going to take it, but they're driving a U-Haul truck."

"Who rented the U-Haul truck?"

"I did."

"What can you tell me about this truck?"

"I don't recall much about the truck. I destroyed the paperwork. I didn't intend to return it."

"What kind of truck was it?"

"It was orange. It had a Dodge engine and four wheels in the back. It was about eight feet wide and eight feet high. It had a roll-back door. Sixteen feet long. I gave it to the Iranians."

"And you don't know where they are taking it?"

"You have reached the end of my knowledge. They were going somewhere on the East Coast. We must conclude this matter. I need to check on Sasha."

"Sasha is not by any chance a nurse?"

"Dr. Carlson, Sasha Ivanov is my granddaughter."

"You must be so proud. Does she play the clarinet?"

Aleksi slapped at the right side of his neck, as if he had been stung by a hornet. He looked to the ground and saw the dart. Staggering backwards, he could not find Andy. He saw the night sky, but only for a short time.

15.

Andy opened the vault door in the mechanic's pit of the garage and ran down the concrete ramp. He called, "Anybody home?"

"Just us chickens," Lindsey answered, running through the doorway from the Grand Chamber, followed by Jack and Ava. Hugs were exchanged.

"Mission accomplished, Dad," Jack said.

"You're not quite through. Don't forget the truck. They must have a truck nearby."

"You really think I could blow it up?" Jack asked.

"If it's there, you can blow it up."

They kissed Lindsey and Ava, hopped in the Kubota and drove to the S-10 Chevy truck parked behind the shed. Andy retrieved the recoilless rifle from underneath the bush hog of the tractor and handed it to Jack. Jack loaded the HEAT round.

Jack lay down on his back in the bed of the small truck, holding the AT4 tube across his stomach.

Andy drove across the covered bridge. After turning right onto South Airport Road, he opened the sliding window behind him in the cab and turned off the headlights.

"Jack, I want you to wait until I come to a complete stop before you move. There will probably be people in this truck, but they will not be expecting us. Steady yourself with your knees and feet. Take your time. The night vision scope will allow you to see well. The safety switch turns on the red targeting laser."

"I got it."

They approached the intersection of South Airport Road and Plank Road.

"My guess is that they're parked within a mile of the farm," Andy said.

He climbed the slow grade up to the intersection. "Look to the left. The truck is parked on that flat spot where the hunting shack burned down. Shoot for the passenger door."

Andy slowly turned the wheel to the right and brought the S-10 to a stop.

The truck was not hard to identify as part of Aleksi's plan. It looked like a surplus Army vehicle, dark green, with a canvas-covered bed, four wheels in the back. The truck was parked parallel to South Airport Road, forty yards ahead and to their left.

Andy saw the red targeting laser on the passenger door and ducked. KABOOM!

"I think I just got a suntan," Jack cried. "My first truck."

"Stay where you are," Andy said.

He sprinted toward the twisted wreckage. The fireball dissipated rapidly after rising a hundred feet in the air. There had been two people in the truck. The only thing Andy could recognize in the twisted wreckage was a tarantula-sized Harley Davidson belt buckle. It was Demetrius and Nadia Popov.

Andy shook his head. Once again he concluded that the best work he did as an emergency physician was invariably wasted on people who refused to change their lifestyles.

Before making a U-turn in the intersection, Andy turned on his headlights. The light flashed across Sasha's house on the opposite corner of Plank Road and South Airport Road.

Andy looked in the rear view mirror. "Sasha got what she deserved. The two in the truck live on the corner of Oak Street and Third Street, across from the ED. They were friends of Aleksi and Sasha, and they've been spying on us. Good job, Jack. You are the fourteenth generation to defend our property."

"Thanks, Dad."

"The Fire Department and the Farmville Police will be here shortly," Andy said. "Did you know that you're supposed to be at least eighteen years old and in the Marine Corps to fire one of those recoilless rifles?"

"Then we better be gettin' on back to the cave."

16.

A ndy found the card with the president's private line on it and turned the laptop screen to face him. "Mr. Umar, this is Andy Carlson. I have good news."

"I need good news."

"I think that the king has located one nuclear warhead."

"Where is it?"

"It's in a container at the Port of Long Beach, and it's twenty kilotons."

"Do you know where in the port this container is?" asked the president.

"I know the specific container. I even have a picture of it. The weapon was sold to two Iranians, who are in a refrigerated container with their hands on a detonator switch. The king told me the Iranians hijacked the container on its way to Long Beach from some legitimate business. They cut a hole in the side of the container and replaced the contents. I recommend that you discreetly locate that container and hope it's not in the middle of a big stack. You would need a clear line of sight to shoot it."

"To shoot it?"

"If you could shoot an appropriate artillery shell or rocket into that container," Andy said, "the warhead would be disarmed. In fact, that's my recommendation. To detonate a warhead, multiple shaped charges around the core must explode at exactly the same time. These timed explosions must compress the plutonium core at the same time that tritium neutrons are boosted into the core from a reservoir. An asymmetric explosion nearby can't do this."

"How do you know?" the president asked.

"My wife told me. I trust her."

"That's great news, Andy," Umar said. "You don't mind if I call you Andy?"

"No sir."

The president asked, "Wouldn't somebody need to look at what's left of that container after we shoot it to tell us if we shot a real nuclear warhead, rather than a container of musical instruments or snowmobiles? Wouldn't you or your wife be the most qualified persons to check this out?"

"You have people who are just as qualified as my wife, Mr. Umar. I just learned that my wife is pregnant. Radiation of any dose would not be good for her. There are very competent HAZMAT people in Los Angeles and Long Beach. They have plenty of Geiger counters and radiation suits. The bill of lading says that you have six days before the ship arrives to pick up that container. Of course, the folks inside could detonate the warhead at any time."

Andy waited for the president to answer. He didn't.

Andy said, "I recommend you call SEAL Team Six. They're one of the few SEAL teams left. They've been trained to defuse old Soviet tactical nuclear weapons. They can assess the situation and choose the best round for the job."

"SEAL Team Six. I've got it," Umar said.

"I'm going to email everything I have on this container, which is labeled as disaster relief supplies for Guatemala. You'll see all of the identification numbers on the bill of lading. The Port Authority can tell you exactly where that container is now. With long range surveillance, you should be able to locate it without stirring up the guys inside. Don't get near it with a helicopter. The SEAL team can determine how large a target area you have. A laser guided weapon is one possibility."

"Send that information right away, Andy, to my personal email address. It's on the card I gave you. I'll get back in touch if I need anything else."

The president hung up.

"Lindsey, I need to make a quick trip into town before daylight," Andy said. "There's an apartment on the corner of Oak Street and Third Street, across from the hospital, that may have phone records of some importance. I'll be back before daylight."

"Breaking and entering, are we?"

"The two occupants of that apartment have been spying on us, along with Sasha," Andy said. "They won't be returning to the apartment. They were in the truck that Jack blew up."

Instead of going through the intersection of Plank Road and South Airport Road and having to deal with the police and firemen, Andy turned off South Airport Road at Pleasant Valley Road. He followed a narrow lane to Raine's Tavern Road, turned left and drove five miles to Highway 15. It was the same route that Robert E. Lee's Army of Northern Virginia had taken in their retreat to Appomattox, after dropping off the gold in the caves under the farm.

Andy parked on Oak Street half a block from Farmville Community Hospital. He looked at his watch. 4:05 AM. In an hour and a half, the anesthesiologists and surgeons would be coming in, followed by the day shift personnel. He sat for a moment in the dark, scanning the street for any signs of life.

From the glove box of his S-10 he retrieved a wallet full of miniature tools. From behind the seat he pulled two disposable size eight and a half surgical gloves from a box of 100. His pickup truck was old, but it had a nice feature. Underneath the light switch was another switch that disabled all the lights. Hunters love this switch. When they get out of their truck, no lights come on. He crossed the street to the second floor apartment.

Yellow tape still surrounded the crime scene. The deadbolt lock was easy to pick. The cell phone records and land line records were in a folder on the kitchen counter. He stuffed these into his pockets.

Demetrius and Nadia had a computer on a card table. He touched the space bar. The screen opened to Yahoo mail. They must have left in a hurry. Andy found the contact list of email addresses and names, scanned the files and recent emails, and sent the files he wanted to his own secure email address as attachments.

Before leaving, he downloaded and installed a program that he learned from Lindsey, who formerly worked for the CIA. As he walked out the door, Andy watched the hard drive being systematically erased. As soon as the police and firemen left the intersection of Plank Road and South Airport road, he would pay a similar visit to Sasha's house. If he couldn't access the data on the computer, he would take it home. Lindsey would be able to hack her way in. There were dots that needed to be connected, but he didn't want to leave any dots that connected to him.

Back at the farm, Andy picked up Sasha's pistol with the silencer and her cell phone from the great room of the farmhouse. He removed the two wooden arrows from her chest by unscrewing the broad heads and pulling the bare arrow shafts out of her back. The broad heads and the arrow shafts were washed off in the kitchen sink and left to dry on the rack next to sink. Before moving Sasha, Andy rolled her body over and took a picture of her face with his own smart phone.

He walked outside to the equipment shed and cranked up his 120 horsepower Kubota Diesel tractor, which had a giant front-end bucket. Sasha's body fit easily in the front-end loader, leaving plenty of room for Aleksi. She had carried no identification and had nothing useful in her fanny pack.

He drove the tractor down to the garage. Aleksi carried no identification, either. Andy took a picture of Aleksi's face before adding him to the front-end loader. He placed the two cell phones and two pistols at the entrance of the garage and got back on the tractor.

As he drove over the covered bridge, Andy wondered if Aleksi had given him enough information about the second warhead. He would look for the U-Haul truck while the SEAL team took care of the warhead at Long Beach.

Why not give the CIA everything he had? Both he and Lindsey had extensive experience working for the CIA. Their standard operating procedure was to use people until they were no longer needed, and then betray them or kill them. Despite their huge database and agents around the world, the CIA was very inept at connecting dots. It took them ten years to find Osama bin Laden, and they found him in the first place that Andy would have looked--Pakistan. The CIA had sent him into Pakistan several times to find and eliminate "terrorists." He was three for three, he recalled. The CIA had been angry when he resigned his commission.

Andy concluded that he was more likely to find the second warhead than the CIA. His connection with Aleksi was unknown to them, and he wanted to keep it that way. Sooner or later they would stumble onto Arco Genetics. It might be a dead end, but he would rather get there first. When he needed help from the president or the CIA, he would ask for it.

Uncle Frank's well was the best spot for the bodies. The dirt had sunk down about eight feet since he had buried the remains of several CIA agents and all of Boris' mercenaries a decade before.

Andy dumped the bodies in the well and covered them up with dirt and sand from the river bank. Driving back to the farmhouse, he wondered how many bodies had been disposed of on the farm since 1743, when his ancestors settled there and discovered the cave entrances.

At the garage entrance to the cave, Andy picked up the two cell phones, two pistols, his camera, and his laptop. He drove the Kubota ATV back to the farmhouse.

17.

"**W**hatcha doing?" Ava asked, watching her dad arrange the cell phones on the coffee table in the great room of the farmhouse.

He plugged his laptop into the receptacle on the side of the table.

"I'd like to recover all of the phone numbers and names stored in these cell phones," he said. "If I spell the names, will you make a list of each name and number I call out?"

"Sure," she said. "I was wondering about Aleksi, the man I shot with the terrible frog from Nicaragua."

"I hope he's the only guy you've shot with the terrible frog."

"He's the only one so far. Mom said he was resting comfortably."

"I'm sure he is, Ava."

Andy was unsure if he should be glad or sad that Ava's concept of death was not completely developed, but he had no regrets about his daughter's courage and poise. He had no doubt that educating his children as warriors was necessary to produce tomorrow's leaders. There would be a better time to explain.

"I want you to make three columns on a sheet of blank paper, turned lengthwise so you have more room," he said. "Make one column for Aleksi, one for Sasha, and one for Demetrius and Nadia. Under each column you will have two more columns, one for calls received and one for calls made."

Ava sprang into action. Andy knew that she remembered numbers far better than he did. He called out the names and numbers from the contacts on Aleksi's cell phone. Ava never required that he repeat anything. Some numbers had no names. He called these numbers out and Ava recorded them.

Andy repeated the process with Sasha's cell phone and Demetrius and Nadia's land line and cell phones. His last list included all email addresses and names on Sasha's computer and Demetrius and Nadia's computer.

"Lindsey, could you help Ava with something?" Andy asked.

Lindsey entered from the kitchen, drying her hands on a towel. She hugged her husband and daughter.

"Could you help Ava research the phone numbers we retrieved from the Ivanovs' phones? Begin by identifying the phone number of each, and any number that more than one called. I'm looking for connections. A top priority would be to find a call to a U-Haul center. Some of your queries may not bring any results, but the research is worthwhile. If Google can't identify a number, just ring it and find out who answers."

Lindsey looked at Ava's columns and opened up her own laptop.

Andy asked, "Ava, do you remember that I had my laptop out on the bench in front of the garage when Aleksi was talking to me?"

"Yeah."

"This plastic thing that sticks out of the side of my laptop looks like a portable Wi-Fi connection device. It has AT and T written on it. Actually, it's a microphone and a recording device. I recorded my conversation with Aleksi. I hoped to get him to admit trafficking in nuclear weapons, and he did. Unfortunately, the conversation reveals too much about us."

"It sounded like you got a lot from where I was," Ava said. "He only gave you this information because he intended to shoot you after he saw the gold, right?"

"That's true. Aleksi used my laptop to pull up the bill of lading for a container at the Port of Long Beach. The president wanted Lindsey and me to go out there and take care of it, but I told them we had other things to do. Lindsey, do you remember the keystroke software you installed on this laptop?"

She looked up from her own laptop. "Yes."

Andy eyed his laptop screen. Ava scooted behind him and wrapped her arms around his neck. She rested her chin on his shoulder.

"That software has allowed us to capture Aleksi's shipping company, his account number, and his password. Here's the picture of the container. I sent this picture to Mr. Umar, but I didn't tell him about Aleksi or Arco Genetics."

Lindsey stood up and took a look. Ava studied the container.

"Aleksi said that two Iranians were inside that trailer with a phone and a detonator switch, and that they would detonate the weapon if anyone came near the trailer," Ava said.

"I tend to believe that," Lindsey said. "He didn't come here with a laptop. Andy forced him to give up that shipping account."

"I want to clarify one thing," Andy said. "We've been teaching SEAL teams for seven years that an artillery shell or a rocket that exploded near a warhead would not cause a chain reaction. Since you wrote most of the manual we gave them on disarming nuclear weapons, I'd like to hear you agree with this again."

She laughed.

"Well, we've never really proved this," Andy said. "You used the pit-stuffing technique to diffuse the warheads in Russia. Do you know of any specific circumstances where a projectile or bomb has been used to disable a warhead?"

"The answer is no," Lindsey said. "Most nuclear physicists would agree with us, but it's theoretical. No one would take such a chance, since disarming those warheads is really fairly simple."

"Fairly simple for you," Andy said.

Lindsey said, "An artillery shell or a rocket would scatter some radiation around, but it wouldn't cause a chain reaction in the nuclear warhead."

"That's exactly what I told the president," Andy replied, "and I used you as a reference."

"Thanks," she said. "Now they have someone else beside the Iranians to blame if they screw it up. I'd say a miss could cost a trillion dollars and a million lives."

"What's the pit-stuffing technique?" Ava asked.

"To disable warheads," Lindsey said, "I unscrew the tritium reservoir and insert a roll of wire into the plutonium core. Every six or eight inches I cut the wire and stuff the end inside with more wire. I keep doing this until the pit, or center of the core, is crammed with pieces of wire. These pieces of wire can't be removed. They prevent the shaped charges around the warhead from compressing the core, so there can't be a nuclear chain reaction. Think of it as stuffing the inside of a coconut with pieces of wire using one small hole. If you cut the coconut, you've destroyed the warhead."

"I'd like to try that sometime," Ava said.

"Aleksi's account with Ready Cargo is bound to be hiding something valuable," Andy said.

"It's certainly worth looking at," Lindsey said, "preferably before the CIA finds it."

"Let's see what he's been shipping," Andy said. "We should be able to access his past shipments."

Andy entered readycargo.com and the website for Ready Cargo appeared on the screen. He entered Aleksi's account number and password.

"Can you cross your fingers, Ava?" he asked.

Ava crossed her fingers and her legs just for good measure.

"Arco Genetics Inc. is a Wisconsin company that sells bull semen," Andy said.

"What's that?" Ava asked.

"I'm going to have to come back to that question, Ava."

"Let's look under History."

"I see only three shipments in the last ninety days," Andy said. "Arco Genetics has shipped three forty-foot containers from Waterview,

Wisconsin, to Long Beach in the past month, one twenty-two days ago and two six days ago."

"I need to know what bull semen is and what it has to do with disaster relief," Ava said.

"As soon as I figure all this out, we can discuss it," Andy said. "Let's follow the clues we have. All three containers have Ready Cargo container identification numbers and Arco Genetics GTINs. The first shipment of twenty-two days ago went to Singapore, and was not refrigerated. This container was loaded onto a freighter eleven days later in Singapore. The freighter was owned by IRSL Group. Google IRSL, Lindsey."

Lindsey tapped on her laptop.

"One container shipped from Wisconsin to Long Beach six days ago was refrigerated," Andy said. "It's Aleksi's disaster relief for Guatemala, and it's still at Long Beach. The second container shipped to Long Beach six days ago was also refrigerated. It left Long Beach four days ago for the Panama Canal."

"Andy, IRSL stands for Islamic Republic of Iran Shipping Lines," Lindsey said.

"Makes sense," Andy said. "That container left Singapore and arrived in Bushehr, Iran, five days later, four days before Ras Tanura was destroyed."

"Oh my God," Lindsey said. "It's a paper trail to Iran."

"I don't understand," Andy said. "We have sanctions against Iran. No container should leave the U.S. and end up in Iran. Google Arco Genetics."

Lindsey scanned the search results for Arco Genetics. "Here's an announcement about the United States approving the shipping of bull semen by Arco Genetics to Iran, compliments of the Bush Administration, in 2007."

"How can that be?" Andy asked. "Google U.S. trade with Iran."

Hundreds of entries appeared on Lindsey's search. She turned the screen toward Andy.

"This is ridiculous," Andy said. He scrolled down page after page. "Here's a policy statement from the U.S. Treasury Department Office of Foreign Assets Control." He clicked on it. "Quote: Our sanctions are targeted against the regime, not the people of Iran."

"I'll bet little or no inspection is done of bull semen leaving the Port of Long Beach for Iran," Lindsey said.

Andy said, "Aleksi could use Arco Genetics' GTIN numbers and ship the unthinkable in a forty-foot unrefrigerated container."

"That seems like an awful lot of bull semen not to be refrigerated," Lindsey said.

"I confess I'm not current on the transportation of bull semen," Andy said. "However, the most important thing is that Arco Genetics has the approval of the United States government to ship containers to Iran."

"How would he get the warheads into an Arco Genetics container?" Lindsey asked.

"Aleksi could have known somebody at Arco Genetics, or he could have known somebody on the trucking line that delivered the truck to Long Beach. He could rent a Ready Cargo Container, slap on a GTIN from Arco Genetics, and ship this container without Arco even being involved if he had someone on the inside to supply him with the GTIN. It's just pasted on the rear of the container."

Ava hopped off the couch. "I'm going to look up bull semen on my own computer. You guys know more than you're telling me. Come on, Jack."

"We already have him on your recording device admitting driving a warhead to the Port of Long Beach," Lindsey said. "We can prove that he shipped unknown cargo to Iran in a Ready Cargo Container using an Arco Genetics GTIN. Shouldn't we discuss this with the president?"

"I don't want to tell the president about Aleksi, his shipping history, or his account," Andy said. "I can't let him listen to my recording, which includes a lot about Confederate gold. Umar only has enough container information to find the Long Beach to Guatemala warhead. I told him the king found out that the Iranians hijacked the container after it was shipped. The president's priority is to disable that nuclear weapon in Long Beach. Arco Genetics probably has hundreds of customers. The CIA isn't nimble."

"I should have some information on the samples from Ras Tanura by tomorrow night," Lindsey said.

18.

A ndy and Lindsey prepared for bed in the master bedroom of the farmhouse.

"I think it's time for us to ease out of the nuclear warhead loop somehow," Lindsey said.

"Do you think America can afford for us to get out of the loop?" Andy asked. "How do you think you're going to feel if warheads explode in American cities? You can't believe that the CIA can locate the other warheads and destroy them without a disaster."

"Most people don't know what we know about our government, Andy."

"Does that release us from our obligation to protect our country? Sure, I hate those imbeciles in Washington. I don't hate them enough to sit smugly in my cave while they stumble around and get millions of Americans killed."

"I understand, Andy. It's my job to be cautious, to protect our family first."

"Let's review some facts about our government before we turn anything important over to them," he said. "The kids need to hear this."

Lindsey left the bedroom and returned with Jack and Ava, both in their pajamas.

"Bull semen is used to impregnate cows," Ava announced as she took a seat on the bed. "Mom, you're pregnant. Does it work like you and Dad and God?"

"Not quite, Ava," Andy said.

"And how do they get those bulls to donate semen for disasters?" Jack asked.

"I really want to discuss that subject fully with both of you, but there's something more important right now," Andy said.

Jack sat down on the bed next to Ava.

"Before you were born, your mother and I worked for the CIA," Andy said. "We had an opportunity to watch how our government works from the inside. It wasn't a pretty sight. Both of us were ordered to do immoral things. We thought that we were serving our country by following the orders we were given. Both of us found out the hard way that our government can't be trusted."

"Be specific," Jack said.

"We found that we couldn't trust our government to tell us the truth," Andy said. "The CIA invented reasons for me to kill people when I was a SEAL. Some of my targets were merely inconvenient to the CIA. Sadly, in some cases my targets were peaceful dissenters in their countries. I was told they were terrorists."

"I can understand why you would feel bad about that," Ava said. "But it wasn't your fault. You were just doing your duty."

"I found out that the CIA considered itself above the law," Lindsey said. "They used me until I knew too much about their activities, and then they tried to kill me right here on this farm."

"Was that the First Battle of Carlson Farm?" Jack asked.

"That's right."

"The more your mom and I studied the activities of our government," Andy said, "the more we became convinced that Washington was unable to set limits on itself or priorities for the country."

"What kind of limits and priorities?" Ava asked.

"Shouldn't it be a top priority for our government to be a steward of the money they collect from us in taxes?" Andy asked. "Shouldn't we expect that they exercise enough restraint in their spending to balance our books and pay off our national debt? Why should we tolerate a government that destroys our currency and wastes our tax dollars?"

"I'd like to know why we're satisfied with a government that lies to us about the reasons U.S. soldiers are sent to war," Lindsey said.

"Are we leading a revolution?" Ava asked.

"No, Ava, we're trying to prepare for an inevitable revolution," Andy said.

"Why is it inevitable?" Jack asked.

"History, Jack," Andy said. "There have been at least six other empires who took the road of involving themselves in multiple foreign wars while debauching their currencies. None of these empires survived. In America, anarchy is only held back by the power grid, the price of oil, and massive government deficits and debt."

"How did things get so bad?" Ava asked.

"The founders of this country had in mind that the brightest people would get together and work out solutions to the problems of the country," Lindsey said. "What we have now is a government that looks out only for itself and those people who are rich enough to pour money into the pockets of politicians. America has been suckered into dependence on government."

"And you don't believe that these things can be corrected by democracy?" Jack asked.

"You give democracy too much credit," Andy said. "It's a form of government that's only effective until the majority of the people learn to vote benefits for themselves out of the treasury and the majority of politicians learn to enrich themselves by pandering to special interest groups and lobbies."

"It's not just in America that democracy is failing," Lindsey said. "Democracies are in trouble all over the globe, and for the same reason. Nobody can control the public's appetite for 'free stuff', which politicians encourage the public to ask for. The politician who offers the most 'free stuff' gets elected. Our Congress is always in gridlock because almost every vote has been bought by lobbyists. Our legislators couldn't compromise if they wanted to."

Andy said, "Our democracy started out with noble goals, but it has succumbed to greed and corruption."

"Do you think Umar is part of the problem?" Ava asked.

"He's disarmed our country unilaterally," Andy said. "He uses the IRS for political purposes. He uses the NSA to spy on American citizens and their phone calls. He lies on a regular basis--about his own life, how he got his ten million dollar net worth, and what our state department and intelligence agencies do. He proposes a federal police force to enforce federal laws, because the military can't legally do this. Where have we heard of this idea before?"

"Nazi Germany in the 1930s," Ava said.

"Let's get back to the current threat, Andy," Lindsey said.

"Any real disaster we have exposes the ineptitude of the U.S. government," Andy said. "A nuclear explosion in two port cities would make Katrina look like a Sunday picnic. We could be on the threshold of this event. It would usher in a new age of martial law in this country."

"I like specifics, too," Ava said.

"The number of patients from such a holocaust would overload available space in hospitals," Andy said. "Most hospitals run at near-capacity already. Emergency departments stay busy. There wouldn't be enough ambulances or helicopters or paramedics or radiation suits in America to respond to hundreds of thousands of radiation-contaminated, burned, and injured patients."

"America has never seen real mass casualties at home," Lindsey said. "When the twin towers collapsed in 2001, everyone left inside was killed. The people who died during Katrina mostly drowned. Flu season fills almost every available bed in American hospitals during the winter. There is no surge capacity in hospitals for hundreds of thousands of complex patients."

"Hospitals would become battlegrounds after any event that produced mass casualties," Andy said. "Our government would have to fight its own people to maintain order. This is the real purpose of a new federal police force."

"How would you feel if a member of your family was dying and nobody came to help?" Lindsey asked. "How would you like to be turned away from a hospital?"

"I read about how many days it took the government to bring water to all those people in the Superdome," Ava said. "And they weren't even injured people."

"Hundreds of thousands of sick and injured people and their families would develop a mob mentality when their government failed to meet expectations," Andy said. "We already have city-wide riots due to inflation and food shortages, and God help anyone who is in an American city when the power goes out."

"So what can we do?" Jack asked.

"The Carlsons are preparing to be part of the solution," Lindsey said. "We stock medical supplies and weapons. We will help those people who can't protect themselves from the mob or the government."

"What do you think will happen to our government?" Ava asked.

"History tells us that oppressive and incompetent governments can't reinvent themselves," Andy said. "They must be overthrown by their own citizens. Google 'revolution' and you will be reading for a long time. No tyrant gives up without a fight. I believe America must start over with a new democracy, but I'm not going to lead this revolution. A national consensus for change must build on its own. I'm not in favor of anarchy. I do see it coming in America."

"Any new democracy must be based on individual responsibility and liberty, as our Founding Fathers intended," Lindsey said. "It can't be based on corruption, greed, and envy. There was nothing wrong with the original Constitution and Bill of Rights. These foundations of our liberty have been ignored, re-interpreted, and forgotten."

"Our Founding Fathers believed that revolution was a good thing," Andy said. "Thomas Jefferson said, 'The tree of liberty must be refreshed from time to time with the blood of patriots and tyrants. It is its natural manure.'"

"That's enough doom and gloom for tonight," Lindsey said.

19.

That night, content and asleep with his arm around his wife, Andy was awakened by the telephone.

"I'm on vacation, so that can't be the hospital," he said. "I know only one person who would call me this time of night, and I'll bet he doesn't have good news. Turn on the speaker, Lindsey. Wake up the kids. We're in this together."

"Andy, I'm sorry to be bothering you this time of night, but we have problems in Long Beach," Umar said.

"It hasn't been destroyed, I hope."

"Not yet."

"Then what's the problem?"

Jack and Ava walked into their parents' bedroom. Lindsey pointed toward the speaker, finger to her lips. The twins sat down on the bed.

"We found this container without much trouble," Umar said. "It's in a stack of five. It's the third from the bottom and has containers stacked all around it."

"There isn't any line of sight?"

"The angle is too steep or too wide," the president said. "The rear doors and identification numbers are only visible from the passageway between double rows of containers. Satellite photographs suggest peep holes at eye level in each door. The Air Force says that it can't target this container without blowing up an area the size of a city block."

"What about the Army?" Andy asked.

"The Army and the Navy agree that there is no smart bomb or cruise missile that can dive between two double rows of containers, make a ninety-degree turn in an eighty foot corridor, level out and hit a target that small. The container is eight and a half feet high and eight feet wide. According to the Navy, any projectile needs to enter the back doors at nearly a level angle to ensure it explodes in the right container, and not in the one below."

"I understand what you're saying," Andy said. "But the right weapon could hit nearby and annihilate the entire row."

"That's another problem," the president said. "I spoke with SEAL Team Six, as you suggested. They have no hands-on experience dealing with someone who has a detonator in his hand. None of the services have any protocols for shooting at armed nuclear weapons. It's never been done, at least not by us. We've never done a test, and we don't have time for a test. I'm the one with the responsibility for what happens if the projectile misses, or the warhead explodes when the container is hit, or the inhabitants of the container survive and detonate the warhead anyway."

"What did SEAL Team Six actually say?"

"They said they were trained by you and that you wrote their manual on disarming nuclear devices."

"My wife wrote most of the manual, but I do give the lectures."

Lindsey closed her eyes and shook her head.

"I must say, when I mentioned your name, SEAL Team Six was very anxious to work with you. SEAL teams usually don't want any help. But you are a SEAL. I did read your file, at least some of it. You and your wife are the only Americans to confront suicidal terrorists with their fingers on a detonator. In fact, you're quite a legend among the SEALs."

"I don't want to be flattered, Mr. Umar, and neither does my wife. We're retired. I was a SEAL a long time ago."

The president went on talking. "These containers are packed so closely together. There's only eight inches between the stacks. It's not wide enough for a man to get through, particularly with a weapon."

"What about climbing the stacks in the next row, facing the front of the container, and shooting a recoilless rifle into the top of the rear doors? Any SEAL could climb a stack of containers and pull up a re-coilless rifle with a rope."

"You're probably right," Umar said. "The larger problem is the Joint Chiefs of Staff. They don't feel comfortable betting the Port of Long Beach, and maybe Los Angeles as well, that one or two or three Navy SEALs shooting shoulder-fired missiles into the back doors would guarantee disabling an armed nuclear warhead inside. They pointed out that success would depend on how the weapon is packaged. What if the container was built to deflect a blast from the rear and protect the men and warhead inside? One of these men would only have to stay alive long enough to press a button. What if the detonator switch is triggered by the blast? We don't have any experience shooting deto-nator switches. Nobody does. Do you understand their reluctance?"

"War is never comfortable, Mr. President, and no one issues guar-antees to SEAL teams when they receive orders. The Joint Chiefs of Staff sound like make-believe leaders trying to cover their own backsides."

"Do you or your wife have any suggestions?" Umar asked. "That's why I called."

Andy stood up. "My only suggestion is to handle this myself."

The president paused.

Lindsey jumped in front of her husband's face and stood on her tiptoes. She shook her head from side to side. She made a thumbs down signal. She crossed her arms over her head as if she were waving off a poor landing approach on an aircraft carrier.

"Will you need anything?" the president asked.

"We'll bring our own gear and provide our own transportation to California," Andy said. "I'll call you when I know our ETA at the Long Beach port. This will be approximately five hours from now."

"What do you plan to do, Dr. Carlson?"

"Whatever is necessary to get the job done, Mr. Umar."

"Thank you."

"A couple of things, Mr. President."

"Yes."

"Don't use my name when you talk to anyone about Long Beach," Andy said. "Tell them my name is Mr. James Lee. Do not circulate my name in this matter to anyone, regardless of whether we're successful. Also, have SEAL Team Six wait for me, out of sight, at the Long Beach Port Authority. They are my back-up and I will have orders for them."

"I understand."

20.

A ndy disconnected the speaker phone. Lindsey exploded. "We?
Your own gear? Have you lost your mind?"

"Lindsey, you heard what he said. They don't have anybody there
with the balls to do the job. I need for you to make me some coffee. I
need for the kids to get dressed and eat some breakfast. I have to go to
the cave and pick up some gear."

"I do have legitimate questions," Lindsey yelled.

"So do I," he called back. "Please call the king's pilot and tell him
to warm up his plane. I know that you love me, Lindsey. Right now I
need for you to trust me."

Andy returned from the Confederate cave through the I-95 tunnel
to the farmhouse. He slipped from the gun closet into the basement,
carrying a huge duffle bag.

Jack and Ava were wide awake, dressed in jeans and T-shirts, and
anxious for their briefing. They sat on the couch. Lindsey paced the
floor of the great room.

"ATTENTION," Andy barked.

The kids stood together. Andy knelt in front of them.

"You kids and your mom are the most precious things in my life,"
he said. "I'm going to ask all of you to go in harm's way with me. I
have more confidence in you than in anyone else. I see no other way
to stop a terrible evil. The President of the United States, whether
we like him or not, has given us a job that no one else wants. We
have everything we need, but there is always risk. I can't guarantee
that nothing bad will happen. We can only be bold and try to do
what's right. I don't like Mr. Umar, but I love this country. I took an
oath…"

He paused, swallowed, blinked his eyes, and lowered his head. A drop hung on the tip of his nose.

Ava grabbed a wad of Kleenex from the coffee table. She stood beside him and covered his nose. "Now blow."

Andy blew his nose and took the Kleenex. He wiped his eyes with his sleeve.

"Thanks," he said.

"Don't mention it," she said, reclaiming her position in front of him.

"Since you warriors were born, I've tried to prepare you for times like today. Success in battle is not guaranteed by having the most soldiers or the most weapons. Success often comes from using the right tools at the right time. Can I have a piece of paper?"

Ava handed Andy her sketch book. Jack stroked his imaginary beard. Andy drew two rows of containers, each with two containers parked front to front, with only the rear doors visible in the pavement between double rows.

"Two very bad guys," he said, "Iranian friends of Aleksi, are hiding inside a container at the Port of Long Beach. Only the rear doors of this container are visible. The containers are stacked so closely together that no adult can squeeze between them."

He looked at Lindsey, who stopped pacing and stared at him. "There are eight inches between these stacks."

"I got that," Jack said.

Andy reached into the duffle bag and pulled out one of two AT4 CS recoilless rifles.

"Do I get to blow something up?" Jack asked.

"You might be the only person who can squeeze through those containers and shoot at an acceptable angle."

"Lindsey, you'll need your disarming toolbox, your radiation spacesuit, and a Geiger counter. Would you wrap up our two old tritium reservoirs in a lead blanket and pack them in your tool kit?"

"I'm not sure why you want the old reservoirs."

"Please, just do it."

"What's the plan, Dad?" Jack asked.

"We're going to ride in the king's Citation X to California. When we get there, Mom and Ava will stay at least twenty-five miles away until I call for them. Riverside might be a good staging area."

"What will you and Jack be doing?" Ava asked.

"We'll sneak around to the double row of containers in front of the row that has the container we want." He pointed to his drawing. "I'm bringing my T5000 thermal imaging binoculars. I should be able to identify bodies and weapons inside that container. There's only a quarter moon. I'll check the local weather in Long Beach after we get in the air. Jack is going to slide between two stacks of containers on the ground, carrying his stick bow, his quiver, and the AT4 with a HEAT round."

He drew Jack's course on Ava's sketch pad. "Jack won't have to do any climbing, so he doesn't have to worry about how high the trailers are stacked. Lindsey, could I borrow one of your measuring tapes?"

"I want to go on record that I don't like any of this," she said, leaving the room. She returned with a yellow tape measure.

Andy took it and measured the circumference of Jack's chest. "Twenty-two and a half inches," Andy said.

"He'll fit easily if he moves sideways," Ava said, doing the math in her head, "and his chest isn't round."

Andy turned Jack ninety degrees and measured his chest from front to back. "Seven inches."

He measured the AT4. "It'll fit, too," he said. "When Jack gets to the place where he can see our container, he'll use the night vision sight on the recoilless rifle to be sure that he's targeting the right container. This recoilless rifle is exactly like the one he used to take out that truck on South Airport road. It can safely be fired in the space between the containers. Water will be discharged behind him."

"And where will you be?" Lindsey asked.

"I'm going to crawl along at the base of the row of trailers that Jack will be looking at. They have peep holes in those doors, but they won't be able to see directly below them. I'll keep moving until I'm standing underneath the right container. I'll try to scan the trailer with the thermal imaging glasses. I'll confirm any identification on the container. When I'm satisfied that we have the right trailer, I'll raise my hand and point toward it. Jack will give me a few seconds to move away, and then he'll shoot for the bottom one third of the rear of that trailer."

"No problem," Jack said.

"I plan to carry the M100 Grenade Rifle Entry Munition (GREM) and an M16," Andy said. "If Jack gets stuck between the trailers or if anything else unexpected comes along, I can take care of that container. The GREM is fired from the M16. I'm taking a couple of hand grenades. This is just a plan. When we get there, I may see something better, or we could be forced to improvise."

"Can we talk about the warhead?" Lindsey asked.

"No need for me to worry about the warhead, Mom," Jack said. "I'm shooting one container."

"That trailer could be full of bull semen, Mom," Ava said. "Let's not get worked up about stuff we can't control. We seem to have a good plan here."

"I appreciate the advice, Ava," Lindsey said.

"You're welcome, Mom."

"Lindsey, do you have any baby oil?" Andy asked.

"Sure."

Andy gave orders. "Jack, put on your darkest hunting shorts, your dark hunting boots, and your black watch cap. Bring your knife, your bow and arrow, and night-vision goggles. Bring plenty of black and dark green camo face paint. You'll need enough to cover your whole body."

"Ava, I want you to wear jeans, a dark shirt, and dark boots. Bring some camo makeup and your Girl Scout uniform. Mom will have your clarinet. You're backup."

Ava smiled.

"Lindsey, how about some bag lunches and suppers?" Andy asked. "There should be Cokes on the plane. Everybody put your personal gear into this duffle bag. Bring an extra set of clothes in case we need to stop somewhere."

"I still don't like this," Lindsey said.

"Then come up with a better plan while we're en route," Andy said. He kissed her on the forehead. "Jack, get a stack of superhero comic books and put them in the duffel bag. I'll explain later."

21.

The combination air traffic controller, groundskeeper, hangar maintenance man, aviation fuel man, and owner of the airport restaurant muttered as he watched the Carlsons load up the Citation X. "Those Carlsons are wearing out the runway lately with those private jets. There's got to be some good reason why they never file a flight plan. They never say where they're going. They're bringing foreigners in here and none of them even buy a cup of coffee. They don't bother to call the tower and let me know they're landing until they line up with the runway. Then the pilot starts yacking in some foreign language. Those kids ask a hundred questions but they won't answer any."

After takeoff, Lindsey worked the phone numbers from Ava's columns. Andy pulled up his secure email account through the Saudi Embassy on his laptop.

To: King Fahd
From: Andy Carlson
Re: On the Trail

I have new information regarding the nuclear explosion at Ras Tanura. I am on the trail of a smuggled ex-Soviet Union warhead that left the United States three weeks ago, bound for Iran. It passed through Singapore, where it was loaded onto an IRSL container ship. The port of destination was Bushehr, Iran. It should have arrived there four days before your disaster.

I recommend that you look into any shipment by any carrier of a container to Ras Tanura or to a nearby port in the week prior to your disaster. I need to know the container number of any shipment. The container number is a 4-letter capitalized prefix, which identifies the owner or operator of the container, and a 7-digit number that identifies the specific container. I also need the GTIN number of the item shipped. This is a fourteen digit Global Trade Item Number, and it is unique to the company sending the item. If you could obtain the bill of lading for any such containers, it would be helpful. Make copies of this information and guard them.

He pressed Send.

"I need to talk with you about superheroes," Andy called to the twins.

"Like Superman?" Jack asked.

"Wonder Woman," Ava said.

"That's right," Andy said. "Don't forget Spiderman and Batman. I've bought superhero comic books for you since you were about two years old, haven't I?"

They nodded.

"There was a reason that I wanted to expose you to superheroes. I wanted to give you time to read about each one before we had this discussion."

Lindsey moved closer.

"Can either of you tell me what all superheroes have in common?" Andy asked.

Ava said, "They're all courageous."

"That's right."

"They do good things," Jack said. "They help people."

"What else?"

"They all have special powers or skills," Jack said.

"Very good," Andy said. "Can you think of anything else that they all have in common?"

Jack and Ava looked at each other.

"They all wear masks," Ava said.

"Ava, that observation is the single most important thing about superheroes. Few people understand why superheroes must wear a mask. I learned the answer to this question from my dad, and I'm going to pass it on to you. I want you to be superheroes."

"Your dad liked superheroes?" Ava asked.

"My dad's favorite was the Lone Ranger, who was a superhero in the Wild West. He wore a mask, too, and for the same reason that all superheroes wear masks."

"The mask is to hide who they really are," Jack said. "Superman is Clark Kent and Batman is Bruce Wayne and Spiderman is Peter Parker."

"Why is it necessary for them to hide who they are?" Andy asked.

"Because people would always be asking them for autographs," Ava said.

"That's close," Andy said. "Superheroes wear masks *to protect themselves from one of the greatest temptations a man or woman has in this world.*"

"You've got my full attention," Lindsey said.

"When a superhero does something," Andy said, "he should do it because it's the right thing to do, not because he's going to get any credit or money for it."

Jack stroked his imaginary beard. Ava twitched her nose.

Andy said, "Most people do the things that they do for personal gain, in the form of money or goods or power, or to achieve the approval of someone else."

"That's true," Ava said.

"Have you ever noticed that Superman or Batman never hang around after they do something courageous?" Andy asked. "You never see them accepting medals or awards. They don't accept money. They don't do good things for selfish reasons. They usually disappear as soon as possible."

"And that's what makes Lois Lane frustrated," Lindsey said. "Superman never hangs around long enough for her to get a kiss."

Andy asked, "Do you understand why politicians and presidents can never be superheroes?"

"Because everything they do is to get re-elected or to please somebody who gave them money," Ava said.

"You're beginning to get the picture," Andy said. "It's so much easier to tell the difference between right and wrong when you don't personally gain from an activity, in terms of recognition or money."

"That's why you don't want people to know who you are, isn't it, Dad?" Jack asked.

"That's right. One more thing. Sometimes I take money from bad people and use it for good. Sometimes money will fall into your hands by accident, like the Confederate gold we have. But we don't spend this money on ourselves. We use it to help others."

"Then we're already superheroes," Ava said.

"Yes, you are," Andy said. "Another word for a superhero is a patriot. A patriot loves his country, but doesn't trust its government. The longer a government stays in power, the more corrupt it becomes. This is the nature of mankind."

"Where have I heard that before?" Jack asked.

Ava giggled.

Andy said, "Now you know why we can't use our real names in California. We don't want any money for what we do. We don't want medals. We won't brag to anyone about what we do, or blame others if we fail."

"What if we're superheroes, but we're not sure what's right?" Jack asked.

"That's simple," Ava said. "Ask Mom."

"Good answer," Andy said. "Works for me."

Lindsey did not comment.

"This plane was built for eight adults," Andy said, "so we have plenty of room to lie down and get some shuteye. We'll be in California in about four hours."

The plane had reached its cruising altitude of 40,000 feet and was traveling 700 MPH.

Lindsey looked up from her laptop. "Aren't you looking for a U-Haul renter, Andy?"

"We are. Have you found one?"

"I've been Googling phone numbers and studying Ava's columns," she said. "Aleksi called a U-Haul Center in Waterview, Wisconsin. Also, Aleksi, Demetrius, and Sasha each called a private number in Waterview regularly."

"Then we have another reason to go to Waterview on our way back east," Andy said. "I'd like to check out Arco Genetics. Can you find the address of the U-Haul place?"

"Sure. I've also got a ten year old picture of Aleksi that might help."

"We can take that picture to the U-Haul Center and Arco Genetics," Andy said. "What we really need are the numbers on that U-Haul truck."

At 1:30 in the morning PST the pilot called Andy to the cockpit. "Dr. Carlson, we'll be landing in Riverside in approximately thirty minutes. The Bell helicopter and pilot you ordered through the king are waiting for you. I understand that your wife and daughter will be staying with me until further notice."

"That's correct. Thank you."

Andy walked back into the passenger compartment of the king's plane. Lindsey glanced up at him, and then wiped her eyes.

"Honey, what's wrong?" he asked, sitting down next to her. "I thought you believed in this plan. Don't forget that hormones can be brutal when you're pregnant."

"Before she took a nap, Ava asked me again if Aleksi was sleeping comfortably."

"Oh," he said. "I'm sorry. Keep in mind that both of us would be dead without their training and courage to do what they don't fully comprehend."

They embraced.

22.

The Bell 525 Relentless helicopter came in low from the northeast and landed on the heliport next to the Port Authority Headquarters in Long Beach. Andy instructed the pilot to return to Riverside and await his call.

Andy and Jack were greeted at the heliport by an over-caffeinated sixty year old Caucasian who motioned for them to follow him to the control tower. The control tower was adjacent to the Port Authority Headquarters. Andy fell in behind him, carrying the duffel bag. Jack brought up the rear.

Andy saw two military officers waiting at the elevator, an Army colonel and a Marine general. Since he had not requested their services, he didn't acknowledge them. Seated to his left at the elevator was a squad of commandos, well-armed but with no insignia. They weren't SEAL Team Six.

The Army colonel and the Marine general got on the elevator to the control tower behind Andy and Jack, who wore their game faces. The ex-SEAL and his son were dressed for battle. Their faces were black with stripes of green. Both wore black watch caps.

Jack wore no shirt. His entire body was painted black. His skin glistened with baby oil. He wore black shorts and black tennis shoes. His bow and quiver of arrows were slung across his body from his right shoulder to his left hip. On his right leg was a knife exactly like his dad's, only his knife extended from his knee to his ankle.

Andy wore a SEAL combat uniform with the trident patch but no name or rank insignia. Every piece of gear that covered his upper body had been modified to accommodate his over-sized neck, shoulders, arms, and chest. Even after ten years on the shelf, the uniform fit well. A .45 caliber Glock pistol was holstered on the right side of his waist. Two fragmentation grenades were clipped to his combat vest. A dark fanny pack held extra ammo, the T5000 binoculars, a monocular night scope, two sets of handcuffs, a knotted rope, and his cell phone, turned off. He carried the GREM M16 and the AT4 in the duffle bag.

As they stepped off the elevator in the control tower, a black male, approximately forty-five years old, approached Andy. He was wearing an ill-fitting blue suit and a tie that didn't match anything else he had on.

"I'm the Director of the Port Authority," he said, "Sam Biggins."

He extended his hand and Andy shook it.

"Mr. Lee," Andy said.

Mr. Biggins introduced the others in the room.

"Could you let us know what you plan to do, Mr. Lee?" Biggins asked.

"I need a radio to get in touch with you when it's done," Andy said. "Can you point out the area where this container is?"

Biggins pointed at a poorly-lit area approximately a quarter mile away. "The container that you want is in the eighteenth row. Each double row has a sign. To see the rear of this container you would have to be in the eighty foot corridor in front of the sign, between row seventeen and row eighteen. You want stack number twenty-six, from the west, on the south side of double row eighteen. The container is on the third level."

He pointed again and handed his binoculars to Andy.

"I see the row signs," Andy said. "I'll need one person in a Humvee or similar vehicle to drive us to row fourteen. We can take it from there. I want no disturbance, no sudden noises, no overflying helicopters, no extra lights. Just sit tight until I call. This should be over in less than an hour."

The military officers looked at each other, but said nothing.

"Where is SEAL Team Six?" Andy asked. "I need to give them orders."

"The president redeployed them," the marine general said. "He decided that he couldn't afford to lose them all if you were unsuccessful."

Jack glanced at his dad, who did not flinch at this news.

"I'd like to speak with my son in private, sir."

Biggins pointed to an office nearby and handed Andy a radio. Andy turned the radio off and clipped it to his combat vest.

He walked into the office, closed the door behind him, and got down on one knee, eye to eye with his son. "Jack, you're the right man for this job. This is why we practice sneaking up on animals in the woods. Take the first good shot. If you see a better opportunity to end this that ensures that the warhead can't be detonated, take it. If you see anyone else besides me outside that container, put an arrow through their chest."

"Yes, sir."

"The HEAT round in the AT-4 must penetrate metal before it will destroy everything inside that container. That means the container doors need to be closed. If you were to fire into an open rear door of that container, the blast would be in the container above it."

Andy looked into Jack's eyes. There is a big difference between being nervous and being anxious to do your job. He liked what he saw. "I'm not going to take anything out of the duffel bag until our guide drops us off. I don't want anyone to know how we do what we do or which one of us does it. Watch for my hand signals. I won't be able to see you, but you should be able to see me with the night vision scope on the AT4."

"I'm ready."

"Do you remember the number of the container, son?"

"RECU6570382."

"It's in the upper right hand corner of the rear door and it's in red letters."

"Got it."

Andy and Jack waited for the elevator to take them back to ground level. The Marine general leaned over to Jack. "I wish that we could have handled this ourselves."

"That's okay, sir, we brought special equipment."

"Special equipment?" asked the Marine general.

"I don't think anyone here has any of these," Jack said. He pulled his dark shorts forward with his right hand and looked down into them.

The general leaned forward, and then stepped back quickly. "What's your name, son?"

"My code name is Batman."

Andy's cheeks elevated slightly, but only for a split second. He stepped onto the elevator with the duffel bag.

23.

Andy and Jack knelt at the end of row seventeen. The air was warm
and humid, more humid than usual for southern California. The
Humvee that dropped them off at row fourteen was out of sight. Andy
opened the duffel bag and handed the AT4 to Jack. He loaded the
HEAT round and checked Jack's bow and quiver. Satisfied, he patted
him on the shoulder. The boy slipped into the shadows of row seventeen and disappeared. Andy looked at his watch.

The ex-SEAL moved like a cat down row eighteen, gliding a few
steps, then stopping with his back to the bottom row of stacked containers. He felt the epinephrine surge. It was a need even a full emergency
department could not satisfy. At some level, he knew he was not invis-
ible or invincible. But a SEAL was. And he was a SEAL again tonight.

At stack twenty-six, he knelt and unzipped his fanny pack. His fingers
found the monocular night scope. The red letters on the target container
were distorted due to the sharp angle. He studied the letters and numbers
for a full minute before putting the scope back in his fanny pack.

The containers in row eighteen were all air conditioned or refrigerated, supplying a comforting amount of background noise. Andy
looked at his watch again, and then looked toward row seventeen.

A creaking sound didn't fit in with the gentle hum of the air condi-
tioners. He looked up. The left rear door of container RECU6570382
was opening.

He held his right palm up toward Jack and relocated to the base of
stack twenty-five, where he squatted. He placed the M16 on the pavement and then stood up, leaning against the rear doors of the bottom
container in stack twenty-five. Plan A was over. Plan B brought its own
surge of epinephrine, even stronger than Plan A.

An explanation landed quietly on the pavement. It rolled several feet on the tarmac between row eighteen and row seventeen. Andy squinted at the object.

So they didn't have all the amenities in there, after all. It was a roll of toilet paper.

A rope flew out of the open door and dangled to the ground. This rope had a knot tied every foot or so.

A young man emerged below the open door, leaning back on the rope, trying to keep his head and body perpendicular to the containers. He was thin and wearing only a white loincloth and headdress. This could be a ceremonial dress related to martyrdom or a practical response to the heat and humidity.

The thin man walked down the container wall one knot at a time. An arm reached out from above him and closed the left-hand door against the rope. When the young man reached the base of the container below RECU6570382, Andy put his right hand on the snap that held his knife in its sheath.

The barefooted man descended to the pavement safely. He turned and walked six steps toward the roll of toilet paper. He leaned over to pick it up. The knife severed both of his carotid arteries, both internal jugular veins, and his airway, in half a second. Andy felt the warmth on his right hand as the body collapsed to the pavement. He looked back to container RECU6570382. The left door was still closed on the rope.

He pulled the body by one leg down the base of row eighteen to the twenty-fourth stack, where he held his right palm toward Jack's position. He knelt to examine the man with the floppy head.

This man was Arab, twenty-five to thirty years old. The knife had penetrated the disc between the fourth and fifth cervical vertebrae. His head was attached to the rest of his body by some skin on the back of his neck.

Jack peered through the night scope of the AT4. His dad took off his boots, his socks, his combat vest, his shirt, his trousers, and his watch cap. He was barefooted, standing in his jockey shorts looking at the man with the floppy head. Jack adjusted the night scope. His dad pulled the loincloth from the dead man and put it on over his own jockey shorts. It looked like a big diaper. Jack put his hand over his mouth. His dad removed the headdress from the floppy head and turned it around several times before he put it on.

Jack identified a potential problem. Dad was taller and far more muscular than the man who had come down the rope. He watched Andy insert his knife and sheath into the loincloth and retie the tip of the sheath to his right thigh.

Andy was looking at the left door of the container with the knotted rope. He held the roll of toilet paper in his right hand. Jack placed the AT4 at his feet. He removed his bow from his shoulder and nocked an arrow. When he looked up, he couldn't find his dad in the shadows of row eighteen. The closest light pole was almost a hundred yards away. He would not be able to identify any target for an arrow unless it moved away from the base of row eighteen. He put down the bow and arrow and picked up the AT4 again. Without the night scope on the AT4 he couldn't even see his dad. He found him again in the scope.

Andy was standing motionless underneath stack twenty-six. Jack wished that he could take a picture. His dad would pay big-time to keep this diaper and headdress out of circulation. On the other hand, Mom and Ava would pay big-time to see such a picture.

After ten minutes, Andy tugged on the rope, banging it against the rear of the containers. When the left-sided door opened overhead, he threw the roll of toilet paper inside.

Jack watched his dad scale the container wall swiftly, hand over hand on the knotted rope, keeping his bare feet flat against the container.

When he reached eye level with the door, Andy saw the other Arab male, seated in a folding chair, also wearing only a loincloth and headdress. A small LED light illuminated half a sheet of plywood, which served as a table. The warhead was underneath the plywood. Food and papers covered the table.

No manual detonator cord was in sight. Andy pulled himself through the door of the container and left the door open. The man in the chair was reading a small book. Andy could see both his hands on the book. He didn't even look up as Andy walked toward him.

Andy's size eight and a half hands had served him well, both as a SEAL and a physician. He disliked gloves in combat, preferring the sensitivity of his fingers to the gloves' protection. It was easier to knock a man unconscious with bare knuckles. No one who wanted to shoot accurately tolerated anything between the trigger and the skin on his index finger.

Andy's right fist lifted the man out of his chair and broke his jaw.

"You have an early flight to Allah," he said, grasping the limp man's neck with his left hand and his loincloth with his right hand. Lifting the wannabe martyr over his head, Andy turned around in the container and launched the body head-first out the open container door.

The floor of the third-level container was seventeen feet above ground level. Andy added another seven feet by holding the body over his head. The ground in row eighteen was an especially hard type of asphalt tarmac, required to support the weight of the containers and the special vehicles that moved them. Andy didn't see the impact, but he heard it. He peered out the door.

The impact had awakened the Arab. He was lifting his head from the pavement between row seventeen and row eighteen. He was trying to get broken arms underneath his body.

Andy stood in the doorway, silhouetted by the LED light behind him. He looked toward Jack's position, extended his left arm, and drew back his right arm. A wooden arrow entered the second martyr's neck below his chin and ended the threat to Long Beach.

Andy lifted up the plywood and carefully placed it on the floor of the container. He pointed the LED light at the warhead and inspected the keyboard used to initiate a timed detonation. The detonator cord, with its switch, was wrapped like a snake in the floor. He followed the cord to its point of insertion in the warhead and pulled it out.

24.

Andy leaned out of the container door and motioned for Jack.
Jack appeared across from him with the AT4 on his right shoulder, his quiver hung on his left shoulder, and his stick bow in his left hand. He walked toward his dad. "Nice work."

"Thanks," Andy said. "Nice work by you. Remove the HEAT round from that rifle, put the rubber covers back on it, and tie it to the rope."

When the knot was tied, Jack held up his thumb.

Andy pulled up the short tube. He rolled up all of the papers he could find in the container and inserted them inside the tube, along with the small book the man had been reading. After replacing the rubber caps he lowered it down to Jack with the rope.

Andy climbed down the rope and embraced his son. "Help me find my clothes, son."

Andy unhooked the radio attached to his combat vest and turned it on, adjusting the volume. "Mr. Biggins, this is Mr. Lee."

"Yes sir, Mr. Lee, go ahead."

"The warhead is in our hands. Two Arabs are dead. We didn't need to destroy the container."

"Thank God."

"I'm going to need an extension ladder for my wife to get into this container and disable the warhead permanently."

"It's not ticking is it?" Biggins asked.

"No, Mr. Biggins. It's safe for now. My wife will be here soon by helicopter. Where can she land that's close to my position?"

"At the end of row sixteen," Biggins said. "We have a big asphalt pad there. It's used to park the machines that move these containers, but it's empty now."

"Can you circle that pad with flares and keep them lit up until my wife's helicopter gets here?"

"We can," he said. "The pad doesn't have any overhead wires or poles near it. It's a good spot."

"Roger that, Mr. Biggins. This is Mr. Lee signing off."

Andy turned his cell phone on. "Lindsey."

"I'm so glad to hear your voice," she said. "Is Jack okay?"

"We're both fine. We surprised two Iranians. We didn't have to fire the AT4. The warhead does need to be disabled permanently. Have our chopper pilot bring you here immediately. We'll have flares out. It's safe to bring Ava. She'll stay with the helicopter pilot while you do your thing. Bring all your gear and spacesuit. I want you to swap the tritium reservoir on this warhead for one of those in your toolbox. I'll keep everybody away. Make it look like there's some radiation risk."

Within five minutes the Humvee with the Marine general and Mr. Biggins turned down the pavement between row seventeen and row eighteen. Andy had almost completed dressing. He held up his hands to stop the vehicle. The two men got out.

"Gentlemen, this should be considered a crime scene for now," Andy said, replacing his watch cap. "And there is some radiation risk. I need at least a couple of hundred yards sealed off. Until my wife gets here to disable the warhead, you shouldn't walk any closer or touch anything. Notify local HAZMAT that we won't need them. The CIA will take care of everything. No modern weapons were fired. Mr. Biggins, there should be no pictures taken here tonight until after we leave."

Biggins shined a bright spotlight past Andy toward the Arab with a displaced head. The light panned to the Arab with a wooden arrow protruding from his neck, and then moved back and forth from one body to the other. The same light followed the knotted rope to the open door of the container.

"Jack," Andy said, "secure the AT4 tube and the HEAT round in the back of that Humvee in the duffel bag. Put both of our knives in there, plus your bow and quiver. Retrieve your arrow shaft. You'll probably have to unscrew it from the broad head. Mr. Biggins, when the CIA gets here, tell them to hold their position at the tower until I call."

Andy opened his cell phone and hit the speed dial for the president. "Mr. Umar, this is Mr. Lee."

"Go ahead, Carlson."

"We got the warhead without shooting it. I killed two Iranians. I disconnected the detonator switch."

"That's great, doctor. Did you find anything related to the other warhead?"

"Nothing so far, sir, but we haven't studied the container thoroughly. You need to limit access to this scene until it's cleaned up. The CIA needs to take control of the weapon when my wife finishes disabling it. Have them wait in the tower until I call. Please don't use my name or release any pictures of this incident."

"Agreed," Umar said.

"I just talked to the king," Andy said.

"Does he know where the second warhead is?" Umar asked.

"The king found a clue to the second warhead. I'm going to check it out."

"Work with the CIA, Carlson. They can help you."

"With all due respect, Mr. Umar, the CIA tagging along would compromise my ability to find the warhead and disable it without tipping off the martyrs."

"It's their job, Carlson," Umar said. "They're good at it."

"Then why couldn't they identify the location of this warhead, sir?" The president cleared his throat.

"One more thing, Mr. Umar. You asked my family to risk their lives for you. I only asked for SEAL Team Six to back me up."

"I'm the president, Carlson. I deploy assets where I please."

"My family is not a government asset, sir. And I can't work with people I can't trust to back me up. Find yourself another boy."

"But Carlson.."

Andy disconnected the call.

The Marine general and Mr. Biggins watched the kid with total body makeup, black shorts, no shirt, greased from head to boots. He was stowing equipment in the back of the Humvee. After all the equipment was covered up, the kid walked over to one of the bodies on the pavement and unscrewed the shaft of the arrow protruding out of the man's neck. He wiped the shaft on the Arab's loin cloth and put it back in his quiver.

When the boy reached the Humvee, the Marine general asked, "Son, where did you get the recoilless rifle?"

"I don't recall, sir."

"Why did that man's head need to be cut off?" asked the general.

"Teddy Roosevelt advised that if you're going to hit your enemy," Jack said, "never hit softly."

The general frowned.

"In the dark, could you tell if that Arab had a remote detonator in his loincloth?" Jack asked. "That warhead could have been detonated by something as simple as a cell phone."

"Good job, Batman."

25.

Lindsey and Ava arrived on the Bell helicopter, which touched down smoothly in the LZ outlined by flares at the end of row sixteen. The family embraced. Andy helped Lindsey put on her spacesuit. He spoke to the pilot of the helicopter. "Would you please entertain my daughter while my wife and I complete our work?"

"As long as we can remain on the ground," the pilot said. "She's already learned everything I know about this chopper. I think she wants my job."

Andy smiled and hugged his daughter again. "Please hop back in and wait for us, darling. There could be radiation hazard here. There's nothing to see."

"Then make sure Mom keeps her lead apron on," she said. "We have a baby to worry about."

"I'll do that. And thanks for your thoughtfulness."

Andy and Lindsey walked to stack twenty-six. He pointed toward the ladder supplied by Mr. Biggins.

"Take your time on this ladder," he said. "I would be glad to carry your lead apron, but I'm not pregnant. I'm right behind you with the toolbox and Geiger counter."

She looked up at the extension ladder and then back toward Biggins and the general.

"Could you guys steady this ladder while we go up?" Andy asked.

The general and Mr. Biggins jumped to hold the ladder.

Andy said. "Mr. Biggins, when we get inside, could you get a tarp or a blanket to cover the bodies?"

They reached the third container safely. "We need a bright light up here," Andy called from the open door.

Mr. Biggins tied his spotlight to the knotted rope and Andy hauled it up.

Lindsey turned on the Geiger counter. The slow, soft chirps indicated an acceptable amount of radiation. She inspected the warhead. "Definitely an old Soviet warhead," she said, opening up her toolbox.

While Andy held the light, Lindsey removed the tritium reservoir from the warhead with a wrench. She held it up. Andy shined the spotlight on it.

"I don't need to take that back to my lab," she said. "It's not forty years old. It's a new reservoir. It has fresh wrench marks at the base. I use a padded wrench to avoid making those kinds of marks. Old reservoirs have unique Russian identifiers. This one doesn't."

"You think somebody besides the Russians manufactured it?"

"Nope. Only the Russians could manufacture a new reservoir that matched an old Soviet warhead. Each warhead has a serial number. Any new reservoir must be manufactured to release neutrons into the plutonium core of the warhead at the exact instant specified by the serial number on the warhead. We're talking hundredths of a second. The Russians never handed over these specifications, since they were not necessary to disarm a warhead."

"Then you're not going to need to finish those soil samples from Ras Tanura."

"No rush."

"Leave one of our old reservoirs next to this warhead, and put the new one in your toolbox."

"Why?"

"I don't know how Umar would respond to the truth."

To complete the disarming process, Lindsey stuffed a roll of wire into the threaded hole in the plutonium core, periodically cutting the wire and pushing the broken piece inside the core with another length of wire. She completed this in fifteen minutes.

"I'm also disconnecting the internal battery for the timer," she said.

"I collected all of the paperwork from their makeshift table and put it inside the AT4 tube," Andy said. "Maybe we can learn something useful from it."

He shined the light around the container while Lindsey searched the container floor with the LED light.

"I stepped on it," she said, holding up a cell phone. "It was under a newspaper."

"Put the cell phone in your toolbox," Andy said. "When we get back on the king's plane we can research every number on it and match the numbers up with our data base."

Two CIA agents were waiting at the foot of the ladder with Mr. Biggins and the Marine general when Andy and Lindsey got their feet back on the pavement. They flashed their credentials.

"You were supposed to wait for my instructions in the tower," Andy said. "You could have exposed yourself unnecessarily to radiation."

"You had a job to do, Carlson," said one agent, "and we have our job."

"My name is Lee," Andy said. "And now you've endangered my family. Please instruct the general and Mr. Biggins to do a better job than you at keeping their mouths shut."

Both agents stiffened.

"Who's going to brief us on what happened here?" the other CIA agent asked.

"Nobody," Andy said. "I don't work with blabbermouths who don't follow orders. Maybe you can do better with the cleanup job."

"We don't take orders from you, doctor," an agent said. "You'll need to file a written report with the CIA if you don't talk to us."

Andy picked up the toolbox, the lead apron, and the Geiger counter. He leaned down until his nose nearly touched the nose of the CIA agent. "I didn't do this for the CIA," he said. "I don't owe you anything. Get out of my way or I will remove you from my path."

The agent stepped backward.

Lindsey took Andy's arm as they walked back to the Humvee, where Jack waited. They left the two CIA agents, Mr. Biggins, and the Marine general at stack twenty-six, row eighteen. Andy drove the Humvee to the Bell helicopter.

On the helicopter ride back to Riverside, Andy pointed out that the president was tracking them using the satellite phone he had given Andy, now on the Citation at Riverside Airport. "If he can track us, he'll send agents to follow us wherever we go. This will only hamper our progress. It may result in some agent tipping off the very people we're looking for. I think it's time to send them off in another direction."

"How are you going to do that?" Jack asked.

"I bought a prepaid overnight FedEx package for the president's satellite phone," Andy said. "I was just waiting for the right time to use it. I'm going to put this phone in the package at the Riverside airport and send it to Bernard Pollard."

"The man from Buckingham who lost his leg in the posthole accident?" Ava asked.

"That's right. I'm also going to send him 5000 dollars in cash."

"Mighty generous of you," Jack said.

"The Pollards are good friends," Andy said. "I think Bernard and his girlfriend deserve to take a vacation, fly around the country, see the sights. I don't care where they go."

"So long as they take the president's phone?" Lindsey asked.

"It's a short-term solution," Andy said. "I need to talk to the king about a better solution."

26.

A ndy approached the king's pilot in the cockpit of the Citation X at the Riverside Airport. "We need to proceed to the closest airport to Waterview, Wisconsin, as soon as possible."

"No problem," the pilot answered, "Give me a few minutes to look at the maps and file a flight plan. We should be underway within fifteen minutes."

"File a flight plan to St. Louis," Andy said. "When you reach cruising altitude, shut off your transponder."

"Roger that," the pilot said.

As the king's plane took off, Andy opened up his laptop to check his email. The king had already responded.

To: Andy Carlson
From: King Fahd
Re: On the Trail

Almost nothing is shipped directly from Iran to Ras Tanura. Ras Tanura was an oil exporting terminal only. It did not usually receive containers. However, we were supposed to receive a container by IRSL on the very day of the explosion. We had been waiting on a shipment of three oversized pipeline valves from Modakhtar Industries for more than a month. Modakhtar said that they would deliver these directly to Ras Tanura on a small container ship. Attached is the bill of lading. Modakhtar is the largest valve maker in the Middle East. We have done business with them in the past, but only

because we could not find another expedient source for a complex valve.

I hope that you can tell me if this was the ship that carried a warhead to Ras Tanura.

King Fahd.

Andy examined the bill of lading. The container had a GTIN number assigned by Modakhtar Industries. But the Container Identification Number matched the container from Arco Genetics in Wisconsin. The bill included a picture of the side of the container and the rear of the container. Andy compared the picture of the container shipped to Ras Tanura to a picture of the container that originated in Wisconsin, gleaned from Aleksi's account with Ready Cargo. They were the same container.

Andy typed his response:

To: King Fahd
From: Andy Carlson
Re: On the Trail

Unless you used a whole lot of bull semen at Ras Tanura, we know who bought the warhead, who sold it, and how it was delivered to Ras Tanura. I have good paperwork to document the path of this weapon to your doorstep. I also have a recording of Aleksi Ivanov admitting that he sold warheads to the Iranians.

Your Citation X and pilot have been very useful to us so far. We have found one warhead at Long Beach and disarmed it. Even though your plane is leased under an

American company name, I am concerned that a bungler will eventually track my movements using its transponder. Currently we have reported that our transponder is malfunctioning. It would be helpful if you would lease another Citation X under another name and leave it at the manufacturing plant in Wichita, Kansas, with another pilot. At some point, we can stop there and switch planes. Ask the Cessna plant to install a new transponder in the plane I leave in Kansas. I am sure that you can do this without anyone connecting you or me to either plane.

Andy pressed "Send."

Lindsey looked up from her laptop. She was holding Ava's list. "Aleksi called Arco Genetics from his cell phone many times over the last ninety days."

"Perhaps I can find his connection there," he said. "Now that we know for sure what was in the first refrigerated container, go back to the second refrigerated container, the one that left Long Beach at least six days ago."

He handed her his laptop.

"I already know where it's going," Lindsey said, working the keyboard of Andy's laptop.

"Where?" Jack asked.

"The letter that the president received from Islamic Jihad said that the British would be targeted also," Lindsey said. "The fact that this second container is refrigerated means that it probably has a warhead and martyrs on board."

Andy sat next to Lindsey and studied the Ready Cargo Account of Aleksi Ivanov. The Citation X cruised eastward at 40,000 feet.

Andy said. "As soon as we have time, we need to warn the British."

Lindsey said, "From Long Beach, the container is scheduled to pass through the Panama Canal. In fact, it should be near the canal now."

"What's the final destination?" Jack asked.

"London, in nine more days," Lindsey said. "We have some time."

"What's the name of the container ship?" Ava asked.

"The *Spirit of Long Beach*," Lindsey said.

"I need to think about how to break this news, and who to break it to," Andy said.

27.

"We've begun our approach to the Madison airport," the king's pilot announced. "Waterview is less than an hour's drive from Madison."

When the plane came to a stop, Andy reviewed his goals for the visit to Waterview.

"I'm going to rent a car and take us all to Waterview. When we get there, Lindsey and Ava will drop Jack and me off at Arco Genetics before going to the U-Haul rental place. Take your laptop with the picture of Aleksi with you. I have the same picture on mine. Call me if you find the truck."

The people at Arco Genetics were really nice. Jack held Andy's laptop as he walked around the room, examining the pictures of prize bulls on the wall while his dad did most of the talking. Andy told the young lady who answered the bell on the counter that he was James Lee, an employee of Ready Cargo in Long Beach.

"I need to talk with someone about a lost shipment of bull semen," Andy said.

He was referred to the shipping department, down a hallway behind the counter. Jack followed Andy to a large office.

The assistant shipping manager appeared to be in his early twenties. He got up from his desk and smiled like a politician when Andy and Jack entered the shipping department.

"I'm John Kirkland. How can I be of help?"

They shook hands and Andy introduced himself and his son, James Junior.

"I'm trying to track down a shipment of bull semen to Iran approximately six weeks ago," Andy said. "It supposedly left here by a refrigerated Ready Cargo Container. A flatbed truck took it to Long Beach. At Long Beach it went to Singapore. From Singapore it was supposedly transferred to IRSL."

"None of that sounds right," John said. "Iran is one of our larger customers, but we ship to them only twice yearly, usually in February and September. We haven't sent them anything since February."

"Perhaps there's some other explanation for this," Andy said. He gestured toward Jack, who handed him the laptop. Andy opened up Aleksi's account at Ready Cargo, which included a picture of the container and a copy of the bill of lading. He showed it to John.

"This is one of our GTINs," John said, "but I have no record of such a shipment in our books. I would remember it. If only Vladimir were here."

"Vladimir?"

"Vladimir Ivanov is our shipping manager," John said. "He took a week off to locate several members of his family who are missing."

"He lost his family?"

"His brother, his brother's granddaughter, and his own granddaughter apparently went to Virginia and didn't come back. His brother had only been there a few days. Vladimir became concerned when he couldn't contact any of them."

"I see. How old is Vladimir?"

"He's about sixty-five. He's training me to take his place when he retires."

"Do you have a picture of Vladimir?" asked Andy. "I think that I know this man."

"I could get one from personnel." John left to get the picture of Vladimir.

Andy didn't recognize the man in the picture. "I believe I met Vladimir when he was younger," he said. "I'd like to reestablish my relationship with him. May I have a copy of this picture?"

"Sure."

"Do you recognize the man in this picture?" Andy asked, showing John the picture of Aleksi on his laptop.

"That's Vladimir's brother, Alex. He's our president and international sales representative. He looks younger in that picture."

"What does Alex do?"

"He travels around the world representing Arco Genetics," John said, "so he's gone a lot. He opens up new accounts, visits current customers, and makes sure that we're meeting the needs of our customers. Alex is the grandfather of this company. He bought Arco Genetics when it only had domestic sales. He's responsible for our accounts in one hundred fifty countries."

"So Alex has visited Iran and might be able to help us clear this up?" Andy asked.

"Alex visits Iran at least once a year. Vladimir usually goes with him."

"Do you sell to Russia?"

"Of course. Alex and Vladimir have old friends there."

"Where does Alex live?"

"Most of the Ivanovs live on a farm outside of Waterview," John said. "Alex and Vladimir's wives are deceased. I don't think they really do much except keep a large garden. At one time they bred the bulls themselves. Vladimir and Alex fish a lot when Alex is home."

"Does Alex have any children?"

"He has a son, Sebastian. He's a professional livestock butcher. Sebastian and his wife Sonja have some kind of import business. They live on the same farm."

"Sebastian doesn't work for Arco?"

"No. He dropped out of school. He was in charge of breeding the bulls on the Ivanov farm at one time. He's an outdoorsman, not a businessman."

"Do Sebastian and Sonja have children?"

"They have three children. Their grown daughter isn't living on the farm anymore. They have a couple of younger kids, twins, in a boarding school in France. Alex is very attached to all his grandchildren. He sees the twins often since he travels through Paris a lot, but I've never met them."

"Is the older daughter named Sasha?"

"Yes. She's a nurse," John said. "Do you know her?"

"I recently met her. Does Vladimir have any children?"

"One daughter named Nadia. She's married to guy named Demetrius. I don't think any of the Ivanovs like him. Demetrius and Nadia are missing in Virginia, along with Alex and Sasha."

"I always wanted to live on a farm in a small town," Jack said. "A place like Waterview, where everybody seems to know everybody."

"Sonja's sister Tasya is married to the police chief here in Waterview," John said. "They live nearby, but I've never visited the police chief's house. Nadia and Demetrius had their own place before moving to Virginia."

"I'd like to visit Alex and Vladimir when they come back from Virginia," Andy said. "Do you have their address, and perhaps a phone number?"

"Sure."

Andy took down the information, and then looked up. "I think this is just a paperwork mistake."

"It's a very big mistake," John said. "Bull semen is sold in small straws of one quarter to one half milliliter each. All of our international shipments go by air, because the semen must remain frozen. One refrigerated package is worth millions of dollars. We usually use UPS."

"Then you don't ship forty foot containers at all?" Andy asked.

"Not for bull semen," John said. "We developed our own insulated liquid nitrogen tank so that our clients could store semen. Did you know that we still have bull semen collected in the 1950s?"

"I didn't know that," Jack said.

"Our liquid nitrogen tanks are shipped in forty-foot containers, but we haven't sold any in several months. We don't use forty foot refrigerated containers for anything."

"You've been very helpful," Andy said. "Somebody goofed."

Andy shook John's hand and walked to the parking lot to wait for Lindsey and Ava.

His cell phone rang. The caller ID said "Lindsey."

He opened the phone. "Is something wrong?"

"No, Andy, something is right. The manager of the U-Haul Rental Center in Madison identified Aleksi and he gave me the license number of the truck."

"That's wonderful. Where are you now?"

"I'm watching that U-Haul truck on Interstate 64 in West Virginia, headed east. Aleksi rented this truck four days ago."

"You're watching the truck?"

"They track all their trucks with GPS, just like we track our containers," Lindsey said. "They want to be sure that their vehicles can't get stolen and their maintenance people can find them when they're disabled."

"Ask the manager if we can call a number and keep track of the location of that truck."

"I already did. They answer twenty-four hours a day."

"Get back here as quickly as you can."

"See you in a few minutes."

"Am I going to get a shot with the AT4 this time?" Jack asked.

"It's possible."

They talked while waiting for Lindsey and Ava.

"We could call the president and tell him where this truck is, and let him handle it," Andy said.

"And Umar would have the same difficulties that he had in Long Beach," Jack said. "We're the only ones with any real experience. They're still not convinced that shooting a warhead is a good way to disable it, and they're worried about the manual detonator switch being activated by any explosion nearby."

"You're right, son."

Lindsey pulled up and Ava shouted out the window, "We cracked the case."

On the drive back to Madison Andy and Lindsey swapped information.

"I know where Aleksi lives," Andy said. "He and his brother work for Arco Genetics. They have a farm outside of Waterview. I have an address and a phone number."

He handed Ava the information.

"It's the same number that Aleksi, Nadia, and Sasha called regularly from Farmville," Ava said.

"But we don't have time to go to this farm now," Andy said.

"We're going to West Virginia, aren't we?" Lindsey asked.

"This is way too important to leave up to the government," Jack said. "The Ivanov farm will have to wait."

"The two of you should keep in mind that this farm will be a risky place to visit," Lindsey said. "We would be at a great disadvantage compared to our farm."

"Funny you should mention our farm," Andy said. "That's where Aleksi's brother is now."

"Aleksi's brother is on our farm?" Ava asked.

"Aleksi's brother Vladimir is looking for Aleksi, Sasha, and Nadia, according to the man I talked to at Arco Genetics. Apparently they aren't too concerned about Demetrius."

"How can we protect the farm if we're not there?" Ava asked.

Andy said, "I'll give Charlie Dodd and Ben a heads-up."

Andy called the king's pilot on his cell phone and advised him of their ETA to Madison.

"We need to get out in front of a U-Haul truck with a warhead in it," he said. "When we're in the air, we can decide where you'll need to land. File a flight plan for Wichita, Kansas, where you will eventually be going to get your transponder fixed."

"Where are we actually going?" asked the pilot.

"Richmond, Virginia," Andy said. "At least for now."

28.

Jack and Ava slept on the luxurious seats in the Citation X.

"Lindsey," Andy asked, "would you check on the shipment from Long Beach that's bound for England? It may have already passed through the Panama Canal. I'm gambling that the canal itself is not their target."

"I feel like I'm losing control," she said, "going deeper and deeper into a dark hole."

"That's normal for combat," Andy said. "Once the action starts, you'll be a warrior again, just like you were when I met you."

She shuddered.

Lindsey no longer needed to look up Ready Cargo's web site or Aleksi's account number and password. She accessed the three shipments in the account and found the most recent shipment, which left Long Beach nine days ago. She clicked on "Locate your shipment."

"Oh Lord," she said. "The *Spirit of Long Beach* exited the Panama Canal six hours ago and is headed to London."

"Then I need an email address for the Prime Minister of England," Andy said.

"I'll see what I can do," Lindsey said.

Andy went to the cockpit. "Could you make a phone call to Virginia for me?"

"You can make it yourself," the pilot said. "Use the blue phone over the co-pilot's seat."

Andy punched in the number for Charlie Dodd, his neighbor on the north side of South Airport Road. "Charlie?"

"Andy, good to hear from you."

"When I left the farm," Andy said, "I sprinkled sand on the farm road just inside the gate. If it hasn't rained, and there are tracks in that sand, someone has broken the lock and is on the farm."

"And you want me to check it out?"

"I'd appreciate it. Give Ben a heads-up and then call me back on my cell phone."

Andy returned to the passenger compartment of the king's plane.

"I think we should talk to the British now," Andy said, "in case something happens to us. Did you find an email address for the Prime Minister?"

She handed him the laptop. "He's now on your contact list. I don't know how secure his end is."

"The British need time to consider my recommendation," Andy said. "They must act while that container ship is far away from London and nowhere near land." He began typing.

To: Prime Minister of England
From: James Lee
Re: URGENT NOTICE OF INBOUND NUCLEAR WEAPON TO LONDON

I am a private citizen of the United States. I suspect that just prior to the destruction of Ras Tanura, you received a letter from Islamic Jihad, as did our president. The president asked me to help locate the warheads in the United States.

Over the past week I have found clear tracks of the movements of several nuclear warheads, including the one that destroyed Ras Tanura.

An armed warhead is on its way to London aboard a U.S. registered container ship named the *Spirit of Long Beach*,

owned and operated by Ready Cargo. It is carrying a refrigerated forty foot container with one twenty kiloton warhead. An identical container at Long Beach had two Iranian stowaway martyrs with a manual detonation switch.

This container is RECU4108265. The GTIN number is 10074652694573. The *Spirit of Long Beach* just left the Panama Canal six hours ago with London as its destination. Confidence that this container has a warhead is very high. This is the only nuclear threat I have identified that targets Great Britain.

The president does not know that I have located the warhead on its way to you. There would be political advantages to both you and the president if you proceed with my recommendation without conferring with Mr. Umar. You have the right and obligation to defend yourself. I'm sure that the president would rather not have the burden of ordering the sinking of a United States vessel.

THIS SHIP MUST BE DESTROYED AS FAR OUT TO SEA AS POSSIBLE, WITHOUT DELAY. It is reasonable for the Iranians to detonate the weapon immediately if they suspect that they have been discovered. They would prefer to be martyrs than to drown in a container.

I recommend that you contact this ship and confirm this container in its manifest, if you do not already have access to this information. It would be fortunate if the refrigerated container was on the outside of the ship, vulnerable to a precision-guided weapon, but this is un-likely, given the number of containers on that ship.

I suggest that you divert this ship from the shipping lane, away from all other traffic and other countries. A submarine could sink the ship, if you have one nearby, but it would probably have to get close to the warhead to ensure proper identification. A large torpedo ex-ploding just under the hull would lift the entire ship in the air and dump most of its containers overboard. The Iranians could survive long enough to detonate the war-head. A large precision-guided bomb delivered from the air would destroy the containers instantly.

Those at greatest risk are the crew of this container ship. It would be worth trying to get the crew to abandon ship just before a precision guided bomb hits, but lowering boats would require that the ship reduce its speed dras-tically. The Iranians may detect any significant change in course or the slowing of the ship. They could panic and detonate the warhead. Rescue seaplanes should main-tain a safe distance from the ship and be aware of EMP.

This communication must be guarded.

Good luck.

Andy pressed "SEND" and looked up from his laptop.

Lindsey walked over to sit next to him. "Do you realize that the children are getting behind in their home schooling?"

"The last time I asked you about school, you said they were ready for Harvard."

"I also said that Harvard wasn't ready for them."

"Then they may as well get some on-the-job training before puberty blows us all out of the water," Andy said.

"Our life is getting a little too exciting, isn't it?" she asked.

"But what a wonderful adventure to tell our grandchildren."

"Along with that crap about the terrible frog from Nicaragua?" Lindsey asked. "I looked that up. In order to get the sweat of one frog they cram a stick down its mouth and out one of its legs. The frog sweats enough poison to kill fifty people. What are you going to say next time Ava asks about how Aleksi is doing?"

"What do you suggest?"

"I think she already suspects Aleksi is dead," Lindsey said. "She's testing you. She's waiting on you to trust her with the truth."

29.

Andy gently shook Jack's shoulder and waited for him to sit up and look around.

"Jack, this U-Haul truck is going to be your job. Tell me how you want to handle it."

"Tell me everything we know," Jack said.

"We know that at least one Iranian is driving a U-Haul truck east on I-64, and we can follow him with a GPS tracker from Madison. He's now in West Virginia. Our weapon of choice is still the AT4 CS. We have two of them on board. The possible targets of the Iranians are Hampton Roads or Washington, D.C."

Jack stroked his imaginary beard.

"Take about ten minutes and then give me your ideas," Andy said.

Jack moved to the front of the plane and sat down behind the cockpit.

"Andy, do you think it's a good idea to let your ten year old son plan an attack on a truck with an armed nuclear warhead in it?" Lindsey asked.

"You can learn a lot about military tactics by reading," Andy said, "but you'll never be any good in the field unless you have real experience. I didn't say that I was sending him out alone. It's important for him to learn how to analyze a situation, plan calculated risks, and choose the right action on his own."

"I know what you're saying, Andy, but he's only a boy."

Andy closed his eyes.

"I know you hate that excuse," she said, "and I know that Jack and Ava aren't normal ten year olds."

"Let me ask you some questions," Andy said. "If I trust him today, do you think he will ever doubt my confidence in him? Do you think he'll have more or less confidence in himself?"

"I'm sure the rest of the mothers and fathers in the world would say we're crazy. On the other hand, they don't know what Jack and Ava are capable of doing."

"Jack and Ava don't know what they're capable of doing," Andy said. "And that is my point. One of our goals is to teach them to think through problems and to trust their own judgment and instincts. Some day they may very well be the greatest hope our country has."

"All right," Lindsey said. "I'll support you, but I reserve the right to worry."

He kissed her. "I want you to worry. I need you to pick up on my mistakes and remind me of dangers I haven't considered. You and I have equal rank in this outfit. No matter what crazy idea pops into my head, I seek your counsel whenever possible, before I proceed."

Jack returned to the table across from his dad and mom and sat down.

"Go ahead," Andy said.

"It's obvious that we need to get out in front of them," Jack said. "We should try to locate some type of funnel, somewhere they will have to stop or slow down. We need a shot from the rear, hopefully not at a moving target."

"Why?" Andy asked.

"If we're in a vehicle on the road, we can get close enough to positively identify the license plate. We're less likely to be identified as a threat and more likely to get off a clean shot from the rear. We should find out if they need to stop for gas. Also, everybody needs to pee sometime."

"What types of funnels have you thought of?"

"Toll booths, possibly."

"That's good. Are there any toll booths near them?"

"I don't know yet," Jack said. "Can we call the U-Haul Rental Center back and get their exact location? We need the size of the gas tank in that truck, how many miles per gallon they use on the interstate, and the last time they stopped for gas. Mom told me that the GPS tracker takes data points every five minutes. The U-Haul center should be able to tell us if these guys stopped last night to sleep, or if they stopped for gas or meals recently. All of that would be good information."

"How would you get the information about toll booths?"

"Call the Highway Patrol and ask them for the locations of toll booths on I-64 in West Virginia."

"Good answers. What would be your best scenario?"

"My best scenario would be for us to fall in behind them in a rented vehicle and follow until they stopped for something. There is less danger to other people if they're not on the Interstate. If they're stopped, the shot would be a piece of cake."

"What would be your backup plan if you're unable to get a clean shot and they get past Richmond?"

"Somebody still needs to shoot that truck," Jack said. "We have to assume that there's a suicidal maniac in the back with a detonator. If we get close enough we could use the T5000 binoculars to look inside it. The local weather needs to be considered. The problem with involving the military is that they are more likely to spook these guys. Ideally, this should be a one-shot battle. We're in a better position to take that shot than anyone else. And we have another advantage over the military."

Andy leaned toward Jack.

"When the president gives an order, he can't vouch for the competence of the few people who carry it out in the field," Jack said. "He doesn't know them personally. In this case, he couldn't find a team with our experience in the field with nuclear warheads. Confidence comes from success. You can't hit a home run if you never swing the bat. Once you hit a home run, you're more likely to hit another one. Nobody in the military could feel confident with a situation like this. They've never been there."

"I think you're right," Andy said. "Lindsey and I will get the information you need, and I'm going to back you up when you shoot."

"I appreciate it, Dad, but I don't intend to miss."

"That's the spirit."

Andy and Lindsey made their calls and announced the results to Jack and Ava.

"This truck has a forty gallon tank, and they haven't stopped in almost 400 miles," Lindsey said. "They didn't stop last night to sleep. The truck gets about ten to twelve miles per gallon."

"Sounds like they'll never make it to Washington or Hampton Roads without stopping," Jack said. "So where are they now?"

"Just going through Charleston," Lindsey said.

"And what's the closest airport out in front of them?" Jack asked.

"The pilot says that Beckley is his choice," Andy said, reaching for his laptop.

Google maps had a great map of West Virginia's section of I-64. They looked it over.

"I would suggest that we fall in behind them at Beckley and hope that they stop before they get to Staunton," Jack said. "At Staunton they could go north on I-81 toward Washington or east on I-64 toward Hampton Roads."

"I'll tell the pilot," Andy said. "He can order a rental car so we're not delayed in Beckley. I want a van with a sliding door and a rooftop rack."

The private jet made a gentle roll and then descended rapidly. The landing was barely palpable. Andy asked the pilot to remain at the airport. He informed him that they expected to be back within a couple of hours.

Fifteen minutes after landing, the Carlsons had stowed all of their gear in a green Ford van with sliding doors on each side and a rack on top.

Andy climbed in and nodded his approval. "What a beautiful spring day. I'd guess sixty degrees." He looked at his watch. 2:05 PM EST. "We need to hurry over to the closest I-64 overpass."

Andy left the airport access road and drove to the I-64 East ramp. After going ten yards down the ramp, he pulled off onto the right shoulder of the acceleration lane. "Lindsey, we need an update on the exact position of that truck," he said. "Call one more time. Be sure that they haven't stopped."

Andy left the engine running, with the transmission in "park." Lindsey sat in the shotgun seat, and Jack and Ava in the single bench seat in the back. Andy looked around the van. The cargo area was huge, more than adequate.

It was time for orders.

"Lindsey, I want you to take the wheel," Andy said, climbing out of the driver's seat.

Lindsey nodded, holding her cell phone in her ear.

"Ava, get up front and take Mom's place. Use your binoculars and watch the traffic as it comes underneath that underpass."

"Jack, take your seat next to the sliding door on the right."

"Ava, look for an orange truck that says U-Haul on the side. It's about half as big as an eighteen wheeler."

"Jack, I'm going to sit in the back next to you. Put your seat belt on. Put your makeup on."

Andy and Jack painted their faces with black camo. Black watch caps hid their sandy hair. Andy tied his knife and sheath to his right calf. Jack did the same. Andy checked the slide on his Glock .45 pistol and put the pistol back in its holster on the right side of his belt.

"When the time comes," Andy said, "you should be outside the van to take the shot. Even the CS model of the AT4 shouldn't be fired inside a vehicle this size. I'm your spotter. Just listen to me."

Andy removed the rubber caps from two AT4 tubes and loaded each with a HEAT round. He handed one to Jack and placed the second in the floor next to his feet.

"The safety is on, but it's otherwise ready to fire," he said.

Lindsey closed her cell phone. "Their last fix was five miles west of here and they haven't stopped."

"Game time!" Ava cried. "I see them."

Lindsey checked the rear view mirror and eased back onto the acceleration lane.

The U-Haul truck shot past them in the passing lane.

"Hang back about 100 yards in the right lane," Andy said. "Check the license, Ava."

She read the plate out loud. "It's a Wisconsin plate, UH7863."

"That's a match," Jack said. "Now we wait for them to stop."

"If any Iranians survive our ambush," Andy said, "we want prisoners this time, not more dead Iranians. Jack, one or more of them might be outside the truck when you shoot. After you shoot, throw the AT4 tube in the back and take out your stick bow. Shoot to wound or disable anyone outside the van. Put these handcuffs in your pocket. I have a pair. Lindsey and Ava will stay in the van until I signal that it's okay to get out. Lindsey, you're going to need your radiation suit and Geiger counter."

Lindsey drove on for about forty minutes.

Ava announced, "They're switching lanes. There's an exit ahead. They have their turn signal on."

"Heads up," Andy said. "Lindsey, take this exit. They're likely stopping for gas at that Shell station."

Andy surveyed the Shell station with his binoculars.

"Expect at least two Arabs to get out of the truck, not necessarily at the same time. We can't dismiss the possibility that someone stays in the back. They might have a peephole. Lindsey, you should try to find a spot where you're facing the back of their truck."

The Shell station had two pump islands, each with two pumps serving both sides of a concrete island. The U-Haul pulled up to the right of the island farthest away from the Shell mini-mart. A white SUV was leaving the lane closest to the building as Lindsey pulled in.

"That's good," Andy said. "It's just us and the Iranians. I hope the AT4 rocket can surgically destroy that truck without igniting the gas tanks underground."

"Lindsey, back over there to that light pole, against the curb."

"Jack, get ready. Your range from that curb is forty-five yards."

An Arab male got out of the passenger side of the truck immediately. He was wearing blue jeans and a short-sleeved T-shirt. He walked across the empty aisle of pumps into the Shell mini-mart. A second Arab male got out of the driver's side and inserted a credit card into the pump. He wore running shoes without socks, khaki shorts, a white T-shirt with a pocket, and a Washington Redskins baseball hat.

"It would be ideal if we could shoot as they pull away from the pumps," Andy said. "They would be farther from the pumps, the underground tanks, and the building."

He reached behind him into the duffel bag and picked up the FLIR monocular.

"Look at the truck and tell me what you see," he said, handing the forward-looking infrared device over the seat to Lindsey.

She studied the truck. "There's too much daylight for the best look."

"Give me what you know for sure," Andy said.

"Confirm warhead in the rear of that truck," Lindsey said. "No one is left inside."

"Ava, roll down your window. Open your door but don't get out."

"Jack, open the sliding door and step out behind Ava's door."

"Rest the AT4 on the window sill of the front passenger door. Your target is just above the license plate."

They watched the driver lean back against the truck while the pump filled his tank.

Ava rested her elbows on the dashboard in the right front seat. She focused her binoculars on the man at the pump. "He's reaching into his T-shirt pocket."

Andy said, "It's a cell phone."

"He looked at us, Dad, and he's gettin' agitated," Ava said. "He's waving toward the mini-mart."

"Stand by, Jack. We can't let him make a call or get back in that vehicle or even stick his arm inside."

Andy reached into the duffel bag behind him and pulled the slide on another Glock .45. He placed the pistol in Lindsey's lap.

"Everybody except Jack concentrate on the guy at the pumps."

"He's putting the cell phone back in his pocket," Ava said. "Now he's staring at us. I think he sees the tube of the AT4 or Jack's legs."

"Jack, take aim."

"Lindsey, open your door and commence firing at the driver. Keep shooting until he's down."

"Say hello to my little friend," Jack said.

Lindsey opened the driver's door, stepped out, and rested her extended arms on the hinge between the door and the door frame. She fired methodically.

Andy opened the sliding door behind the driver, dropped to a prone position on the pavement at Lindsey's feet and began firing his Glock .45.

"Here he comes with a gun," Ava called.

"Ava, get in the floor," Lindsey yelled.

The driver of the U-Haul truck ran straight toward them for five yards with his head low, arms extended, his gun obscuring his face. At forty yards he began to zigzag. His Washington Redskins hat flew off. Running and zigzagging made it more difficult for him to control the muzzle of his pistol. It also made him a poor target for Andy and Lindsey.

Lindsey and Andy sent a hail of bullets toward the target. But .45 caliber pistols are not designed to hit moving targets at thirty-five to forty yards, even if the shooter is an expert marksman. The average policeman couldn't group six .45 rounds inside the three inch center of a stationary target at ten yards at a firing range. Under stress, like someone firing at him, the average policeman would be lucky to hit a beach ball at fifteen yards.

The Arab staggered at thirty yards, but kept on firing and moving toward the van. Two bullets penetrated the windshield, shattering the rear view mirror and the dashboard Garmin. Other bullets ricocheted off the pavement underneath the van. The left front tire blew. The van shook.

At twenty-five yards, a .45 hollow point caught the driver of the U-Haul in the face. He collapsed to the pavement.

Andy stood up and ran toward the crumpled body. The Arab was lying on his right side with his arms extended toward the van. Andy kicked the pistol out of his right hand. He rolled the driver to a supine position with his foot and squatted to examine his face, chest, and belly. The cellphone was still in the his T-shirt pocket. Andy picked it up and rolled the body face down.

"Nice shooting, sweetheart," he called back to the van. "Four wounds in the torso and one in the head."

"Jack, put the safety back on the AT4 and lay it on the seat," Andy yelled. "Take your bow and arrow and shoot that other man in the legs as soon as he comes out of the mini-mart."

Lindsey dropped her pistol next to the brake pedal and slumped behind the wheel.

Andy sprinted toward the driver's side of the U-Haul truck.

Lindsey leaned toward Ava in the floor. "Are you okay?"

"I'm fine, Mom."

"Stay in the floor," Lindsey said. "I feel nauseated." She gripped the wheel to control her shaking hands.

"Do you think it's morning sickness, Mom?" Ava asked.

"I don't think so." She lowered her head to the top of the steering wheel.

A loud cry prompted Lindsey to open her eyes and look for Andy and Jack. She peeked over the dashboard. The second Arab was down to his knees with an arrow in his right medial thigh.

Andy was running from the front of the U-Haul truck. He jumped on the Arab's back, crushing him prone to the pavement. Using his knees and weight to hold the man down, Andy pulled the man's wrists behind him and snapped on the cuffs. With shackles secure, he rolled him over and searched his pockets. There were no weapons, keys, or remote detonators.

Jack ran toward Andy.

"Watch him, Jack, while I find the key to the roll-back door on that U-Haul."

The key was hanging on the small chain attached to the ignition key. Andy pulled up the door and stared at the beast. Another Russian tactical nuclear warhead. He estimated twenty kilotons.

Andy motioned to Lindsey. "Put on the spacesuit and lead apron and bring your Geiger Counter and tool kit."

"Ava, you can sit up but stay in the van for a few more minutes," Lindsey said.

Andy crouched next to the wounded man while Lindsey dressed to disarm the warhead.

Jack muttered, "That's the second time I've been cheated out of my shot."

"It's better this way," Andy said. "Battle is fluid. Opportunities arise. We wouldn't want to see innocent people injured in secondary explosions here. We knew there was no one left in the vehicle. We could have been injured ourselves if the tanks in the ground blew."

Andy looked at Jack's arrow. "You hit the femur and missed the femoral artery and vein. Otherwise this arrow would have passed clean through and he would be bleeding out."

He spoke in Arabic to the wounded young man. "If you'll hold still, I'll unscrew this arrow. It'll be less painful when you move around.

Eventually an orthopedic surgeon will have to pull the broad head out of the bone in your thigh, but he can do that under anesthesia."

The Arab watched as Andy unscrewed the shaft from the broad head.

"We've got all the warheads in the U.S. now," Jack said.

The wounded Iranian smiled.

Andy said, "Jack, put the weapons back in the van and wipe off your face."

The mini-mart attendant stood in the doorway. "What happened? I heard shots."

Jack said, "These Iranians are terrorists. They had some kind of bomb in that truck."

"Are you kiddin' me?"

"No sir. You better call the local sheriff."

"I'll do that." He ran back into the mini-mart.

"Andy, there's no significant radiation hazard here," Lindsey called from inside the U-Haul. "I removed the tritium reservoir. I'm stuffing the pit."

"New reservoir?" Andy asked.

"You guessed it."

"Then switch it with our other old one," Andy said.

"Ava, you can get out," Lindsey called after finishing her work.

30.

The Carlson family sat in the van and waited on the local police.
"Jack, what did you say when your dad ordered you to take aim?"
Lindsey asked.

"Say hello to my little friend."

"And where did you hear that?"

"On *Scarface*."

"Where did you see a violent movie like that?"

Ava said, "I think you and Dad were in the bedroom meeting with
God. It was a long meeting."

Andy punched the speed dial on his cell phone and then the speaker button. "Mr. President, this is Andy Carlson."

"Where have you been?" the president asked.

"We found the second warhead, sir, in West Virginia."

"West Virginia?"

"Two Iranians in a U-Haul truck were headed toward Washington
or Hampton Roads. I'm not sure which."

"What happened?"

"The warhead is disabled. We had to kill one Iranian. The other
one's wounded in the leg, but he's handcuffed."

"I need more than that."

"My wife and I were exchanging gunfire with the dead man. Not
sure which one of us killed him. My son shot the second one in the leg
with an arrow. I thought we needed a prisoner to interrogate. These
details are only for you."

The president cleared his throat.

Andy said, "You better get somebody over here to the Lewisburg
Exit where Highway 219 crosses I-64, about forty-five miles east of

Beckley, West Virginia. Send a helicopter to take my family to Beckley. There's a good LZ behind a Shell Station at this intersection."

"Is there any radiation hazard there?"

"Not much, Mr. President, but you need to send the CIA's nuclear weapons team."

"Then we have all the loose warheads, don't we?"

"Maybe not, sir."

The president cleared his throat again and coughed. "The Jihad letter said there were two warheads in the U.S."

"Could have been a head fake."

"How did you come up with this conclusion, Carlson?"

"It's just a hunch, sir,"

"What kind of a hunch?"

"Can't say yet."

"Carlson, you're very close to insubordination."

"Not possible, sir," Andy said. "I'm not in the military. This is a courtesy call."

"If there are other warheads, you'll need the CIA's help."

"Like I told you before, my wife and I have been on the receiving end of CIA help. I can assure you we don't need them and we don't want them following us."

"I don't understand why you're so uncooperative."

"Then you haven't read enough of my file, Mr. President. When I was a SEAL, my CIA contact in the Middle East illegally bought warheads for one of your predecessors. The CIA sent me into countries to kill people who were not enemies of the United States. They tried to use me in a fake terrorist plot. They tried to kill me more than once, and they tried to kill my wife."

"I don't know anything about that," Umar said.

"I don't believe you, sir, but it doesn't matter."

"Why do you say that?"

"I'm not risking my life or my family's lives for you, Umar. I think my country would be better off without incinerated cities. The world would be better off without another Middle East war. If you want to give the CIA something to do, let them interrogate the prisoner here. If you want something to do, then urge anyone who calls you to cooperate with Mr. James Lee."

"And you're not going to tell me where you're going?"

"I'm going to the bathroom next. Then I plan to wash my hands and have some ice cream from the Shell mini-mart here. Could my daughter charge some ice cream to you?"

The president sighed audibly and hung up.

"That sounded like a 'yes' to me," Ava said.

"Andy, perhaps you're being a bit disrespectful to Umar," Lindsey said

"Think of us in a foxhole with Umar," Andy said. "We stay awake and watch his back while he sleeps. Umar goes to sleep on his watch. He can't shoot worth a damn. He knows nothing about strategy. He says he's going to do something, but he doesn't follow through. I wouldn't tolerate such a man in my foxhole."

"Now that we've got that cleared up," Lindsey said, "tell me about your hunch."

"It's the wounded Iranian."

"Did he tell you anything?"

"Not in words," Andy said. "Wounded and defeated men don't smile unless they know something that you don't know."

"Like what?"

"He could know that there were other warheads in the United States."

"I doubt if he knows what happened in Long Beach yet," Lindsey said. "Nobody has called the cell phone I found in that container. Perhaps the smile was for Long Beach."

"We can't assume that," Andy said.

"But we've followed every lead that Aleksi left us," she said.

Andy said, "When you were in Madison, did you consider that Aleksi rented more than one U-Haul, perhaps from another dealer?"

"There are no other U-Haul Centers in Madison."

"We need to consider a rental under another name from the same address, as well as rentals from businesses other than U-Haul. We should check car and truck dealerships. Look for recent vehicles of any kind that would carry a warhead. What if Aleksi bought a new truck or SUV for the Iranians? What if we've missed a warhead already on its way to an American city?"

"My God," she said. "That was stupid of me."

"No, we reacted to the obvious threat, which needed immediate attention. Now we need to go back and make sure we haven't missed anything. Call the U-Haul Center and thank them on behalf of the president. Tell them the president is likely to give them a citation for helping us. Ask them about any other rentals at the same time. Ask them about local new vehicle dealerships. Check for any other truck rental companies and crosscheck for any information that would tie a rental or sale to Aleksi, a member of his family, or his address. Let's try everything rented or sold in the last thirty days within a hundred miles of Madison. When we get back on the helicopter, you work on the truck and SUV rentals and I'll call the DMV for Wisconsin and throw the president's name around."

The local sheriff arrived and Andy filled him in on the disabled warhead transported by the Iranians. The sheriff took charge. The injured Iranian went by ambulance to a local hospital, accompanied by a deputy. The dead Iranian went to a crime lab. The sheriff unrolled a yellow crime scene ribbon around the entire Shell Station and minimart. He called another deputy to block off interstate access to the Shell Station.

A dark brown helicopter with no markings arrived after forty minutes, landing 115 yards behind the Shell Station. Andy walked toward the chopper and gave a brief report to the officer in charge, who carried CIA credentials. They had trouble communicating due to engine and rotor noise. Andy asked who would fly him and his family to Beckley. The agent pointed to a smaller helicopter, which had picked out an LZ in the grass between the access road and the interstate.

Andy walked toward Jack. "Be sure that the AT4s are secured and unloaded," he yelled. "Put all our weapons inside the duffel bag. Take everything over to that helicopter before the CIA has time to think of more questions."

The president had apparently ordered ice cream for everybody, or at least Ava thought so. She distributed ice cream sandwiches to the sheriff, the deputies, the attendant, and the CIA personnel.

Andy urged Lindsey to turn the site over to the CIA. He picked up her toolbox and Geiger counter and walked toward the van. Lindsey's Glock .45 was in the floor on the driver's side. He picked the pistol up and inspected the rest of the vehicle. Nothing was left behind except the keys in the ignition.

On the helicopter flight back to Beckley, the CIA pilot asked, "Dr. Carlson, the president wondered if you still had the satellite phone he gave you. You've been calling him on your own phone."

"Oh yes," Andy said, "I think I left it on the plane."

"Which plane?"

"Back at the airport."

They landed safely in Beckley in twenty minutes. The king's plane was parked seventy-five yards away from the helipad.

"Is that your Citation X?" the CIA pilot asked.

"It's one of those leased planes that multiple companies share," Andy said. "The pilot shuttles other people around in between my flights. That's probably why the satellite phone moves around a lot. I'll try to keep it with me."

"Must be expensive renting a plane like that."

"I'm thinking about sending the president a bill."

Back on the king's plane, Andy instructed the pilot to file a flight plan to San Francisco.

"Turn the transponder on and notify the tower that you found the problem," he said. "When you get to cruising altitude, turn the transponder off again and land in Wichita, Kansas."

"The king has instructed me," the pilot said. "The new Citation X at the Cessna plant has different colors, a different lease name, and of course, a different transponder. All of the paperwork has been taken care of. The king is having the transponder in this plane replaced. When it leaves Wichita, it will look like a different plane on radar. We have another pilot in Wichita who will fly it back to Farmville."

"That sounds good," Andy said. He returned to the passenger compartment. "Lindsey, I'm concerned about this farm in Waterview. Whatever is there, I want to get to it before the CIA."

As the plane climbed westward toward Kansas, Andy found the phone number for the DMV in Wisconsin on Google. When the receptionist answered, he asked to speak to the supervisor. Lindsey worked the rental and new vehicle dealerships in their search area.

"This is Lawrence Crane, supervisor, Wisconsin DMV."

"Mr. Crane, this is Mr. James Lee, a member of the president's task force on domestic nuclear threats. I need information about recent purchases and registration of vehicles in the Madison area. I'll give you the phone number of the president himself if you're uncertain if you should help me. Time is critical."

"What sort of information do you need?'

"A suspected terrorist in the Madison area may have bought a new vehicle within the last two weeks. This could be an SUV or a mid-sized truck with a camper top. The suspect may be transporting radioactive material with this vehicle."

"Like the stuff they use to make dirty bombs?"

"Exactly," Andy said. "He may have used the name of Aleksi Ivanov, or the vehicle may have been purchased by a relative with the last name of Ivanov or another Eastern European or Russian name. Please look for any purchase from Waterview or Madison with such a name, or any purchase from the address 106 Guernsey Lane in Waterview."

Andy could hear Mr. Crane rustling papers.

"What do I do with this information, Mr. Lee?"

"Call me directly if you find anything. I will personally see that the president acknowledges your contribution to preventing a disaster."

"This shouldn't take too long," Crane said.

"One more thing," Andy said. "If you find a suspicious vehicle, I'll need to know everything about it, including the VIN, extra features, color, license plate."

"Got it."

After giving his cell phone number to Mr. Crane, Andy hung up and turned to his family. "I'd like to visit Vladimir and Aleksi's farm outside of Waterview next, but we can't do that if there is another warhead on the road. Hopefully we'll get some answers before we reach Wichita."

"We showed 'em how to kick ass, didn't we, Dad?" Ava said.

"That's true, Ava, but we don't usually say it like that."

"It's better than kissing ass, isn't it?"

"Yeah, I guess you're right."

"Mom did say you were a good ass-kisser, too."

"It's important to be well-rounded," Andy said.

"Do you mean that Mom's ass is well-rounded, or do you…"

"Ava," Lindsey said, looking up from her laptop, "we are not discussing my rear end anymore on this mission. Is that clear?"

31.

"Dr. Carlson," said the king's pilot, "I have a call for you and a call for your wife."

"Can we take them at the same time?"

"Sure. Your call is in the co-pilot's seat. I'll route your wife's call to the phone next to the first seat in the front of the cabin."

"Mrs. Lee," said an employee from U-Haul, "we couldn't find any rentals in the Madison area within the last ninety days that fit your criteria."

"You've been very helpful," Lindsey said. "I'll see that the president recognizes you for looking." She hung up. "That takes care of rentals," she said aloud. "No luck."

"Mr. Lee, this is Steven Crane from the Wisconsin DMV. I think we've found something."

"Go ahead."

"A Mrs. Sonja Ivanov bought a new Chevrolet Suburban seven days ago in Madison. She wrote a check for the full amount. She listed the same address that you gave us."

"Can you fax me a copy of the DMV registration with the VIN, color, current license, and other features?"

"Yes, I can."

"Mr. Crane, don't all Chevy Suburbans come from the factory with OnStar already installed?"

"That's correct, since 2010," Crane said. "But the system isn't activated unless the buyer requests it and pays the three-year fee. I don't have that information about this vehicle, but it would be in the sales contract."

"Can you give me the name of the dealer and his phone number?"

"Yes. This car was bought at Madison Chevrolet. Give me your fax number and I'll send you a copy of everything I have, including the address and phone number for Madison Chevrolet."

"Thank you so much for helping the president."

Andy returned from the co-pilot's seat. "Listen up," he said. "We have a suspicious vehicle. If this new vehicle is in Waterview, it's not likely to be carrying anything. It could be a getaway car. We can check it out when we get there. On the other hand, if this vehicle is somewhere on the interstate system, we may have another job to do."

"Do you think there's a chance I could shoot this one?" Jack asked.

"There's a chance, but so far we have no way of tracking it. I should know in a few minutes if we can activate the OnStar feature on this car and locate it. I suspect that it's not at its target city."

Lindsey said. "I've been wondering why the Iranians set this whole scheme in motion and destroyed Ras Tanura before placing all the warheads at their targets."

"Good question," Andy said. "Let's try to get into the mind of our enemy."

Jack and Ava moved closer.

"Iran wants to strike Israel before detonating any warheads," Andy said. "They are counting on Umar not interfering for fear of losing two American cities. They need some time to gauge the president's immediate response to the letter they sent him. In their mind, there's no way for the United States to know about Aleksi Ivanov. The Iranians anticipated that Umar would frantically search for warheads in our ports and in Washington. A moving target is much harder to find than a sitting duck. Thus, I believe that the Iranians planned for these warheads to be moving while Umar searched for them in target cities. That's probably what the FBI and CIA are doing."

"That makes sense," Jack said.

"I suspect that Iran intends to detonate all warheads after the war with Israel begins," Andy said. "Umar could hardly be faulted for concentrating on America's nuclear disasters and domestic security once two cities were incinerated here."

"This boy's got talent," Ava said, smiling at her dad.

"Also," Andy said, "moving an army from the continental U.S. to the Middle East would be nearly impossible if two of our most important ports were destroyed. One of these warheads must be for Hampton Roads. The Atlantic fleet is stationed there. It's the largest Navy base in the world. All the nuclear aircraft carriers were built there. Three carriers are mothballed there, and two more may be in port now. Half of the remaining SEALs are stationed there."

"What should we do?" Ava asked.

Andy said, "There's almost always a way to outsmart an evil person."

"Why's that?" Ava asked.

"Evil men make mistakes because they're arrogant," Andy said. "Anyone can make a mistake, but evil people often do downright stupid things under the mistaken impression that they're smarter than everybody else. For example, Aleksi and Sonja should never have rented or bought vehicles under their own names. Their assumption was that the vehicles would be vaporized and they would be long gone from Waterview."

The pilot called back into the cabin over the intercom, "There's a fax for you, Dr. Carlson."

Andy studied the information in the fax. "Call Madison Chevrolet, Lindsey."

He handed the fax to Jack.

"Madison Chevrolet, how can I direct your call?" an older woman asked.

"This is Mr. James Lee, a representative of the president of the United States. I need to speak with your sales manager."

"Is this a joke?"

"No ma'am."

"I'll connect you with Mr. Gallop."

"Gallop. I can sell you a new car today."

"Sir, this is a very important call," Andy said. "I'm a member of the president's task force on domestic nuclear threats. If you need to bother him to confirm that this call is legitimate, by all means do so."

"What can I do?"

"Seven days ago, someone at Madison Chevrolet sold a new Chevy Suburban to a Sonja Ivanov."

"I sold it. What's the problem?"

"We suspect that this vehicle will be used by a suicidal bomber. Do you recall if Sonja Ivanov activated the OnStar system?"

"She didn't want it."

"At the request of the president of the United States, please call OnStar and activate the system in this vehicle by satellite. Do you have the VIN?"

"I've got everything I need right here."

"What I need is the current location of this vehicle," Andy said. "I need its direction, speed, and fuel status. And I need it immediately and confidentially."

"You are correct that OnStar would only do this at the request of law enforcement. I'll call OnStar and get the information."

"I'm going to give you my personal cell phone number. Give it to OnStar. Tell them that this is a request from the president. Ask them to call me directly with the data I need."

"What did you say your name was?"

"James Lee."

Andy gave Mr. Gallop his cell phone number.

32.

The king's plane descended as it approached Wichita and landed smoothly. The pilot assisted in the transfer of gear to the new plane.

While the last of the gear was stowed, the pilots chatted on the runway at the Cessna plant. Andy sat in the copilot's seat. His phone rang. "Mr. Lee, this is OnStar. We spoke with Madison Chevrolet. A man named Gallop assured us that you worked for the president. I understand that this vehicle is carrying something radioactive. I have the information you need. This is a silver four-door Suburban currently traveling east on I-64 forty-five miles west of Covington, Virginia. Its average speed is sixty-one miles per hour. It stopped a half hour ago and now has a full tank of gas. It has a temporary tag T-WIS 5846."

"Thank you," Andy said. "That's useful information. When they get to Staunton, please call me back and tell me if they go north on I-81 toward Washington or turn east toward Hampton Roads."

"Sir, we can do that. Were you aware that we can slow this vehicle down or stop it by satellite?"

"I've read that," Andy said, "but I don't want to use those features at this time for fear of spooking the occupants. What I need is to know what the driver does at Staunton. It's imperative that you not give any information to anyone else while we're tracking this vehicle. Many lives could depend on your discretion."

Andy motioned the king's pilot to return to the cockpit. "How fast can you get us to Richmond's airport?" Andy asked.

"Buckle up," he said, "and we'll see."

Once airborne, Andy explained his concerns to the pilot. "Our target is thirty to forty miles west of Covington, Virginia on I-64," he said. "Just like before, there're two possibilities. They could go to Washington, D.C., or Hampton Roads, Virginia. We should know their destination within one hour. Either city is three hours by car for them."

"I can go from Kansas to Hampton Roads or Washington in less than three hours," the pilot said.

"That's what I wanted to hear," Andy said. "We'll need to pick out an airport in front of them, like we did in Beckley, and get into position. We won't have much daylight to work with."

Andy returned to the cabin. Everybody was asleep. He sat down to consider what he could be overlooking.

An hour later, his cell phone rang.

"This is OnStar, Mr. Lee. Your target vehicle has just turned east from I-81 to I-64. The next metropolitan area is Charlottesville, Virginia."

"Thank you, OnStar. We'll stay in touch. Let us know if this vehicle leaves I-64 East."

He consulted a Google map in the passenger cabin and walked to the cockpit. "Our target is apparently Hampton Roads instead of Washington. I think Williamsburg should be our destination. We'll have to stop them between Williamsburg and the Hampton Bay-Bridge Tunnel."

"Where are they now?"

"They just left Staunton."

"Williamsburg will only require a minor correction in our course," the pilot said. "I can probably get you on the ground in Williamsburg at least a half hour before the target vehicle."

"Close enough."

"ATTENTION. Everybody wake up," Andy announced in the cabin. "We have new information. The target is Hampton Roads. We're landing in Williamsburg. The driver has plenty of gas to get there. We have a temporary tag on a Chevy Suburban. It's important that we intercept them before they reach the tunnel between Hampton and Norfolk. By now they may know about West Virginia and Long Beach."

Jack and Ava rubbed their eyes and absorbed the information.

"Lindsey, I need a van waiting for us at the runway in Williamsburg. I want one with sliding doors, one bench seat behind the front seats, just like before, and a ladder on the back door leading to the luggage rack. Try a local hotel van that shuttles people from the airport to Busch Gardens."

"This situation isn't like the one in West Virginia," Jack said.

"A good observation," Andy said. "Tell me how."

"The vehicle in question will be moving, probably sixty-five to seventy miles per hour," Jack said. "You said they have plenty of gas to get to Tidewater. It may be dark by the time we engage this vehicle. Identification will be more difficult."

"Weapon selection is critical," Andy said. "It's unlikely that we'll be able to use AT4s. We can't fire them in front of us from a moving van, and we can't pull up next to them. We would be too close to the target."

"Could the GREM could be the right tool?" Jack asked.

"That's the one with the shaped charge that knocks down doors?" Ava asked.

"GREM stands for grenade rifle entry munition," Andy said. "It comes in two pieces. When screwed together, the projectile looks like a spear with a fat biscuit in the middle of the shaft."

"This is the one that's fired from an M16?" Lindsey asked.

"I had it with me at Long Beach, as a backup," Andy said. "But we didn't need it. One end of the spear has a bullet trap. You just slide that end into the muzzle of an M16 and the standard 5.56 millimeter cartridge propels the spear when you fire the rifle. The spear doesn't have to go very fast or very far."

"Its best feature is the shaped charge, the biscuit, in the middle of the shaft," Jack said. "When the point of the spear hits the target, the shaped charge explodes one foot away, concentrating all the high explosive biscuit forward, away from the person who fired the M16."

"How would we use it?" Lindsey asked.

"Before the GREM was invented," Andy said, "a soldier had to run up to a door or bunker and plant an explosive charge. Now he can flatten any door from forty meters away without exposing himself."

"What does it do to the folks behind the door?" Ava asked.

"That depends on how big the room is," Andy said. "We have two of these, and two M16s. The M16 has a laser sight that activates when the safety is turned off. Jack fired one GREM on the farm. I've fired a bunch."

"Would you use one GREM or two?" Ava asked.

"Two would be best," Andy said. "But we would have to be in the left lane. The Suburban would have to be in the right lane. If we could pull up beside the Suburban and shoot the driver's door and the door behind it at the same time, the vehicle would be lifted off the road and thrown away from other vehicles. Everything in it would be destroyed. Some radiation contamination, but no chain reaction."

Lindsey asked, "Are you thinking they won't detonate their warhead until they get to the Norfolk side of the Hampton Bridge Tunnel?"

"At this point it would be prudent to suspect that whoever is coordinating the delivery and detonation of these warheads is concerned about communication with his martyrs."

"I'll bet the warhead we stopped in West Virginia was meant for Washington," Jack said.

"Likely," Andy said. "This coordinator could panic and order those people in the Suburban to do as much damage as they can without waiting on the Middle East war to get underway, especially if they are discovered. A detonation on the other side of the tunnel would do the most damage to our Navy, the ports of Hampton Roads, and the shipyards."

"You guys are forgetting something," Ava said. "We have the Iranian cell phones from Long Beach and West Virginia. They're stowed in the back of this jet, on the universal charger, close to the engines. It's possible we didn't hear them ring. Shouldn't we look for missed calls?"

"Good thinking, Ava," Lindsey said.

Jack ran to the storage compartment in the rear of the plane and returned with the cell phones. "No missed calls on either phone."

"That's still good information," Lindsey said. "It means the coordinator of this Iranian scheme likely doesn't know about the status of either warhead. The safest thing for him to do is make no contact until he's ready to order detonation. Cell phones aren't very secure."

"I agree," Andy said. "I'm struggling with how to be at two farms at once, after we deal with this Suburban. We may have to split up."

"I don't understand how you can be thinking about splitting up before we even intercept this Suburban," Lindsey said.

"When facing an enemy," Andy said, "you have several choices: Plan for success. Plan for failure. Make no plans. Be nervous."

"I vote for success," Ava said.

"Whenever you feel anxious waiting for something to happen, plan for a successful outcome," Andy said. "After a while, this becomes a reflex. Why be nervous? Use your supercharged brain to anticipate your next move."

"If I was going to be nervous about anything," Jack said, "It would be how many miles we have to work with from the time we identify this Suburban until it reaches the tunnel."

"That's certainly worth thinking about, but it's a factor we can't control," Andy said. "The king's pilot will get us to Williamsburg as quickly as possible. Put your spacesuit on, Lindsey, and get your gear. Everybody dress for battle."

"Am I the driver again?" Lindsey asked.

"You're the driver," Andy said. "Jack should be lying in the bench seat when you pull up next to the Suburban. I'll be in the floor. I'll take out the front door. Jack will shoot the passenger door behind the driver. Both of us will fire on my command. Ava will sit in the passenger front seat and describe the driver and any other occupants of the vehicle. We should scan the vehicle with the FLIR monocular when we get close enough. The Geiger counter might even be useful at that range."

"All this could change if a better way of disarming the warhead presents itself or we can do it without the loss of life," Jack said. "It's possible we won't be able to pull up alongside this Suburban. I'm thinking about alternatives."

Andy smiled.

The Citation X made another rapid descent to the Williamsburg-Jamestown airport. "Every time he does that it feels like this airplane is dropping faster than my butt," Ava said. "I would prefer to travel at the same speed as my butt." They taxied to the gate.

"I see the van," Jack said. "How did you pull that off, Mom?"

"I told them Justin Bieber was on board and that he needed a van. He's giving a surprise show at Busch Gardens. You don't look much like Justin Bieber, Jack, but we won't be here long enough for you to talk to your fans."

"That's too bad," Jack said.

Andy examined the luggage rack on top of the van and the ladder on the right rear door. The green vehicle was labeled "The Williamsburg Inn."

They transferred their gear to the van. Lindsey followed the signs and accelerated down the ramp onto I-64 eastbound toward Tidewater.

"We need a fix from OnStar," Andy said.

32.

"Your Chevy Suburban is traveling eastbound on I-64 just west of Exit 234," OnStar said. "Speed is sixty-six miles per hour. Do you wish us to intervene?"

"Negative, OnStar," Andy replied. "Please stand by."

"I think the driver of this Suburban is more likely to be an Iranian than Sonja," Andy said. "Sonja has no reason to be a suicidal Jihadist. Either way, we can't predict what the driver's response would be to interrupting the fuel line. So far all these warheads have had manual detonators."

"Exit 242 is coming up," Ava said.

"Then we're about eight miles ahead of the Suburban," Andy said. "Reduce speed to forty-five miles per hour and wait for them to pass us."

Lindsey reduced the speed of the van. Other cars streamed around them in the left lane. Andy adjusted the FLIR monocular and scanned the vehicles as they passed.

"I'm trying to focus so that we can detect human body outlines and warheads clearly from a range of ten feet," he said. "We only have about thirty minutes of daylight left. Jack, turn on your mom's Geiger counter and put it on the dashboard above the speedometer, to her left. That way we can compare readings with vehicles as they pass us."

"Can you tell what color underwear a person has on with that FLIR monocular?" Ava asked.

"Superheroes never concern themselves with those kinds of details, Ava," Lindsey said. "We're looking for weapons and body outlines. The FLIR monocular is great at looking through walls at objects with different temperatures. Colors don't show up very well, but other details are remarkable. We can even take a picture of what we see. And it has a rangefinder."

About fifty cars passed the van with no response from the Geiger counter.

"The sun's already down," Ava said. "Twenty minutes of shooting light left."

"Maybe we're going too fast," Andy said. "I'm guessing we have twenty miles to the entrance of the Hampton Bay-Bridge Tunnel. In another seven or eight miles the interstate will widen to four lanes on each side, and there will be streetlights. The light might help, but the extra lanes would give them more room to maneuver."

He scanned the cars approaching from their rear with his green Zeiss binoculars.

"The Suburban is ninety meters behind us," he said. "Jack, zoom the license plate with your binoculars and read it."

"T-WIS5846," Jack said.

"That's a match for the Suburban bought by Sonja Ivanov," Ava said.

"Heads up," Andy said. "No weapons needed as the vehicle passes on our left."

Lindsey took her foot off of the accelerator.

"Everybody look straight ahead," Andy said. "Listen to the Geiger counter. I will count bodies and try to identify a warhead."

The Suburban gained on them rapidly. The Geiger counter began to chirp slowly. The chirps increased in frequency and volume as the vehicle approached. The chirps of high radiation readings were sustained while the Suburban was directly opposite the van, and diminished in frequency and volume as it pulled away.

Andy scanned the Suburban with the FLIR monocular. "There're two occupants in that vehicle. The driver is a young man. A second person is lying in the floor in the back next to the warhead. I have a picture."

He reached over Lindsey's left shoulder, grabbed the steering wheel and handed her the FLIR monocular with his right hand. "Take a look at the picture on the quick view screen before another car gets between us."

Lindsey studied the picture. "I agree with you. The warhead is Russian design. We must assume that the guy in the back can detonate it whenever he chooses."

She handed the monocular back to Andy and took the steering wheel again.

Andy said, "Speed up. Jack, load both M16s with GREMS. Check the magazine and make sure there's a shell in the breech of each rifle."

He looked at Ava. "Check your seat belt and keep your binoculars on the Suburban.

Lindsey, start your approach. Take up a position directly beside the Suburban in the left lane. Everybody listen to me. I'm the spotter."

Jack took up his position lying prone on the bench seat, his GREM spear pointed toward the sliding door on the right side. Andy reached over him and opened the sliding door completely. He squatted in the floor next to Jack and held his M16 with both hands.

When they pulled alongside the Suburban, Andy said, "Safety off."

Two dancing red laser sights came on.

"Aim."

The eastbound lanes of I-64 switched from asphalt to concrete. The Williamsburg Inn van hit the horizontal pothole between the first two sections of interstate concrete. A red laser targeting light bounced across the driver's face and into the cab of the Suburban. Another targeting light penetrated the window behind the driver.

The driver snapped his head toward the Williamsburg Inn van. He had wild eyes. He lowered his head and tucked his chin. The Suburban jumped ahead of them.

"We've been made," Lindsey said.

They watched the Suburban race away, weaving between other vehicles.

"Do everything you can to stay with him," Andy said, closing the sliding door.

"The accelerator is on the floor," Lindsey said. "That Suburban has a hundred more horsepower than this van."

"I-64 will be four lanes in about half a mile," Andy said.

"Should I tell OnStar to stop them?" Jack asked.

"Get them on the phone but tell them to stand by," Andy said. "How far are we from the Hampton Bay-Bridge Tunnel?"

The vehicle bounced on another horizontal pothole between two sections of concrete. Lindsey swerved as she switched lanes. Traffic was picking up. "About five miles," she said, regaining control.

"We can't let them get to the tunnel," Andy said. "OnStar signals won't work in the tunnel. Now that they know we're chasing them, they'll detonate on the Norfolk side of the tunnel."

"They're pulling away," Ava said, looking through her binoculars. "And they're weaving all over the place."

"OnStar says it will take five minutes to shut off the fuel to the Suburban," Jack said.

"We don't have five minutes," Andy said.

"This looks like a good time for flexibility," Ava said. "You said there was always another way."

"Jack, I'm climbing that ladder in the back that leads to the luggage rack," Andy said. "When I get up there, hand me a loaded AT4. Make sure the safety switch is on."

"The rear doors won't open from the inside while we're moving," Lindsey said.

"The one on the right will," Andy said. He pulled his Glock from its holster. "Hold your ears."

Bang. Bang. Bang.

The right rear door lock disappeared.

Andy holstered his pistol and jumped behind the bench seat. He kicked the rear door on the driver's side firmly with his combat boots.

It popped open. Crawling on his knees, he reached outside to his left and grabbed the ladder.

Lindsey looked in the rear view mirror. Andy was gone.

His head appeared upside down in the open rear door. "Jack, keep the door open with your foot and hand me the AT4. Lindsey, I need you and Ava to roll down your windows so you can hear me."

The van bounced every time it hit the divider between concrete sections.

"I'm sorry about the ride," Lindsey called. "This concrete section of I-64 has been a rough ride for at least twenty years."

"Ava, look through the infrared monocular and give me range readings to the Suburban," Andy yelled. "Call out the distance in meters every five seconds. Use the scan mode."

Jack placed the recoilless rifle into the hand dangling from the open rear door.

"I can feel him bouncing around on top," Lindsey said, "but I can't do anything to smooth out the ride."

Ava unbuckled her seatbelt, stuck her head out the right passenger window, and screamed, "They keep moving from lane to lane."

"Do the best you can," he yelled back. "Just call the distances that you're sure of."

Andy's head appeared upside down in the driver's window. "Lindsey, use all four lanes to get me a clear line of sight. Try to straddle the white lines between the lane you're in and the lane to your left."

"One hundred twenty meters," Ava screamed.

"How far to the tunnel entrance?" Andy called.

"Three miles," Lindsey yelled.

"One hundred thirty meters."

Lindsey straddled the two lanes and held the accelerator to the floor.

Andy assumed a prone position with the barrel of the AT4 on the front of the luggage rack. The street lights provided more visibility, just enough to make the night vision scope worthless.

"Move two feet left," he called.

Ava unbuckled again and leaned out of her window. "When we move, they move," she yelled. "They're hiding behind other vehicles in the right lane. And they're getting away."

"Lean forward, Ava," Jack said.

Jack unbuckled his seatbelt and wiggled his head and chest through Ava's window.

He yelled, "Go for the red ball on top of the coyote, Dad."

"Lindsey, slow down gradually," Andy called.

"Slow down?"

"Yes, slow down, and get in the right lane," Andy called. "The interstate will narrow to two lanes at the tunnel entrance."

"Two hundred meters," Ava called.

Lindsey eased off the accelerator.

"How far to the tunnel entrance?" Andy called.

"A quarter mile," Lindsey yelled.

"I see the concrete top of it," Andy called.

"Two hundred fifty meters."

"Hold this speed," Andy called. "I don't need any more ranges."

"I see the tunnel entrance," Ava said. "Why doesn't he shoot?"

SWOOSH.

A spectacular ball of fire erupted at the tunnel entrance.

"He hit something," Ava said.

"Hold on, Andy," Lindsey yelled. She stomped on the brake. The AT4 tube jumped off the van and struck the rear end of a Jeep Cherokee in front of them.

Hundreds of tires screeched behind her. Dozens of bumpers, fenders and grills lined up to kiss each other.

She guided the van onto the right shoulder of the road.

Andy's head appeared upside down in the driver's window. "I think

I hit the little red ball on the coyote's head. Move up the right shoulder as far as you can." His head disappeared.

"What's he talking about?" Lindsey asked.

Jack said, "Dad waited until the Suburban was far enough ahead of us to lob the rocket over the car they were hiding behind. He could see where they were hiding because the interstate descends to the tunnel."

"Why did he wait until the last second?" Lindsey asked.

"I think he wanted the rocket to fall at the tunnel entrance," Jack said. "Those big concrete walls narrow down like a funnel. All that concrete would concentrate the blast effect. Even if he missed the vehicle, a hit on those walls would destroy anything in the mouth of the tunnel. It's only two lanes."

The van could go no farther. Other drivers had pulled onto the shoulder. Andy jumped off the passenger side and looked inside.

"Everybody okay?" he asked.

"We're fine," Jack said. "Can I go look?"

"Not yet, son," he said. "Let me take a look first."

He leaned in the window and kissed Ava. "Thanks for the ranges."

"I've been through this tunnel hundreds of times," Andy said. "I was stationed here when I was a SEAL. I met Lindsey here. Jack made the correct call for a lob shot. I think the rocket fell next to the Suburban at the tunnel entrance. Lindsey, put on your space suit and bring the Geiger counter. Jack, stow all the weapons out of sight. Everybody but Lindsey wait here until we know about the radiation hazard. Call 911 and say that something exploded at the western entrance of the tunnel between Hampton and Norfolk."

Lindsey approached the flaming wreckage in full radiation gear, and Andy followed. The Geiger counter began to chirp ninety meters away from the flames. She stopped at seventy-five meters. The counter was purring. She turned toward Andy. "You shouldn't go any farther."

"I'm going to check on as many drivers as I can until the cavalry arrives," Andy said. "It looks like fender benders. Tell everybody in front of us to move away from the flames. Somebody's gas tank could cook off from the heat."

Lindsey walked ahead.

After another thirty meters she heard a vehicle behind her. A motorcycle policeman was weaving between cars and pickups along the right shoulder. She placed the Geiger counter at her feet and held both her hands up. The policeman stopped and took off his helmet.

"There is a radiation hazard here, officer," Lindsey said, picking up the purring Geiger counter. "Do not approach the tunnel entrance without proper gear. Call your HAZMAT team. Mobilize as many Hampton police as possible. We'll need lots of ambulances and lots of radiation suits. I will tell all these people getting out of their vehicles to move away from the tunnel entrance. I want a secure perimeter of at least 200 meters. Shut down traffic in both tunnels and divert to the Monitor-Merrimac tunnel. There's no reason for anyone from Norfolk to come over here and get radiated."

"And who are you, ma'am?" the policeman asked, putting his helmet back on.

"I'm a nuclear physicist, working for the president of the United States on a classified mission. The vehicle on fire at the tunnel entrance was carrying radioactive material." She held up the Geiger counter.

"Please stick around while I call this in," he said. He backed up the motorcycle and gunned it away from the tunnel.

Lindsey returned to the van and advised Jack and Ava to remove their combat clothes and wipe their faces. They sat in the van while emergency vehicles converged on the scene.

Andy jogged up to Lindsey's window. "Nobody seriously hurt that I could find," he said. "Lots of whiplash. It's a great day for lawyers, and a bad day for EMS crews and emergency departments."

"The motorcycle policeman didn't hassle me much," Lindsey said, "and neither did any of the people in front of us."

"You don't look like Santa Claus in that suit," Jack said. "Let me guess. The purring Geiger counter suggests that you're not here on vacation and you're not selling ice cream."

Lindsey and Ava laughed.

33.

"Go ahead, Carlson," said Mr. Umar. "I was wondering if I would hear from you again."

"I just blew up a vehicle carrying a warhead on I-64 at Hampton Roads," Andy said. "We're at the tunnel entrance, on the Hampton side. There is some radiation contamination, but no chain reaction."

"So there was another warhead loose in this country. Hmm. What else will you tell me?"

"There were two Arab males in a Chevy Suburban. Correct that. One was lying in the floor, so I can't say for sure that he was Arab. I think they intended to detonate this warhead on the Norfolk side of the tunnel. We were chasing them from the west. Lots of vehicles sustained minor damage but no serious injuries. There have been no secondary explosions. My wife told a motorcycle policeman that the vehicle I shot at the tunnel entrance was carrying radioactive material, which is true."

"What did you shoot this vehicle with?" asked the president.

"Something private citizens aren't supposed to have," Andy said.

"What do you want me to do this time?"

"We've already asked a policeman to call the local HAZMAT team, but you should send some of your CIA people here," Andy said. "We now have a bona fide example of an armed nuclear warhead disabled by an explosive projectile. The scene needs to be studied."

"I agree," Umar said. "Do you think you can hang around until the CIA gets there?"

"If they ask for Mr. Lee," Andy said, "and they give me a ride out of here, I'll speak with them."

"Are you ready to stand down, Carlson, or do you have more hunches?"

"Sir, I have a solid lead to follow that might clarify the role of the

Russians," Andy said. "We really need to know if these Iranians had the help of the current Russian government in this blackmail scheme or if some ex-KGB agents were just looking to profit from warheads they've been sitting on for forty years."

"I'm guessing that you don't want any help with your lead."

"I need a few more days before any stories break about nuclear weapons," Andy said. "The Iranians don't know how far their plans have unraveled. The CIA can help you come up with some cover story about radioactive materials being transported with chemicals that leaked, causing an explosion."

"Do you think that we have control of all of the loose warheads in the United States?" Umar asked.

"I should know the answer to that question in about forty-eight hours, sir," Andy said.

"Then carry on, Carlson," Umar said. "Try to check in every now and then."

"You're welcome, sir."

Three CIA helicopters arrived within fifteen minutes, too quickly to have come from Washington. Andy surmised that the choppers came from Langley Air Force Base in Hampton, which had a CIA communications facility. They landed in a makeshift LZ cleared by Hampton police in the center of eastbound I-64, about 200 meters behind the Williamsburg Inn van.

"Are you Mr. Lee?" asked a CIA agent.

"Yes, sir," Andy said. "I'm sure the president told you about the accident here today."

"We brought radiation suits and Geiger counters," the agent said.

"Can someone escort me and my family to the Williamsburg airport?" Andy asked. "We're in that Williamsburg Inn van." He pointed.

The agent turned around and motioned to a Hampton police officer, who drove toward them on his motorcycle.

"Can you escort a van to the Williamsburg airport?" the agent asked.

"I'll try, sir," the policeman said. "We'll have to go by some back roads. The interstate from here to Busch Gardens is filling up with people looking for Justin Bieber."

"It's nice to see so many of my fans," Jack said as they followed the motorcycle policeman to the Williamsburg-Jamestown airport.

They transferred the gear to the Citation X.

Andy saw Jack toss the AT4 tube into the luggage compartment of the plane.

"I don't like leaving stuff like this lying around," Jack said. "It has both our prints on it."

"Where to?" asked the king's pilot.

"Back to Farmville, where we drop off Lindsey and Jack," Andy said. "We need to switch planes there. I would like for you to take Ava and me to Madison, Wisconsin. If we need Jack and Lindsey, the other pilot can bring them to Madison."

"I'm glad we're getting out of here," the pilot said. "I've never seen so many people fighting to get to one gate at one small airport."

The king's Citation X made the hop between the Jamestown-Williamsburg airport and the Farmville Municipal airport in twenty-five minutes. They pulled up alongside another Citation X. The pilot shut down the engines.

"I haven't gotten to put anybody to sleep with the terrible frog since Aleksi," Ava said.

Lindsey closed her eyes.

"You can take your clarinet with you on this trip to Madison," Andy said. "I wish we didn't need to split up. We can't leave Vladimir wandering around our farm, but I need to get to the Ivanov farm in Waterview before the CIA does. Even a blind hog occasionally finds a nut."

Lindsey asked, "How do you plan to approach this farm?"

"Ava and I will start at the local courthouse," he said. "We want to know how large it is, when it was purchased, what buildings are on it, and what geographical features might be useful to us. It's possible that this farm contains a cache of nuclear weapons."

"I understand," she said. "Now might be the best time to investigate the Ivanovs, since their new patriarch is on our farm."

"We'll spend some time observing before we make any attempt to enter it," Andy said.

"What do you need in the duffel bag, Dad?" Jack asked.

"I'll need Lindsey's tool kit and Geiger counter," Andy said. "Take the AT4 tubes out, along with the HEAT round we have left. Make sure I have my battle dress and clean civilian clothes. Ava should pack her Girl Scout uniform, her battle dress, and clarinet. We should have our black diving suits and watch caps. Take the bag to the other plane."

Jack unzipped the duffel bag.

"Jack, let me explain why you're going with your mother."

"I know why," Jack said. "If Vladimir is at the farm, we could be walking into a trap. I'm already working on how we'll get into the cave system, but we sure won't be driving across the covered bridge."

"I think that you understand your mission perfectly," Andy said. "If you have tactical advantage to eliminate this threat, you're authorized to do so. This man comes from a family of evil people. He would like nothing better than to take one of you hostage. Don't hesitate. You have plenty of weapons at your disposal. Take care of him as soon as possible. Call Ben when you get inside the cave."

"I'm on it," Jack said.

"Your mom should not be put in jeopardy," Andy said. "It won't be necessary for either of you to show your faces above ground right away, certainly not until you know where your target is. You have the monitors in the cave. Charlie Dodd is watching for more visitors at our gate. I'll have my cell phone on vibrate. You do the same. I wrote the address of that farm in Waterview on the back of the president's card. I've got his numbers already in my phone."

He handed the card to Jack.

Andy's cell phone vibrated. It was Charlie Dodd. "Somebody cut the chain on your gate, Andy. One vehicle drove through. This person replaced the chain link he cut with a threaded link. Didn't see but one set of human tracks. I've already talked to Ben."

"Thanks, Charlie. We should have a picture of this intruder. Each morning when you get your mail, check the gate. Lindsey and Jack are on their way back home, but they won't be entering the farm through that gate."

The combination air-traffic controller, restaurant owner, ground-skeeper, and fuel man in the Farmville tower shook his head. *Those Carlsons are beginning to piss me off. Two multi-million dollar private jets sitting in front of my restaurant. Carlsons jumping off one plane and onto an-other. Carlsons driving off. Nobody tells me anything. Nobody buys a sandwich, or a Coke, or a cup of coffee. They gas up in Richmond or Dulles or anywhere but here. The pilot waits until he's lined up with the runway before he calls the tower. And then he starts jabbering in some foreign language, every time. He knows I don't speak French. And I bet they take off without filing a flight plan or requesting permission to depart.*

The Carlsons hugged each other. Ava and Andy fastened their seatbelts as the king's pilot taxied toward the north end of the single runway at the Farmville airport.

"Dr. Carlson," the pilot asked, as the Citation X climbed away from Farmville, "do you know any reason why that guy in the tower would shoot me the bird?"

34.

Andy drove the rental car, a Ford Escape, from Madison to Waterview. The courthouse in Waterview wasn't high tech, but he had experience searching records in low tech courthouses. His general rule of thumb was to locate the oldest person in the records room, almost always a lady, and tell her that he needed to look at the public records of a local property he was interested in. Coffee and a box of Dunkin Donuts never hurt. The elderly lady could usually supply a county map of roads and a wealth of general information unavailable from a computer data base. Ava could ask this lady questions that would seem strange coming from an adult.

Ava and Andy sat in the courthouse reading room and studied the documents and maps available. This particular farm was 158 acres. It had been bought by Vladimir and Aleksi in 1977. The plat showed a farmhouse, a dairy barn, a garage, and a shed. The entire property was protected inside a loop in a river. There was only one road in. The farmhouse was 135 yards off the road.

"This farm has some of the same natural security features that we have, Dad," Ava said. "I hope they don't have a cave system."

"Caves aren't common here," Andy said. "Too many lakes. Not enough limestone. While we're waiting for darkness, let's ride past the entrance."

Andy pointed out their location on the county map. He scanned the list of local roads and found the one he wanted.

"Here it is," he said. "Guernsey Lane."

Andy drove the Escape while Ava guided him outside the city limits of Watertown to Guernsey Lane. Ava disagreed with the best route recommended by the female voice from the windshield Garmin, which came with the rental car. Guernsey Lane turned out to be a wide gravel road with only an occasional driveway and mailbox.

"The next mailbox on the right," Ava said. "The last box said 104."
The lady in the Garmin agreed.

Andy pulled off of the road opposite the entrance to 106. They looked at the one-lane gravel driveway, the locked gate with heavy chain, the condition of the road, and the mailbox.

"Ava, could you bring me any mail in that mailbox?"

A hunting magazine and a catalog of knives were addressed to Sebastian Ivanov. A local newspaper was addressed to Vladimir Ivanov. Aleksi had a bill from Suburban Propane. A personal letter was addressed to Sonja Ivanov. Andy recognized the handwriting.

"Vladimir and Aleksi Ivanov were brothers," Andy said. "They lived here with Aleksi's son Sebastian and a woman named Sonja Ivanov."

"She could be Sasha's mother," Ava said.

Andy opened the letter.

Dear Mom,

My computer is on the fritz, and I don't want anyone here to look at it. I hope this is my last week in this God-forsaken town. Grampa should be here tomorrow. I'm fine. Demetrius is improving. Nadia should have aimed higher. Dr. Carlson is trying to make us think he is out of town. Think lots of gold and me coming home.

Love,
Sasha

Andy reinserted the letter into the envelope and threw the mail in the back seat.

"Dad, isn't it a federal crime to steal mail?"

"Technically, it is," Andy said. "But we're working for the government today, and the government has a license to steal."

35.

Captain John Smathers sat in his chair on the bridge of the *Spirit of Long Beach*. He tapped his pipe in an ash tray.

The radio operator buzzed. "Captain, could you come to the radio shack?"

"Something we can't discuss over the intercom, Mr. Schwab?"

"Yes, sir."

Captain Smathers twisted his mouth and rolled his eyes. "Helmsman, maintain current course and speed."

"Aye sir, maintain current course and speed."

The radio shack was one deck below the bridge on the stern of the container ship. Smathers stood in the doorway, chewing on his empty pipe. He looked down at Mr. Schwab.

"All right, Schwab, what is it that you have that makes modern communication between the bridge and the radio operator useless?"

"I have a communication from the Port of London that's marked TOP SECRET, sir," Schwab replied.

He handed the Captain the printed message.

To: Captain Ralph Smathers, *Spirit of Long Beach*
From: Port of London, at the direction of the Prime Minister of England
Re: ARMED NUCLEAR WARHEAD ON YOUR SHIP

We regret to inform you that your ship is transporting a nuclear warhead in one of its containers. We have confirmed from your manifest that this refrigerated container is on board. Do not go looking for it. We sus-

pect that the two stowaway terrorists in this container have the ability to detonate the warhead at any time. The container is RECU4108265. The GTIN number is 10074652694573. Please advise us if this container is in a stack facing the water and vulnerable to a projectile.

The Captain's pipe hit the floor in the door way of the radio shack.

"Do you have a location for this container, Schwab?" Smathers asked, picking up his pipe.

"I already looked, Captain. It's surrounded on the bow. There are other refrigerated containers above and below, front and back, both sides."

"Send this message to the Port:

Regret to inform you that the container in question is surrounded on the bow, with no visibility. Await further instructions.

Captain Ralph Smathers, *Spirit of Long Beach.*

Within sixty seconds of sending this satellite communication, the maritime radio spit out a reply. Smathers could tell by the length of the message and the speed with which it arrived that it had been prepared in advance.

To: Captain Ralph Smathers, *Spirit of Long Beach*
From: Port of London, at the direction of the Prime Minister of England and the Royal Navy.

We cannot allow the *Spirit of Long Beach* **to endanger London or other ships. You are directed to divert your ship east to maintain a heading of 100 degrees. This will**

take you out of the shipping channel. No other ship is currently within 150 miles of your position.

When you commence your turn, lower your speed to fifteen knots. Allow thirty minutes to reach your new heading, then reduce your speed gradually to five knots. When your speed is five knots, call all of your crew to the bridge and inform them of the need to abandon ship. Pass out life jackets. You are authorized to shoot anyone who tries to leave the bridge or attempts to use a communications device before entering the lifeboats. You may reduce your speed further at your discretion in order to safely lower the lifeboats. After you have notified us that your lifeboats are in the water, you will have twenty minutes to get away from the ship before we destroy it. Make sure that you have adequate fresh water, food, and communications gear on your lifeboats. We have your GPS position.

A precision-guided bomb will target the bow of the *Spirit of Long Beach*. Seaplanes will stand by at a safe distance.

Good luck.

Captain Smathers returned to the bridge.

"Helmsman, set a new heading to 100 degrees. Turn to starboard slowly over thirty minutes. Reduce speed to fifteen knots."

The helmsman answered, "Aye, aye, Captain, new heading of 100 degrees, slow turn to starboard, reduce speed to fifteen knots."

36.

Andy and Ava sat in the Ford Escape at McDonald's in Waterview, studying the county map they had been given at the courthouse, waiting for darkness.

"Ava, find our route around to the opposite side of this river, across from the farm."

Ava stood on the bench seat of the booth to get a better view.

"We should turn around and go back to the last intersection where we turned right," she said. "From that intersection turn left onto State Road 607. After about a mile, turn east onto State Road 650. State Road 650 goes north over a bridge." She pointed with her finger. "We'll travel about four miles on 650, then east on River Road. We want Park Avenue. If there's really a park, that might be good for us. The water could be shallow, since the river is making a lot of turns."

"I agree. Good job. Let's go."

He checked his watch. 8:15 PM.

"Set the GPS for Park Avenue and we'll see if that lady agrees with us," Andy said as they pulled out of the McDonalds.

"She's generally reliable," Ava said, "when she's not stupid."

"Check your mom's tool kit. Make sure we have the wire cutters."

Ava leaned over the front seat and opened the tool kit. "Good ones."

"Does she have that ratchet screwdriver with the snap-in hex heads and screwdriver heads?"

"She does. Also one knuckle buster, a pair of needle nose pliers, a box of .45 caliber shells, a couple of electronic bugs, two earpieces, and a flashlight."

"Good," Andy said. "Put the toolbox in your backpack along with my night vision binoculars, your clarinet, my Glock, my knife and belt, two black watch caps, some face paint, and the Geiger counter."

"Are you trying to drown me?" Ava asked.

"You're going to ride on my back," he said. "Just hold onto my shoulders, and let me do all the swimming. Keep the gear dry."

He handed her his cell phone. "Put it in the toolbox. Why don't you hop in the back seat and change into your diving suit?"

There was a park on Park Avenue. Andy pulled into a small parking lot on the north side of the river. A grove of trees. A few picnic tables. A swing set for kids. A garbage can.

"Not exactly Central Park," Ava said. "Might be a good place to make out with your boyfriend."

"Ava, you're much too young to be thinking of things like that."

"You told me to plan ahead."

Accustomed to eating his own words, Andy considered other implications of Ava's mental preparation for being sixteen years old. The safest thing to do was shut up and put on his diving suit. Ava organized the backpack. Both smeared black camo paint on their faces. They wore dark running shoes to protect their feet.

"Hand me the night binoculars," Andy said. He looked south, scanning the terrain from behind the Ford Escape.

"The river is about fifty yards across," he said. "I can see a tall steel fence on the opposite side, a large barn, and a farmhouse. There's only one light outside and it's on a pole between the barn and the farmhouse. Looks like sparse cover on the other side of the fence. The wind is blowing right to left, so we'll try to approach downwind from the left. The river flows that way. That's good."

It was an easy crossing for a muscular ex-SEAL doing a breast stroke. Andy let the current carry them downstream. When they reached the opposite bank, he removed the backpack from Ava's shoulders and slung it over his right shoulder.

"I hardly got wet," Ava said.

They sat down at the fence. Andy strapped on his knife and Glock .45. They pulled back the head covers of their diving suits and tucked their hair underneath the watch caps.

"Do you think this fence is hot?" Andy asked.

"Probably only the two barbed wire strands on top," Ava said. "It would be difficult to electrify an entire eight-foot fence. You only have two hot wires on our fences on the farm, and we have free electricity."

Andy reached into the backpack, found the knuckle buster, and handed it to Ava.

She tossed the wrench against the fence, and then picked it up. "Told you, so. Even a tiny spark would be visible in the dark."

"What does the eight foot fence with barb-wire on top tell you?" Andy asked.

"They have something to hide," she said, "like us. Most cows couldn't jump a three foot fence. Besides, I don't see any cows."

"Trust your nose, Ava. We're downwind. There're no cattle or horses here."

Ava adjusted the night vision binoculars to fit her eyes. She concentrated on the lighted area between the farmhouse and the barn. "There's a dog dish on the porch, Dad."

"Good pick-up. How many dog dishes?"

"One."

"Where's the dog?"

"He's sleeping on the porch. Looks like a Rottweiler."

"Let's get your clarinet ready."

Andy dipped a dart into the tiny chamber that held the sweat of the terrible frog from Nicaragua. He tamped the dart in place and handed the clarinet back to Ava. "Are you ready?"

"Ready."

"I'm going to move fifteen yards to your left, so that the dog will come to me when I call," he said. "He won't be able to smell us because of the wind, so he'll have to come and investigate. You should have a broad side shot through the holes in the fence. Test your angle of fire."

Ava stuck the clarinet through a hole in the fence and determined how close the animal would have to come to the fence before she no longer had a clear shot. She signaled okay.

Andy lay prone and yipped.

From across the river, near the park, a coyote answered back.

Ava said, "He hears you. He's up."

Andy yipped again.

The Rottweiler ran directly toward Andy. He stopped about six yards from the fence.

The clarinet spoke softly. The dog staggered and collapsed.

"Good shot," Andy said.

"He'll have a nice nap while we do our scouting," she said.

Andy reloaded the clarinet and handed it back to Ava. He worked on the fence with the wire cutters. The fence was typical chain-link construction. Cutting four feet up from the bottom was enough for them to push the backpack through and slip in behind it. Their diving suits protected their skin from the sharp edges.

"We're going to key in on that big barn, the building with the long cupola on top," he said.

"Like our plantation house?"

"That's right. Our cupola was more of a lookout for Indians, the British, or the Yankees. Theirs has a weather vane on top and helps to ventilate the barn. It's a lot bigger than our cupola, larger than necessary for that size barn. I wonder why."

Andy repacked the wire cutters and the wrench, adjusted the straps, and put on the backpack. "Let's crawl toward the barn," he said. "There's a big rig tractor and container parked on this side."

Lying in the orchard grass fifty yards from the barn, Andy pointed out the features of the building. "Notice the loading platform on the left side of the building," he said. "That means there's a drive-up ramp on the inside, probably for a forklift. We'll go for the right side. Can you see why?"

"Even though the pole light is on the right," she said, "that eighteen-wheeler is parked so close to the building that we'll be in the shadows. We can't be seen from the house if we crawl underneath the container on the trailer."

"Good assessment."

They crawled underneath the trailer and crouched next to the metal barn.

Andy examined the metal panels of the barn. The panels were thirty-two inches wide, sixteen feet high, mounted vertically with standard one quarter inch hex head screws. The vertical rows of screws every sixteen inches represented the metal studs of the wall. The horizontal rows of screws every four feet up the wall represented metal nailers between the studs.

Using the ratchet screwdriver, Andy removed one vertical row of screws, as high as he could reach. Next, he removed a row of horizontal screws in the sole plate and the row of horizontal screws four feet above the sole plate. Before bending the panel back, he loosened the screws on the right side of the panel. This would allow him to open the panel without creating noise or bending the panel.

He crawled to the end of the trailer and inspected the lighted part of the yard. Ava waited at the panel while he crawled past her to the rear wheels of the rig. He returned with a chock, a stop block used to keep the trailer from moving while parked. Andy propped the panel open with the chock.

The Geiger counter had a bonus feature, a flashlight. Andy pushed the Geiger counter in front of him and stuck his head inside the opening. He turned the flashlight on. The barn was cavernous. A pair of twenty foot electric rollback doors on each end of the barn allowed a tractor-trailer to be driven through the building.

The center of the barn looked empty, except for two rows of metal poles, far enough apart so that a tractor-trailer could be driven between the rows. There were four boxes on the far side of the room, each covered with a tarp, and another three boxes on the near side of the room, also covered with a tarp. Each covered box was the size of a washing machine. The seven boxes were mounted on pallets. He located the forklift. Rows of five gallon metal buckets and boxes were stacked against the far wall. Stacks of dog food and garden fertilizer were close to the new opening in the metal wall. The far right corner of the barn was packed with square bales of alfalfa.

Andy backed out of the panel. "Ava, I smell chemicals in this barn, something like acetone."

"What's the plan?" Ava asked.

"If I can get inside and confirm radiation from those boxes," Andy said, "all we need to do is get out and call the CIA. They may have followed us here. If warheads are under those tarps, this find is probably too big for us to handle by ourselves."

He picked up the Geiger counter again and gave Ava final instructions. "Stay here with your head inside this panel, so you can see if anything happens. The Ivanovs probably have alarms, just as we have on our farm. Let's hope their alarms are at the small door facing the farmhouse or at the electric rollback doors."

"How can I help if I'm just sitting here?"

"You're the lookout. The lights may come on suddenly. An alarm may go off. We don't know how many people are home. They could have infrared trip wires that I can't see. We can be fairly sure that they don't have explosives on a trip wire. Warheads are too valuable. Those chemicals would explode. They have a dog that could accidentally trip an explosive alarm."

"Anything else I should know?"

"Don't be surprised if I'm discovered or captured," he said. "These things happen. It's how you react that's most important. I've been captured more than once. You must resist the urge to yell or rescue me. If I can't come back to you, learn as much as you can about the situation before leaving."

"This ain't my first rodeo, Dad."

"I love you."

"I love you, too."

Andy entered the metal barn on his knees, pushing the Geiger counter-flashlight in front of him. The Glock .45 was in his right hand.

Ava watched the circle of light from the flashlight. The beam moved toward the center of the barn. She heard fluctuating volume and frequency of chirps from the Geiger counter as the light moved from box to box on the near side of the barn. The flashlight beam turned to the row of boxes on the far side of the building.

Andy stood up. He shined the light at his feet and eased across the center of the floor in the barn. A metal-on-metal squeaking noise from overhead prompted him to duck his head and attempt to flatten out on his stomach. Heavy steel bars drove his body to the concrete floor. The crash of metal on concrete left his ears ringing. A lightning bolt of pain tore through his left shoulder, surging into his neck and head. He couldn't move his left arm. The lights in the barn came on. An alarm tone sounded from the direction of the house.

Ava saw her dad lying on his stomach, his left arm twisted behind him. He was trapped in a steel cage, about eight feet by eight feet, five feet tall. He tried to pull himself up the wall of the cage using his right arm. His left arm hung limp at his side as he pulled himself to his knees. He was looking outside the cage. Blood trickled from the left side of his watch cap and ran behind his ear to his neck. The Glock was on the concrete floor outside the cage. He slid down the steel wall to a prone position and reached for the pistol. The .45 was more than two feet away from his extended right hand. His head flopped to the concrete floor. He stopped moving. Pieces of the Geiger counter littered the floor inside and outside of the cage.

Ava backed out of the opening in the metal wall and pushed the panel back in place. More lights came on inside the house. She tilted the wooden chock against the panel.

37.

Andy rolled over and inspected the cage he was in. He pulled himself into a sitting position and leaned back against the steel bars. The cage was cleverly designed. The walls and top were one inch diameter welded steel rebar. He estimated the cage weighed at least 2000 pounds. He palpated the shattered pieces of his left clavicle and scapula with his right hand.

A painful lump was growing on the left side of his scalp. As an emergency physician he commonly measured lacerations using the lengths of his own fingers. This laceration in the center of the lump in his scalp was seven centimeters in length, full thickness to his skull. He looked at his bloody right hand, and wiped it on the thigh of his wetsuit. The blood was from his scalp. The hand was okay. When he took a deep breath, he felt no pain in his chest, only his left shoulder. He moved his legs and twisted his torso. Turning his head evoked a sharp pain in his neck, but he palpated no wound or deformity in his neck. He was able to unzip the back of his wetsuit eight inches with his right hand.

There were no doors in the cage, only six inch openings between horizontal and vertical rebar. Two steel cables attached the cage to electric motors overhead. The entire cage had been hidden in the cupola. He had walked through an infrared tripwire. A magnetic switch released the cage. The squeak came from the steel cables rolling over two pulleys.

There were switches next to the two rollback doors on either end of the barn. He followed the wires from the fluorescent lights and the wall switches to a breaker box on the wall next to the small metal door. A third "up" and "down" switch was next to the breaker box. A large red Craftsman toolbox on wheels was located under the breaker box.

His scalp touched a vertical bar in the cage wall. He winced. The cage was not high enough to stand up, even if he could stand up. Had he been fully erect when the cage fell, his neck would have snapped like a twig. Shattered pieces of the Geiger counter littered the floor in the cage. His scalp throbbed, but took second place as a source of discomfort. His left shoulder was on fire, and swelling rapidly. When the dizziness began, he tried to lie down on his right side. He forgot to put his right arm out. He palpated the new lump on the right side of his head, but found no laceration. He was forgetting something important, but he had been preoccupied with his injuries. Lying flat improved blood flow to his head. He jerked his head toward the wall where he had entered the barn. The sharp pain in his neck reminded him not to do this again. Ava was gone.

Andy absorbed the pain as he waited for his captors. After twenty minutes, a fiftyish year old lady entered the small door carrying an automatic shotgun. She was wearing a trench coat. At fifteen yards, Andy knew who she was. He pulled himself back to the sitting position, facing her.

"You're the first rat we ever caught," she said. "Vladimir and Sebastian will be pleased. Sebastian is a pretty good welder, isn't he?"

"I can see that," Andy said. "Will I meet him soon?"

"Soon enough," she said. "He's working a twelve hour shift in the slaughterhouse. This is important information for you. He's a butcher. His nickname is 'the Whittler.' He will whittle parts of you off until he finds something that you want more than the information you are hiding."

She was tall, like Sasha, and still quite attractive.

"But I have nothing to hide," Andy said. "As you can see, I can't reach my pistol. My left shoulder was crushed by the cage. I think I have a migraine."

She looked at the limp left arm and the dried blood on the left side of his painted face.

"Why are you here?"

"I came to check out your merchandise."

"What kind of merchandise were you looking for?"

"Aleksi told me that there were more warheads. I would like to buy your inventory."

"Why do you want to buy warheads?"

"Aleksi never asked me a question like that," Andy said, "and I never asked him what he did with the money I gave him. It looks like you have seven warheads left. Let me make an offer for all of them. I can transfer the money to any account that you like. You can confirm the transfer immediately."

"What did you say your name was?"

"I didn't. Aleksi calls me Mr. Lee."

Her eyebrows shot up. "You're not from Virginia, are you?"

"I am, but I've not been home in a few days."

"Vladimir is already looking for you."

"Perhaps I can help. What does Vladimir want with me?"

"He's looking for Aleksi and my daughter. We've not been able to contact my niece and her husband, who also live in Virginia."

"And Vladimir thought that I might know where they were?"

"Aleksi went to Virginia to do business and didn't come back," she said. "I've not heard from my daughter in more than a week. Vladimir has not heard from his granddaughter in more than a week."

"I know your daughter well," Andy said.

She squinted at him. "How do you know her?"

"We work together. We have saved lives together. She's a great nurse. She's a friend to my children and my wife."

"To whom are you referring?"

"Sasha Ivanov," Andy said, "although she didn't use that last name in Farmville.

"When did you last see her?"

"About a week ago, when I left Farmville."

"Do you know Demetrius and Nadia?"

"Sasha and I saved Demetrius' life after Nadia shot him."

"The police said it was an accident." She studied his face. "Have you met Vladimir?"

"Not yet."

"This is an interesting story you've told," she said. "Sebastian will review every part of it when he gets home and has breakfast. Whatever you know, you will tell him. I must call Vladimir and tell him that you're here. My sister and her husband will want to talk with you about their daughter."

She picked up Andy's Glock and turned toward the door.

"I'll be glad to help you, Sonja," Andy said.

She looked back at him. "Then we shall see you in the morning, Dr. Carlson."

"I'm looking forward to it. I don't want to spend too much time in here. I was hoping to have more children someday. Before my Geiger counter was damaged, I realized that I wore the wrong kind of under-wear tonight."

She smiled and closed the door behind her.

Andy looked at his watch. 9: 55 PM.

38.

Ava crouched underneath a window outside the Ivanov farmhouse. She lifted her head slowly and peered into the room. A land line telephone was on a small lamp table next to a wooden rocker. She crawled around to a side window next to the rocker. The window was already cracked. She nudged it up a half inch.

Sonja opened the door and went straight to the lamp table. She removed two keys from a drawer and inserted each into a keyhole in the wall next to the front door. She turned both keys ninety degrees to the right and left the keys in the switches. She sat down in the rocker next to the window and punched a number into the phone. Ava leaned against the wall outside the window. Not enough numbers to be long distance.

"Tasya, the doctor from Virginia is here at the farm, the one with all the gold. He's caught in Sebastian's cage."

Ava heard the rocking chair creaking.

"Yes, he is. I'm not sure why he's here. He says he wants to buy our inventory. He was wearing a wetsuit. He probably came across the river and cut a hole in the fence."

More rocking.

"I think the cage broke his shoulder and hit him in the head. The dog is missing. He must have done something to it."

More rocking.

"I think he knows what happened to Aleksi and Sasha and Nadia. He may know why Vladimir didn't check in tonight."

More rocking.

"Sebastian will cut it out of him," Sonja said. "Tell Nicolai what has happened. It would be helpful for both of you to drive a squad car around to the park on the opposite side of the river. This doctor must have left a vehicle. There may be someone waiting on him. You should be prepared to take care of anyone there now and anyone who shows up before morning."

More rocking.

"Tell your husband to put drugs and chemicals in this car. No loose ends. Both of you drive over here after daylight. Dr. Carlson will be very glad to tell you about Nadia."

More rocking.

"I think I'll be fine until Sebastian gets home at 7:30 in the morning. Tell Nicolai to have a police car drive by my front gate every hour. Arrest anybody who looks suspicious. The front gate is the only part of the perimeter that's not electrified now, and it's locked. I turned the electric fence on and activated the sensors in the front gate."

More rocking.

"And good luck to you, Tasya."

39.

J ack led his mom to a small rowboat that he left hidden on the south
side of the Appomattox River, across from the canal where his dad
built their independent power station. They left Andy's S-10 Chevy
in the employee lot of the tri-county prison. Jack had their gear in his
backpack. He held Lindsey's hand as they walked through the woods
toward the river. The aluminum boat was upside down, chained by a
seat in the bow to a tree ten yards from the river. He kept it covered
with a camouflage net. Jack dialed the numbers into the combination
lock and removed the chain.

They rowed across the river in the dark and walked up the north
bank of the canal to the undershot waterwheel. Underneath this building was the access tunnel to the I-40 East section of the Confederate
cave system. They followed the I-40 tunnel to the I-95 tunnel and
arrived in the Grand Chamber in thirty minutes. Jack went for the re-
frigerator while Lindsey reviewed the security tapes for the past three
days.

Since the covered bridge was the only vehicular entrance to the
farm, each car or truck that passed over it could be automatically
photographed and the driver's face identified. Vladimir had passed
through the covered bridge twelve hours earlier in a black F-350. The
large pickup had a dark camper top. He was by himself.

Lindsey switched to real–time and scanned the farmhouse from
the cameras in the shed and barn. The F-350 was parked in front of the
farmhouse. Switching to the great room camera, Lindsey found him
lying on the same couch where Sasha had tied her up. She zoomed in.
Sasha's blood was still on the floor. Vladimir was apparently tired from
exploring the farm. She noted the pistol on the coffee table.

Jack peeked over her shoulder while wolfing down a sliced turkey sandwich. "I've got two things for you, Mom," he said. "A turkey sandwich and a plan."

She took the plate. "I'm glad somebody understands that pregnant people have to eat. What's the plan?"

"I can get to his truck from the magic stump in the front yard," he said. "You can go with me as far as the farmhouse. We can take a C4 charge and a remote timer. I'll attach the C4 to his gas tank." He looked at his watch. "In twenty minutes I can start the big Kubota tractor in the shed and drive down the road toward the covered bridge. You should choose a weapon and hide behind the smaller tractor in the shed, just in case."

"In case of what?"

"Vladimir will know that he can catch me easily with the truck," Jack said. "I'll wait until he makes the left turn toward the covered bridge to press the remote. If the truck hasn't exploded by the time he completes this turn, something has gone wrong. In that case use the recoilless rifle underneath the bush hog on the back of his truck."

"I don't like the AT4 here. You might be in the line of fire."

"If my charge fails, then I'll jump off the tractor into the ditch next to the road."

"I still don't like it," Lindsey said. "I'm not firing something powerful enough to destroy a tank in your direction. Get me an AK-47 with a night vision sight and a banana clip. There's a nice ledge to rest the rifle on. I'll move to the side so I won't be firing down the road."

"I'll get the AK ready."

Lindsey's cell phone vibrated. "Mom, Dad's in a steel cage and he's hurt," reported Ava.

Jack watched his mom pace the floor of the Grand Chamber with the cell phone at her ear. She sat down on the couch and pointed at Jack. Still listening, she made a circle with her free hand.

Jack ran to the weapons storeroom behind the cabinet in the bathroom.

"I'll call you back when we're airborne," Lindsey said. "I love you, Ava. Be fearless."

Lindsey called the king's pilot and advised him to warm up the jet in preparation for an emergency flight to Madison, Wisconsin.

Jack returned to the Grand Chamber with the AK-47 slung over his shoulder. His fanny pack held a magnetic C4 charge and a remote detonator. He dragged a duffel bag with more gear.

"What happened, Mom?"

"Your dad's been caught in Wisconsin. He's hurt. Your sister is in way over her head. We've got to take care of Vladimir quickly and get on the king's plane."

"Don't underestimate Ava, Mom. She's the smartest kid I know. Dad has been training us for times like this."

"I see you've already picked up a few things," she said. "I've got a list of my own."

She knew that Jack could recall any list verbatim. "Once Vladimir is out of the way, load up my SUV with your bow and arrows, your knife, at least two AT4s, two GREMs, two M16s, our diving suits, and a couple of C4 charges and remote detonators. Get several different kinds of detonators, some timed, some remote. We also need makeup, watch caps, gloves, a couple of flashlights, a Glock, and extra clips of .45 and M16 ammo. Get an extra-large shoulder immobilizer and pack your dad's emergency medical kit. Pack an inflatable raft and two paddles."

"I've got most of that stuff already," he said. "I'll go back and get the raft, the paddles, and the shoulder immobilizer."

He handed Lindsey the AK-47 and ran back toward the weapons storeroom and the medical supply room.

Lindsey called after him, "Please hurry."

They exited the Grand Chamber and moved quickly down I-95.

Lindsey led the way, the Russian assault rifle with the banana clip and the night scope slung over her shoulder. Jack dragged the duffel bag behind him by the end strap. In nine minutes they were underneath the magic stump in front of the farmhouse. Jack dropped the duffel bag at the base of the ladder and tied a rope to the end strap while Lindsey started up the ladder.

She opened the hinged top of the stump and looked around. A 150 year old white oak tree blocked the light from the single pole lamp between the shed and the farmhouse. She listened for thirty seconds while watching the farmhouse. Vladimir was not stirring. She climbed out. Jack followed with a rope in his teeth. Together they pulled the duffel bag to the top of the stump and lowered it to the ground. Jack closed the top of the stump.

Lindsey pointed Jack toward the F-350. She dragged the duffel bag toward the shed while Jack crawled underneath the intruder's truck and attached the C4 charge to the metal band holding up the gas tank. He pulled the safety strip to arm the charge. A red L.E.D. light confirmed that the device was armed. Lindsey left the duffel bag behind her SUV and took up a position in the back of the equipment shed. She leveled the AK-47 on the rail of the side wall, pointed toward the alfalfa field and the road to the covered bridge. It was a good shooting window, about four feet high. The 7.62 mm rounds in the banana clip packed a bigger punch than an M16.

Lindsey had spent hours at this same spot with the twins, when they were younger, watching deer in the alfalfa field. The road to the covered bridge dropped off fairly rapidly from her position. Jack should be far below her and to the right if she fired at the truck from this angle. She checked her weapon and made an okay sign to Jack.

Jack warmed the plugs of the Kubota tractor, started the engine, and backed out of the first slot in the shed. He shifted the shuttle transmission into forward and moved the gear shifter to second gear. The tractor lurched forward. He turned down the road toward the covered bridge.

After moving twenty yards down the road he looked over his shoulder. The light came on in Vladimir's truck in front of the farmhouse. He shifted into third gear, gunned the accelerator, and continued down the road next to the alfalfa field. At fifty yards he mashed on the brake and the clutch, while shifting into neutral. The remote detonator shot out of his lap and fell onto the gravel road underneath the tractor. Jack looked back toward Lindsey. He pulled the parking brake on the tractor.

Lindsey saw Jack jump off the tractor and dive into the ditch on the left side of the road. As Vladimir's truck pulled in front of her position in the shed and turned toward the covered bridge, she put her finger on the trigger of the AK-47. The crosshairs of the night scope could not find Vladimir's head or body. The camper top obscured the driver.

A fifteen round spray of armor piercing .50 caliber bullets riddled the right side of the truck. Lindsey ducked under the rail of the sidewall, anticipating an explosion that never came. She peeked through the gaps in the vertical siding below the rail. The black F-350 had nosed into the ditch between the alfalfa field and the gravel road to the covered bridge.

Lindsey looked toward the camouflaged concrete bunker on the far side of the alfalfa field, at its high point. From this same bunker Ben Carlson had saved her and the twins on the day the twins were born. The Confederate army had placed a cannon at the same location to protect their retreating army 150 years before. Ben was running toward her.

"You did it again, Ben," Lindsey yelled. "Stay back. There's a C4 charge under that vehicle." She ran to meet him in the field.

"Glad to be of service," he said. They embraced. "I've been watching him since he got here. I could see what Jack was trying to do. I'm just backup."

"You're the greatest backup of all time," Lindsey said. "I still need your help. Andy got caught in Wisconsin on a farm, and Jack and I need to leave right away."

"Then go on."

"Something went wrong with the C4 charge under that truck," she asked. "We need to drive around it."

"No problem."

"Please dump Vladimir, the driver of that vehicle, in Uncle Frank's well."

"Sure."

They looked toward the rear lights of the tractor. Jack was running toward them.

"Thanks Ben," Jack said, extending his hand. "I'm sorry, Mom. The detonator fell off my lap and went underneath the tractor. I had one hand on the steering wheel and I was trying to put the tractor in neutral with the other. There wasn't time for me to find the remote in the dark, but I got it now." He held up the remote.

"You didn't run up here with a live remote detonator?" Ben asked.

"Of course not," he said, handing the device to Ben. "I try to limit myself to one stupid mistake per day. I took out the batteries."

'That's why we have backup," Ben said. "Learn from it. You should have had the remote inside your belt."

"Why didn't the armor-piercing shells ignite the gas tanks on that F-350?" Jack asked.

"Diesel fuel is not as explosive as gasoline," Ben said. "You can't count on it blowing every time from an armor-piercing shell. Your C4 charge would have done it. You two get going. I'll take care of this. Call me if you need my help."

"I'll do that," Lindsey said.

Jack hoisted the duffel bag into Lindsey's SUV.

On their way to the airport, Jack said, "I owe Ben for that one. Sometimes I feel like he really is a relative of ours."

"He is a relative, Jack."

"But he's black."

"His ancestors were slaves on the Carlson plantation for hundreds of years. He and your dad have a common ancestor."

"A common ancestor. I'm not sure I understand."

"Andy will explain it to you," Lindsey said. "Right now all you need to know is that he's your dad's best friend and he's saved your bacon twice from that same bunker."

40.

Sonja turned down the television set to be sure that the alarm from the front gate was really sounding. She stared toward the gate from the living room. Someone with a flashlight was climbing over the gate. She watched as the flashlight made its way toward the farmhouse. The person pointing the flashlight was actively shining the light back and forth on either side of the gravel driveway, clearly making no effort to hide his approach.

She checked the shell in the chamber of her shotgun and took a seat in the dark on her front porch. When the flashlight was about seventy-five yards away, she realized that the owner of the flashlight was singing. Yes, singing some song about coming around the mountain. It was a young girl's voice.

She was an adorable sight in the light from the pole, dressed smartly in a Girl Scout uniform. Her brown hat was cocked to the side. Two blonde pigtails bounced behind her head. She wore a brown purse attached to her waist. A clarinet was slung like a rifle on her left shoulder. She shined her light around the yard. The light ended up on the door of the farmhouse. Sonja leaned the shotgun against the house and stood up.

"Hi, my name's Kaitlin," the Girl Scout said. "My dad told me that the people who lived here probably were asleep and didn't need any Girl Scout cookies. He said he'd wait for me at the gate, but he didn't think it was worth the walk. I told him that these cookies were going to support an orphanage in Russia. I think people should care about little children who don't have a home, no matter where they live, don't you, ma'am?"

"I think you're a brave girl to walk down a strange road at night," Sonja said.

"I'm not afraid of the dark."

"I have a watch dog out there somewhere."

"You mean that Rottweiler?"

"Have you seen him?"

"He likes the chocolate chip cookies. I had to give him my last five before we made friends."

"You made friends?"

"Animals like me, ma'am. I guess it's because I'm small. Your Rottweiler weighs a lot more than I do."

"Where is he now?"

"He's waiting for me at the gate. I told him to keep my dad company while I sold you some cookies."

"You told him to wait for you?"

"Most dogs understand what 'stay' means, ma'am. Your Rottweiler knows I'm no threat to him. We're friends now."

"Where are you from?"

"We moved to Waterview three months ago from Kentucky," the Girl Scout said. "My dad hopes to sell real estate here. He's trying to learn the area while driving me around to sell cookies."

"You said these cookies were for an orphanage in Russia?"

"We don't have many orphanages in this country anymore," the child said. "Kids usually go to foster homes. But in Russia there are large orphanages and nobody wants the children. My cookies will buy warm coats and shoes for kids my age."

"That's admirable."

"I can't imagine anyone not caring about their own children. My mom says she worries about me every day. Do you have a daughter?"

"Yes, I do, and I worry about her every day."

"Is she home tonight? Maybe she would like to buy some cookies, too."

"I'm afraid she isn't home." Sonja wiped away a tear.

"Maybe you could give her some Girl Scout cookies the next time she comes home. I have a catalog that you can look at. You don't have to pay me a thing until I bring the cookies the day after tomorrow." She handed Sonja the catalog.

"It's too dark here on the porch," Sonja said. "And I need my reading glasses. Why don't you step inside while I look at your catalog?"

"Thanks, ma'am."

Sonja led the way into the house. She offered a chair to the child and sat down in a rocking chair next to a lamp table. After locating her reading glasses in the drawer of the table, she studied the selections while the child smiled and swung her legs.

"What would you suggest, Kaitlin? That was your name—Kaitlin?"

"Kaitlin Saunders, pleased to meet you," she said standing and extending her hand. "I was named after my grandmother, who came from the old country."

"The old country?"

"She was a Russian immigrant. Her name wasn't Kaitlin, but it sounded like Kate."

"That's remarkable," she said. "My name is Sonja."

"So you can understand why I want to do something for Russian children."

Sonja wiped away another tear.

"I would recommend the macaroons, ma'am."

"Why don't you put me down for four boxes of macaroons," Sonja said.

"Would you mind writing your name and address down on this order form for me?" the Girl Scout asked.

Sonja filled in the order form and handed it back to the child.

"Could I ask you for one favor, ma'am?"

"Sure."

"I've gotten thirsty walking to all these houses tonight. Could I have a glass of water before I go?"

Sonja smiled and went into the kitchen. "How about a Coke?" she called. "You can take the can with you."

"You're so kind, ma'am. Do you want me to send your doggie back to the house?"

"That would be nice of you. I understand why my dog likes you."

The girl took the opened can of Coke and said, "It's been a pleasure meeting you. I'll be back the day after tomorrow with your cookies."

Sonja stood in the doorway and watched the girl skip down the gravel road with her flashlight. She sat back down in her chair and smiled. The sensors would alarm again when she climbed over the gate. She sat down on the porch and waited for her dog.

The alarm never sounded and the dog didn't return. Sonja got up to check the gate alarm. The gate alarm was turned off. The key was missing. The electric fence was turned off. Its key was missing. Blood rushed to her head. Her heartbeat pounded in her ears. Her face hardened. She considered what had just happened. She picked up her shotgun and marched to the barn.

Andy's eyes were closed. He was lying on his right side, absorbing the pain from his left arm, left shoulder, neck, and head. He heard the small door open. The lights temporarily blinded him. Sonja strode toward him with the shotgun.

He pulled himself back to a sitting position.

"Dr. Carlson, do you have a daughter?"

"Yes, I do."

"I can't believe you are so stupid that you would bring her here with a clarinet and a Girl Scout outfit to sell me cookies."

"Is she okay?"

"I will keep her safe until I find out what happened to my daughter and my dog."

"My daughter is only ten years old, Sonja. She couldn't hurt anybody."

"You and I have something in common, doctor," she said. "We will both worry about our daughters tonight. It's clear that your daughter is expecting someone to come and rescue you. She tried to disarm our fence and motion detectors. Fortunately, I have other keys to replace the ones she stole. Sebastian will get to the bottom of this in the morning, but I want you to know something for sure tonight. If you have harmed my daughter, your own daughter will never leave this farm alive. Currently, she's tied up in my house. Rest assured, we will be ready for anyone who comes to rescue either of you."

She stalked toward the door. The lights went out. The door slammed.

Andy tasted bile and stomach acid from his throat. He wiped the sweat from his brow with his right hand, and then leaned on his right forearm. More sweat trickled down his face and puddled on the concrete floor in the dark. An icicle of fear plunged into his heart. The cold spread from his chest to the rest of his body. He could not remember the last time he was afraid. He had invited his entire family into harm's way, and he could lose them all. He had done exactly what he had cautioned his children not to do. He had allowed his own need for danger to cloud his mind. He had taken risks for selfish reasons. This disaster was about his own pride. He enjoyed it when Jack and Ava admired his skills. He wanted to be a SEAL again. He should have given the president and the CIA everything he had days ago. He had forgotten what was most important. He should have listened to Lindsey's words of caution. God was judging him for his pride.

41.

"Dad, I'm okay. Stop worrying."
The pain was making him delirious. Ava was tied up in Sonja's farmhouse. He was lying on his back next to a wall in the steel cage. His pain and fear and self-loathing were distorting reality.

A familiar, soft hand wiped his forehead. He knew the hand wasn't real, but he grabbed for it anyway. He squeezed tightly.

"Dad, calm down," she said. "You've already got enough broken bones for the whole family. You don't need to add my hand to the pile."

"I didn't hear you come in," he said.

"That's because you taught me how to move quietly."

"Keep your head and body low when you move around in here," Andy said. "They have motion sensors."

"Why do you think I crawled in here, Dad? I watched you trip an alarm."

"Ava, thank you so much for coming back and for trying to help."

"You taught me to be fearless. Did you think I wasn't going to do my job?"

"I'm sorry. I got hit in the head. I haven't put everything together yet."

"I was listening outside when Sonja called Sebastian and her sister Tasya."

"It was a nice try, stealing the arming keys for the fence and the gate," Andy said.

"Nice try? Come on, Dad. That was a misdirection play. You keep forgetting that you taught me this stuff. I knew she would notice the missing keys when the dog didn't come back. Of course she has spares.

The purpose of the visit to her house was to plant a bug on her trench coat and one underneath the table."

She handed her dad his molded earpiece. "You will be able to hear anything said in that house for the next twelve hours."

"Did you get in touch with your mom?"

"You're not talking to an amateur. They're on their way. Sonja's brother-in-law is a policeman. His name is Nicolai. He and his wife Tasya will be waiting for Jack and mom in the park."

"What about the front gate?"

"A police cruiser will be driving past that gate every hour tonight. The gate isn't electrified, but it has a motion sensor."

"Do you smell the chemicals now?" Andy asked.

"It smells like dog pee in here."

"That's ammonia," Andy said. "There are other chemicals in bulk on the far wall. I think the Ivanovs have another business—selling the ingredients required to make methamphetamine."

"Why would they take such risks if they have warheads here?"

"It wouldn't be much of a risk to store the chemicals if a family member was the chief of police," Andy said. "Most of the ingredients of crystal meth are now controlled substances in the United States. But all of them are readily available in Canada, only a short drive from here."

"Do you think they make the stuff here?"

"Too risky, even for an inside job," Andy said. "Some of the chemicals used in manufacturing crystal meth are highly explosive. Labs blow up all the time. They could make a fortune selling the chemicals to cookers in the United States."

"Do we really need to get involved in a corrupt police department or the crystal meth trade while we're here trying to find nuclear warheads?" Ava asked.

"The chemicals are an important find. I don't know what we can do with them yet."

"Sonja told her sister to put chemicals in the rental car in the park."

"That means they intend to make killing your mother and Jack look like a drug deal gone bad. You can help us even the odds."

"I've got my own ideas, but I'm willing to listen to yours."

"Cut the phone line with the clippers in the backpack," Andy said. "She may have a cell phone, maybe not. The box will be attached to the house."

"I know what a phone line looks like. What next?"

"The main power line to this farm goes to the barn first," Andy said. "Remember the transformer on the light pole outside? You need to turn off the electricity at the breaker panel."

"What's to keep her from just coming out and turning it back on?"

"If she comes out in the dark, she'll be very vulnerable," Andy said. "She won't know who is here or how many people are here. Besides, you can fix the electrical panel so that she can't turn it back on."

"How?"

"Over there between the small door and the rollback door is a red Craftsman toolbox. That's where you need to go. The electrical panel is above the toolbox. When the lights were on, I found the motion detectors. They're the same color as the steel poles. They're on the inside of the two rows of poles in the center of this barn, three feet high. That's how I got caught. If you work your way on your tummy around the sides of the building, behind the pallets of warheads and chemicals, you'll be fine."

"Do you want me to shoot Sonja with the clarinet, Dad?"

"If she comes back into this barn before morning, you'll have to shoot her. They intend to kill us all."

"I understand that, Dad, but I wanted to hear you say it."

"I have a confession to make."

"What do you mean?"

"It was wrong for me not to correct you when you said that Aleksi and the dog were sleeping. Nobody shot with the terrible frog wakes up. I wanted to protect you from the reality of what you were doing."

"You're talking about Aleksi being dead?"

"Yes, and you did the right thing by shooting him."

"Some evil people have to die in order that good people can live. That goes for evil Rottweilers, too."

Andy said, "I've felt guilty not telling you exactly what you were doing. The truth is that you saved our whole family, and you're going to do it again."

"Who do you want me to shoot first?"

"Nobody yet. When the time comes, you'll know it. Just like when you shot Aleksi."

"How do I turn off the power at that breaker box?"

"Find a hammer or a twelve-inch knuckle buster in the toolbox. Climb on the toolbox and hold your Maglite in your mouth. The panel door opens with a hinge on the right. You put your finger in the latch on the left side of the panel door and lift up."

"I've seen you do it."

"The main switch will be at the top of the panel and it will be labeled. This switch is nothing but a piece of plastic. Flip the switch to the left, and then smash it from the right side until there's nothing left that a finger can work with. Keep hitting it until you're satisfied."

"That's all there is to it?"

"If Sonja is bold enough to come back in here with a flashlight, you'll have plenty of opportunity to shoot her in the dark. It's not an easy job for a woman to remove the face of an electrical panel. Six long screws, at least two over her head. She would need a ladder, someone to hold a light, and a screwdriver or portable drill with the right bit."

"She would have to put her shotgun down," Ava said. "And she would be facing a wall."

"Even if she can get Sebastian on a cell phone," Andy said, "he would be walking into an ambush in the dark as well. It's much more likely that they won't enter this building until daylight. They don't want to kill me until they can get information about their lost family members in Virginia."

"Should I start on the electrical panel now?"

"Cut the phone line first."

Andy saw nothing and heard nothing for twenty minutes. A small circle of light appeared on the electrical panel. He heard the switch close. The dim light from underneath the small door disappeared. She hit the switch three times. There was a pause. She hit the switch again. The circle of light at the breaker box disappeared. Andy waited for Ava to come back to the cage. She didn't come back.

42.

"Ava said to park at a veterinarian's office on the left," Jack said.

"I see it," Lindsey said.

"She said it was less than a mile from the park."

"I really don't like Ava's idea of blowing up two strangers in a police car," Lindsey said. She turned into the small lot at the vet's office on Park Avenue.

Neither do I," Jack said, "but these two people are waiting to kill us. And their relatives plan to kill Dad and Ava. We didn't go out looking to kill Ivanovs. They came to kill us. The president has got to back us up because we're doing all the hard stuff. Whenever you feel guilty about killing our enemies, think about Dad in that cage. When we leave this farm, we can't leave anyone alive."

Lindsey blinked her eyes several times. "You've learned a lot from Dad."

"Ava said to get rid of the rental car," Jack said. "She wants us to put a C4 charge under both the police cruiser and the rental."

"Do you have them ready?" she asked.

"They're ready. The first one is activated by engine noise. It's for the police cruiser."

"What if their engine is already on?" Lindsey asked.

"Nobody with a brain would sit at a stakeout with the engine on," Jack said. "Even if they were that stupid, I would just switch to a standard timer to blow at daylight. That's what I'm doing with the rental."

"I hope you don't plan on moving around with a remote timer in your lap."

"We don't have to tell Dad everything."

"I'm glad you're beginning to understand such things."

"Thanks, Mom. I'm learning discretion."

Lindsey said, "Ava said that after we leave the charges, we should move a hundred yards down the river and use our inflatable raft to cross."

They climbed into their wetsuits next to the car in the vet's parking lot.

"How come we're not blowing this car?" Jack said.

"I didn't rent it in my name," she said. "Your dad produces his own driver's licenses."

"How does he do that?"

"He hacks into the DMV and substitutes his picture or my picture for somebody else in Virginia. You can bet he didn't rent the car in the park under his own name."

"I'm going to ask him to teach me that. I could use a fake ID."

"Wipe everything down in this car," Lindsey said. "You don't have to blow everything up to cover your tracks."

"It's easier," he said, "and it's more fun than wiping down the interior of a vehicle."

Jack stuck his head and right arm inside the string of his bow and slung his quiver over his left shoulder. They walked on the shoulder of the gravel road toward the park, stopping often to look back over their shoulders. Jack dragged the duffel bag.

At 6:50 AM Andy heard an explosion in the distance, from the direction of the river and the park. He swallowed. There was a second explosion. Daylight was coming from underneath the door. He wondered if Ava had actually come back, or if she was tied up in the farmhouse. He remembered an experience in the first Iraq war. A mortar shell had exploded nearby. He talked to his dead parents before he woke up. Even today, he could remember exactly what they said to him. He looked toward the wall where he had entered the building. There was no sign of a cavalry. Ava had given him an earpiece. He reached for his ear. There was nothing there. He could find no earpiece in the floor of the cage.

43.

At 7:58 that morning the small door opened. Sonja was dressed in her trench coat, black jeans, and boots. The shotgun was tucked under her right arm. She was followed by Sebastian. Even in the poor light inside the barn he was a powerful man with tree-trunk arms. He wore a full beard to compensate for his receding hairline. Andy guessed he was fifty years old.

Sonja locked the door.

As Sebastian walked closer to the cage, Andy saw some resemblance to Sasha, especially in the nose. A long knife was attached to the right side of his belt. He smelled like sausage.

"Good morning," Andy said. "You must pardon me for not standing. My shoulder's broken."

They stared at the painted man in a wetsuit, seated with his legs crossed, leaning against the back of the cage, his left arm hanging from a deformed left shoulder. Dried blood was caked on the left side of his face and scalp.

"Sebastian," Andy said, "you did a fine job on this cage, but it needs to be at least a foot taller. Had I been wearing a cowboy hat, you could have done some real damage to it."

"When I was driving in," Sebastian said, "I heard explosions on the other side of the river. My sister-in-law and her husband were over there in the park, waiting on whoever was coming to rescue you."

"Have you ever noticed that two people can hear the same noises, but have entirely different opinions about what they mean?" Andy asked.

Sonja and Sebastian looked at each other.

"Your daughter told us about your family coming to rescue you," Sebastian said.

"She's just trying to help me," Andy said. "Just like your own daughter Sasha would help you."

"My wife has told me your story," Sebastian said. "She has probably told you already. If you have harmed my daughter, or my father, there is no amount of money that can buy these warheads. I will carve you up into a shish-kabob and feed you to the pigs, after you watch me do the same to your daughter."

"You don't own any pigs, Sebastian, but you do smell like one."

"I'm beginning to develop a dislike for you, Dr. Carlson."

Andy leaned forward. "I heard that you were good with a knife, Sebastian. Is this true?"

"You've heard the truth. I've never lost a knife fight."

"It would be difficult for you to do much to me with a knife while I'm in here," Andy said. "You're too tall to stand in this cage. I wonder- -if you have the door locked, and your wife has a shotgun, and you have a big knife, and I have a broken shoulder, and you're as good as you say—why are you afraid of me?"

The veins popped out in Sebastian's face. He glared at Andy, who leaned back against the wall of the cage again.

"Tell me what happened to my daughter and my father, you smartass."

"Why don't you raise this cage and turn on the lights?" Andy asked. "You could hurt yourself with that knife in the dark."

"Do it, Sonja. Lock it in the 'Up' position and turn off the sensors."

Sonja looked at the electric panel. "The girl smashed the main switch."

"Silly girl," Andy said. "If you have a metal pick or a punch you can close the switch without taking the face of the panel off."

Sebastian walked to the toolbox, found the right tool, and flipped the switch.

The barn lit up. Andy looked around at the pallets of dog food, the chemicals, the alfalfa, and the boxes on pallets. He saw no Carlsons.

Sonja pressed the "Up" button on the switch next to the panel. The cage slowly began to rise. Andy leaned forward. The electric motors stopped when the cage disappeared into the cupola. She turned a breaker off.

"Is it locked up there?" Sebastian asked.

"Yes."

Andy stood up and steadied himself. "Sonja," he asked, "do you believe in magic?"

Sebastian's eyebrows converged. He looked at Sonja, who squinted at Andy.

"I once saw a magician's trick," Andy said. "There was a young woman. She looked a lot like you. She was standing with a gun in her hand, just like you. She looked down and saw an arrow sticking out of her chest. It was a wooden arrow, and it was tipped with a bloody hunting broad head. I wish you could have been there."

Nothing happened.

"He got hit on the head," Sonya said.

"Step forward, Sebastian," Andy said, "and I will teach you something about knife fighting."

"You will teach me?"

"I will teach you," Andy said. "Since you have two arms and I only have one, you might have a chance."

"I can't stand this man any longer," Sebastian said.

"Don't kill him until he tells us what happened to Aleksi and the girls," Sonja said.

"His tongue is the last thing I'll cut off."

Sebastian crouched and tossed his knife from his right hand to his left hand without looking down.

"That's very good," Andy said. "I believe it's time to start your education."

Sebastian moved closer to Andy. He was smiling.

"First of all," Andy said, circling to his right, "most knife fights are decided by the first cut. The person who loses doesn't even know that the winner is there. In other words, you have lost the element of surprise in this fight."

"I don't need to surprise," Sebastian said, continuing to throw his knife from one hand to the other without looking at his hands.

"We'll see," Andy said, widening his stance. "My second point is that you must determine if your opponent, the person you are trying to carve up, has a knife of his own. In this case, I do."

Andy reached behind his right shoulder and pulled his ten inch knife from the sheath in the back of his wetsuit. He held it next to his right ear with the blade pointed up.

Sebastian's eyes widened.

"I apologize if you only have experience cutting people who are unarmed," Andy said.

"It doesn't matter whether you have a knife, Dr. Carlson. No one has ever cut me."

"If you didn't have information about our relatives," Sonja said, "you would already be in pieces."

"The last part of your lesson," Andy said, "is to know your enemy before you pick a fight. It's not a good thing to learn about your enemy after you are already engaged."

"I'm going to enjoy slicing you up," Sebastian said, tossing his knife back and forth, moving toward Andy six inches at a time.

"Stop," Andy said, holding up the knife. "I'll give you a hint. You're twelve feet from me. This knife will rotate one complete turn in the air before it reaches you."

The throw was instantaneous. A dull thud announced that the hilt of Andy's knife had struck Sebastian in his epigastrium, that triangular space with the breast bone at its apex and the rib margins of the left and right anterior chest wall descending like a tent on either side. Both the aorta and the vena cava, the largest blood vessels in the human body, pass through this triangle. Sebastian looked down, and his head carried him forward to the concrete floor.

Sonya didn't see her husband lose his first knife fight. Andy's knife had only completed 180 degrees of its 360 degree rotation when a wooden arrow, tipped with a three-blade razor-sharp hunting broad head, entered Sonja's left chest, exited her right chest, and came to rest in a stack of twenty-five pound bags of Purina Dog Chow.

44.

"I wanted you to tell Sonja a story about a little Girl Scout with a clarinet," Ava said.

"But Sonja had already heard that story," Andy said.

"You're right," Ava said. "Nobody likes to hear the same story twice."

"Jack, cut a tarp off of one of these weapons and throw it over these two bodies while your mom and I look at these boxes."

Lindsey fitted the shoulder immobilizer on Andy's left arm.

"Ava, start gathering everything we brought in the duffel bag and backpack," Lindsey said.

Andy cut the ropes that held the tarps over the boxes. Each box was draped with a lead blanket.

"Put on your spacesuit, Lindsey," Andy said.

Jack helped Lindsey into her radiation safety suit. She moved from pallet to pallet. Andy stood behind her and made adjustments to his shoulder immobilizer.

Each warhead was lashed to a pallet. The tritium reservoirs were packed separately in lead cases, also lashed to the pallet.

"The tritium reservoirs are new," Lindsey said. "I can count the neutrons in my lab, but these are just like the reservoirs at Long Beach and West Virginia. There are no batteries in the electronic timers."

"Where do you think the old reservoirs are?" Andy asked.

"They must be close by," Lindsey said. "They wouldn't keep them in their farmhouse."

They walked around the building.

"Andy, why does Aleksi need all of that alfalfa stacked up over there if he doesn't have any cattle or horses?"

They walked toward the stacks of bales.

Lindsey said, "I noticed the Geiger counter's broken. It could have helped us here."

"Blame that on me," Andy said. "Jack, we need your help."

Ava joined in. At least she tried to. Each alfalfa bale weighed twice what she did.

"What are we looking for in this pile?" she asked.

"A box the size of a foot locker," Lindsey said.

Jack walked around the stacks of alfalfa bales, kicking the bottom bale in each stack with his shoes. He found a bale that didn't move at all. He climbed on top of an adjacent stack and kicked the top bale. The entire stack toppled over. He dragged the bottom bale backwards.

Ava leaned over and looked in the space behind this bale. "Like that box?"

"It doesn't look like we can move it easily," Jack said.

"That's because it's lead-lined," Lindsay said. "Knock over all the stacks around it and brush it off."

The box had a key lock hanging from a pair of clasps.

"Jack, bolt cutters are on the wall near the toolbox," Andy said. "See if you can hold the lock in the jaws while I press down with my good arm."

Jack arranged the jaws of the bolt cutters so that one handle was against the floor while Andy pushed down with his right arm on the other handle. The lock snapped.

"Kids, please step back while your mom looks inside," Andy said.

After a few minutes, Lindsey yelled, "It's the old reservoirs. Seven of them."

"Lindsey, would you switch the old reservoirs in that locker with the new ones on the pallets?" Andy asked.

"You've never explained why we are switching these reservoirs," she said.

"I'd like to leave two warheads here, both with old tritium reservoirs," Andy said. "When the Feds find forty year old tritium reservoirs next to two warheads they will conclude that Aleksi hasn't received any recent help from the Kremlin."

"But he obviously did," Lindsey said. "These reservoirs on the pallets are all new. They're loaded with neutrons and ready to boost a chain reaction."

"But the president doesn't know that," Andy said. "I want the president to believe that the Russian government is not involved. Two is more convincing than one, don't you think?"

Lindsey shook her head. "You want me to stuff the pits of the two we're leaving?"

"Yes," Andy said. "After we're gone, I'll call the president and tell him where to look."

"I don't see where you're going with this," Lindsey said. "Why would you want to make the Russians look less guilty?"

"Consider the possibility that we've missed a warhead," Andy said. "What if some other Iranian with a Russian warhead detonates it in one of our cities? Wouldn't politicians want revenge? What good does it do for us to risk our lives to stop warheads from destroying cities in America and Britain, only to hand over evidence to politicians who might demand retaliatory nuclear strikes against Russia? Umar would certainly rather bomb Russia than an Islamic country."

"New tritium reservoirs are powerful evidence for active, current Russian involvement," Lindsey said.

"A man at Arco Genetics told me that Aleksi visited both Iran and Russia regularly," Andy said. "We have been calling Boris and Aleksi ex-KGB. Is there such a thing as ex-KGB?"

"I don't know."

"The Russians who are helping Iran do not represent the Russian people," Andy said. "The KGB doesn't represent the Russian people. I don't want to facilitate any more Nagasakis or Hiroshimas in any country."

"I don't either, but you're getting ahead of me again."

"We can no longer afford to look at the problems of this world only through American eyes," Andy said. "Our own government is an ever-growing monster. We can't blindly say we're always on America's side or the president's side. We must be on the side that prevents war and loss of life. There is only one city in the world whose destruction would prevent war and loss of life. I would like to deal with it now, before the Middle East war starts."

"Don't tell me you're planning your own nuclear strike," Lindsey said, laughing.

"This could get interesting," Jack said to Ava. They sat down on bales of alfalfa to listen.

"I think it could be done without anyone else but King Fahd knowing where the warhead came from," Andy said. "And it could stop the coming Middle East war in its tracks."

"No, Andy," Lindsey said.

"Natanz is a military target, not a population center," Andy said. "Think about it. Let me talk to King Fahd. Time is critical."

Lindsey faced Andy. She put her right hand on his cheek. "I'm almost speechless," she said. "There is no way for you and King Fahd to pull that off by yourselves. You're injured, for crying out loud."

"Lindsey, do you remember how this all got started with the nuclear explosion at Ras Tanura?"

"A girl usually remembers all of the nuclear explosions in her life."

"We now know where that bomb came from and how it got to Ras Tanura, right?"

"Yes, we do," Lindsey said. "The same container that left Wisconsin was delivered to Ras Tanura on the day that the explosion occurred, by ship. The warhead could have been remotely detonated."

"Then the Iranians have shown us the way," Andy said. "This evil was masterminded by the Iranians. Natanz is where Iran has 3,000 centrifuges purring along, enriching uranium. We still don't know the status of their nuclear weapons program. It's all underground. The president has shown that he has no stomach for decisive action against Islamic countries. U.S. or NATO inspectors have never seen the insides of that bunker, thanks to Umar's endless negotiations and sanctions. If not for Umar, the Israelis would have dealt with Ahmadinejad and his nuclear weapons program years ago."

"Andy, private citizens from the United States are not authorized to bomb other countries," Lindsey said. "We do have an elected government for those kinds of decisions."

"Might I remind you that the Iranians are the Islamic Jihad," Andy said. "They have planned the destruction of Israel, to begin in days. Iran arms Hezbollah, Hamas, and Al Qaeda. They back insurgents in Iraq and Afghanistan. They incite civil war in Syria and Egypt and Africa. Iran is the first country in the twenty-first century to use a nuclear weapon against another country--its own neighbor, Saudi Arabia. Iran concocted this entire nuclear blackmail scheme for the U.S. and Britain."

"I'm fully aware of all that now," she said. "It's you I'm worried about. That was a great speech you gave to the kids on the plane about superheroes. Search your own heart. Why must you be the one to do this? Convince me that you're the only person who can eliminate the threat of Natanz without precipitating Armageddon."

"Thank you for the opportunity," Andy said. "I had some time to think more clearly in that cage after Ava came back. Think about the reasons why we should *not* involve our president."

"I'll try to keep an open mind," she said, sitting down on a bale of alfalfa next to the twins.

"First, consider what would happen if the United States actually hit Natanz with a bunker buster."

He waited.

"The Iranians would certainly strike back at us in some way," Lindsey said. "I can still remember the Iranian hostage crisis. If not us, then they would take their frustration out on Israel. They're poised to do this already."

"What if the Israelis strike Iran unilaterally?" Andy asked.

He waited. Lindsey frowned.

"If the Israelis bombed Natanz on their own," Andy said, "they would be inviting war with all their Islamic neighbors. With King Fahd's help, we can make the entire world safer without doing any harm to innocent people. There are no innocent people in the Natanz bunker. There are no children playing in the bunker. It's a factory for WMDs."

"Andy, do you remember about ten years ago when I thought that exploding a nuclear weapon was a good thing?" Lindsey asked. "Do you remember that I almost killed you trying to do it?"

"I recall, Lindsey, but you've more than made up for it."

"That's very sweet of you, but I'd like to stay on the job as your wife. I'm retired from the CIA."

"All you need to do is fly with me to Riyadh," he said. "We can transport one of the warheads that we bought from Boris ten years ago from the cave. We could use any of the new tritium reservoirs in this barn. None of us have to go to Iran. I think the king and I can figure out a way to ship Iran a present."

"I knew the first time you had me switch a reservoirs that I would regret it," she said. "What weapon size were you hallucinating about sending to Natanz?"

"The facility at Natanz is supposedly fifty feet underground, with a concrete reinforced roof," Andy said.

"The top layer is fill dirt," Lindsey said. "A fifty kiloton warhead delivered to that site would crush the bunker. But it would also throw that loose fill into the air, probably scattering radiation contamination to God knows where. If you could put a warhead inside the bunker, radioactive fallout would be minimal. But that's impossible."

"It's not impossible," Andy said. "I just don't know how to do it yet.

I agree with your assessment. Detonating a warhead above ground is not the way to go."

Jack asked, "Would blowing up Natanz fall under our Second Amendment right to bear arms?"

"That's a legitimate question," Andy said. "Our Founding Fathers wanted the citizens to be as well-armed as the government. They envisioned that our government could one day become as oppressive as England. They wanted the people to have the means to topple their own government."

"So you think everybody in the U.S. is entitled to their own nuclear warheads?" Lindsey asked.

"No," Andy said. "While I hate gun control, I'm in favor of WMD control, especially for madmen in Iran. The Soviet Union manufactured thousands of small warheads. Some of them fit in a backpack. It's naïve to think that anybody knows where all of these are now. The Ivanovs are a wake-up call."

"Please talk to King Fahd, Andy," Lindsey said. "Tell him that something very heavy recently fell on your head. Maybe he can talk you out of this. Anyway, what would we do with the kids while you and I launch a warhead?"

"Now wait a minute," Ava said, standing up. "We haven't needed babysitters for a long time. We're in training to be superheroes. We've been in this together since Aleksi and Sasha tried to kill us."

Andy and Lindsey stared at their daughter.

"You've got to stop protecting me," Ava said. "I shot Aleksi. He's dead. I was protecting my family. I'm not going to be treated like a glass princess. I take my chances just like the rest of you. You can't expect me to be fearless one day and a chicken the next."

"She's right," Jack said. "However, it does seem somewhat inconsistent that we're planning the detonation of a nuclear weapon in one country after preventing the same in our own country."

"That's called critical thinking, Jack," Andy said. "Robert E. Lee spoke about this kind of paradox in the nineteenth century. Lee said that true patriotism sometimes required a man to act contrary at one time to what he had done at another time. In his case, he once fought for the United States. He ended up fighting against the United States because he was a Virginian under attack by a Federal army. In our case, the proper motive should be the same as General Lee's—the desire to do what is right for the circumstances we are now in."

Jack said, "I think Ava and I can accept that."

"What are we going to do with five more nuclear warheads?" Lindsey asked.

"Save them for the future," Andy said. "To give Jack and Ava options."

"I should be shocked by that statement," Lindsey said. "How do you intend to get five warheads back to the Confederate cave?"

"I can still handle that eighteen-wheeler next to the barn," Andy said. "The shoulder immobilizer lets me use my left hand."

"That's ridiculous," Lindsey said.

"Jack's feet aren't long enough to reach the pedals of that rig," Andy said, "but he knows how to shift the gears. We've practiced this while driving containers from Farmville to the ports in Hampton Roads."

"My real specialty is avoiding inspection and weighing stations," Jack said.

"Did you hear the siren on the other side of the river?" Andy asked. "We need to move along before some local connects a dot to the Ivanov farm."

45.

A ndy sat down at a desktop computer in the sitting room of the Ivanov farmhouse. The computer had pathetic security features. He accessed his own secure email through the Saudi embassy, and requested a chat conversation with King Fahd. There was a brief pause between exchanges.

Andy: *We have made great progress finding and disarming Russian warheads in the U.S. I believe that it is imperative that we deal with the Iranians as soon as possible, before they start a war or detonate any more warheads.*

King Fahd: *What do you have in mind?*

Andy: *Do you remember my asking about an ex-KGB agent named Boris, a man who tried to sell you nuclear weapons?*

King Fahd: *This is the man you disposed of in your own kingdom. We have found no current information about his successor, the man you called Aleksi.*

Andy: *I was able to capture two of Boris's nuclear warheads ten years ago. These are stored in my cave. They are currently dismantled and cannot explode, but my wife could re-arm one quickly. Besides my family, you are the only person who knows this.*

King Fahd: *President Umar does not know this?*

Andy: *Especially not Umar. I feel that you and I can improve the possibilities for peace in the world if we act on our own as soon as possible. If the Iranian nuclear weapons facility at Natanz were to explode, for example, America could righteously deny any involvement, even though they would be happy. The Israelis could righteously deny any involvement, but they would be happy. You would be happy. Much of the world would be happy.*

King Fahd: *Your suggestion is intriguing. I do owe Iran a nuclear weapon. You must be the only man in the world who has a personal stockpile of nuclear warheads.*

Andy: *I feel better with mine locked in my cave than I do with such weapons in the hands of Iranians. It remains to be seen whether I am the only private citizen who has a nuclear warhead.*

King Fahd: *If Natanz were to disappear from the map and you have found all the warheads in America, Iran would think again about launching a war. They would not know who to go to war against. There would be no reason for the United States to be reluctant to help Israel.*

Andy: *What if my wife disassembled a nuclear warhead and shipped it in pieces from my farm to the palace where you usually receive our containers? Would you allow her to come to Saudi Arabia and re-arm the bomb inside that palace?*

King Fahd: *Could she guarantee that it would not explode in Saudi Arabia?*

Andy: *Absolutely. I understand that your country and my country don't look at the roles of women in the same way. It would be a tremendous risk to you to let anyone handle a nuclear weapon in your country. I suspect that most of your subjects and your family would object to my wife performing this task.*

King Fahd: *Neither my subjects nor my family are the King of Saudi Arabia. I must do what is necessary. I appreciate what you are offering. I also believe that time is critical. Let me fly to Farmville and pick up this warhead.*

Andy: *Consider it a gift. You recently told me about your limited trade with Iran. Doesn't much of your container traffic go through Ali Jabayl?*

King Fahd: *This is true.*

Andy: *Do you have trusted contacts in Pakistan?*

King Fahd: *I have contacts in every country.*

Andy: *Pakistan does not export nuclear warheads, at least so far as we know. They do export nuclear technology. How hard would it be for one of your contacts in Pakistan to ship a container to Iran, one that stopped at Ali Jabayl?*

King Fahd: *This could be done.*

Andy: *You must help me solve one problem. What can you offer from Pakistan that the Iranians would want transported to Natanz?*

King Fahd: *In some respects, the Iranians are quite predictable. I know of* one thing that would make their mouths water. A container will leave Pakistan within twenty-four hours.

Andy: *We track our containers shipped to you with GPS already. I could install the proper antenna on this container from Pakistan when it arrives in your port of Ali Jabayl, at the same time we add the warhead to its cargo. We should be able to monitor its journey to the bunker in Natanz. You would be able to detonate the warhead by satellite phone.*

King Fahd: *There are risks to this plan, but these risks are worth taking.*

Andy: *How do you propose to avoid security measures at Dulles?*

King Fahd: *My planes have refueled at Dulles many times. If I'm on board, no one ever enters my personal jet. Your government and I have differences, but I am not considered a security risk. Likewise, I do not search American planes carrying only diplomats.*

Andy: *There is one person who could prevent us from proceeding with such a plan.*

King Fahd: *Who would that be? Your president?*

Andy: *No, the real boss, my wife Lindsey.*

King Fahd: *You are a persuasive man, Dr. Carlson. I have faith in you in this regard.*

Andy: *Please advise me when you have a firmer timetable.*

King Fahd: *Thank your wife for everything. Tell her my wives would like a broader selection of black bras, all sizes.*

46.

Andy walked out of the Ivanov farmhouse. "Jack, let's back the trailer up to the loading dock. The warheads are already on pallets and we have a forklift. While I load the container, I want you to inspect the diesel engine on that rig. Check the oil, the airbrakes, and the air pressure in all tires. Look for a log book in the cab. You can make it look good in case we do get stopped. Ava, start searching the house."

After loading the warheads and the lead-lined foot locker into the back of the forty foot trailer with the forklift, Andy and Lindsey returned to the farmhouse.

"I want every record here," Andy said. "Anything that would tell us if this is the entire inventory in the United States or if there are other warheads. Perhaps we can learn the name of the KGB contact who supplied the new tritium reservoirs."

He turned around. Lindsey had walked into another room.

"Come in here, Andy." She pointed to a huge safe pushed against the wall of a home office.

"It must weigh a thousand pounds," Andy said. He walked over to the window and looked outside.

"No problem," he said, walking out of the farmhouse. "Stay here. Open that window."

He returned to the yard of the farmhouse driving the forklift.

"Lindsey, tell me when the forks are pointed underneath the floor that supports that safe."

He maneuvered the forklift and adjusted the forks to be parallel to the floor of the home office. Lindsey guided Andy to the wall behind the safe. He positioned the two forks inside the width of the base of the safe and Lindsey marked their targets with a chalk line on the outside wall of the farmhouse.

"Everybody out of the house," Andy called.

Lindsey and Ava stood in the yard and watched.

After backing the forklift six feet, Andy shifted into forward and stomped on the accelerator. The forks rammed through the wall underneath the safe. He tilted the tips of the forks upward and raised the forks six inches, ripping the floor away from the floor joists. As he backed up, the wooden shingles around the safe snapped. The safe was outside, leaving a rectangular hole in the farmhouse wall.

"I should say I'm impressed," Lindsey said, "but I'm really not. Anybody who plans to nuke another country ought to be able to move a safe around."

"You're going to have plenty of time flying home with Ava to think about backing out of this opportunity to stop war and save lives," Andy said, turning the forklift toward the tractor-trailer.

"Backing out?" Lindsey said, walking along beside the forklift. "I don't remember agreeing to anything."

"Well, the king thinks it's a fine idea," Andy said. "He's bringing his personal jet to Farmville to pick us up, as well as the warhead and reservoir we discussed. We need a safe remote timer and detonator, one that can be actuated by satellite phone."

Andy lined the forklift up with the open doors of the container on the trailer.

"That's all the king said?" Lindsey asked.

"He did say to thank you for everything you do, and he wants a broader selection of black bras for his wives, all sizes."

Lindsey shook her head. "I've been thinking about the child I'm carrying. Should this child grow up in a world that's threatened by Natanz if I can prevent it? You're right about Umar. Once he is sure that all the threats to America are gone, he will lose his stomach for taking out Natanz."

Andy lifted the safe just above the height of the floor of the trailer, inserted the forks, and tilted them down. The safe slid into the container. After backing up, he switched gears and used the forks to push the safe completely inside. The section of the farmhouse wall behind the safe fell out of the trailer as he backed the forklift away. He dismounted the forklift.

Jack ran to his dad, carrying a packet of Arco Genetics GTIN numbers.

"I found these in the shed," he said. "These two match. We can peel the backing off and paste them over the number on the container. The Ivanovs had a supply of locks for the container's rear doors."

"Good work, Jack," Andy said.

"Ava stripped every kind of record from the house while you were loading the warheads," Lindsey said. "She found one laptop and their phone records. I'll get the desktop computer. No telling what's inside the safe."

"I'll bet Aleksi's records are in the safe," Andy said. "I know somebody in Virginia who can open it. We may be able to find their bank accounts. Put the records in a suitcase and take them with you on the king's plane. Put the desktop and the laptop in the container."

"Do you have any idea what roads you should travel over?" Lindsey asked.

"Did you bring my laptop from the plane?"

"Yes."

"Use it to find a Wi-Fi connection. Look under MapQuest or Google and locate the best directions from Madison, Wisconsin to Farmville. Specify "avoid all interstates" and save the file under Jack's name. Also check the Department of Transportation for the location of truck inspection and weigh stations on this route. Save that file under Jack's name. Put the laptop in the cab of the tractor-trailer along with the charger. Jack can compare results with the map and GPS app on my cellphone."

Jack was standing on a ladder pasting the new GTIN number on the back door of the trailer.

"When you're finished up there," Andy called. "Disable the GPS receiver and transmitter on top."

"Do you plan to clean out the Ivanovs' bank accounts after you open the safe?" Ava asked.

"We'll have to see what's in them first, who the money belongs to, and what it's used for. No one but us knows that the Ivanovs are dead."

He turned to Lindsey. "I will advise Umar how to handle the two explosions on the other side of the river. We're all riding out of here in that big rig. I'll drop you and Ava off at the Madison airport at the king's plane. You'll fly back with the suitcase of records. Jack and I will drive the rig home."

"What if you get stopped," Ava asked, "and somebody wants to look in the container?"

"The president owes us a few favors," Andy said. "I think he would be able to get any kind of law enforcement off our backs."

Ava said, "So far all we've gotten out of him is some ice cream."

"What are you going to do with the farmhouse?" Jack asked.

"They have propane heat," Andy said. "Go take a look at it. I'll help Lindsey drag the two bodies onto the forklift. I'll insert them in the new hole in the side of the farmhouse."

Andy tilted the forklift inside the rectangular hole in the Ivanov farmhouse. Sebastian and Sonja rolled off the forks.

Jack returned. "I looked at the propane. No problem."

"Before you put a C4 charge in the house," Andy said, "I want you to turn off the main power switch in the barn. You'll need a pick. There's one on top of the red Craftsman toolbox. Set your fuse for ninety minutes. The last thing you should do is open the largest propane line you find. There's a knuckle buster in the toolbox in the barn. We're going to leave the barn standing."

47.

After leaving the Madison airport, Jack and Andy began the long drive back to Farmville. Driving with his right arm and left hand, Andy was able to keep his left shoulder in the sling.

"Jack, there's hardly anyone on this road," Andy said. "Could you connect your cell phone to the speaker so I can talk hands-free? I want to pull over in a few minutes. We don't want any highway noise. Your phone doesn't have a GPS chip, but if we stay here long enough we could be triangulated."

"You're connected," Jack said.

Andy pulled onto the shoulder of the two lane highway and parked underneath an overpass. He killed the engine. "Punch in the president's number from the card I gave you."

"Mr. President, we have some more good news."

"Go ahead, Carlson."

"There's a farm in Waterview, Wisconsin, 106 Guernsey Lane. It's owned by the Ivanov family. The patriarch of this family is Aleksi Ivanov, an ex-KGB agent who travels the world as a bull semen salesman, with the blessing of the U.S. government. This farm is where all of the loose warheads have been coming from."

"How did you find out about this?" the president asked.

"I've been following leads from the king and from the sites where we've disarmed warheads."

"What's at this site now?" the president asked.

"There're two warheads at this farm in a barn. My wife has disarmed them using the pit-stuffing technique. What we really need is a cleanup operation."

"I can arrange that."

"The Ivanov family were also involved in the importation of chemicals for the manufacture of methamphetamine," Andy said. "They probably trucked the chemicals in from Canada, the same way they trucked the warheads in during the Cold War. The Ivanovs put up quite a fight. They had so much firepower in their farmhouse that we had to put a couple of HEAT rounds in it.

"And where did you get these?"

"We used the same shoulder-fired rockets the Army and the Marines use, AT4s. This is the same weapon I used at the mouth of the tunnel in Hampton. It's the same weapon system you have sold to several Islamic countries. That's where I got mine. King Fahd bought them for me. I think they had chemical accelerants in the house or their propane lines ruptured. The whole building went up like the Fourth of July. Let me give you a list of the Ivanovs that we observed going into this farmhouse before the fight started."

"Go ahead."

"Aleksi, his brother Vladimir, his son Sebastian, his daughter-in-law Sonja, and his granddaughter Sasha perished in this explosion. You'll find plenty of evidence in their barn. The local sheriff was a member of the family and involved in everything. I've been injured."

"How badly?"

"My left shoulder is broken, but I'm otherwise okay."

"Can we get you a doctor?"

"I'm on my way to see a doctor."

"Do we have control of all the loose warheads yet?"

"I believe that we do. Of course, the CIA needs to pick up the two left in the barn in Wisconsin."

"I'll take care of it."

"I don't think the people in Waterview know anything about the warheads or the methamphetamine," Andy said. "Somebody needs to come up with a good explanation for the sheriff's car blowing up on the opposite side of the town with him and his wife in it. A rental car also blew up nearby. It had chemicals in it. Since the Ivanovs were involved in everything, perhaps you could stress the methamphetamine ring and leave out the nuclear warheads."

"That sounds very prudent, Dr. Carlson," said the president. "But I need more documentation from you."

"We'll have time for that," Andy said. "I still have a bit of investigating to do."

"The British just informed us that a ship bound for London, the *Spirit of Long Beach*, was a victim of a nuclear terrorist act."

"I'm so sorry," Andy said.

"I'm curious, Dr. Carlson. According to the British, it was James Lee who sent them warning of the warhead on the ship and allowed them to steer it out of the shipping lanes and away from Britain."

"I regret that I didn't have time to discuss it with you, sir," Andy said. "After I learned about the container ship I was injured and captured. I was locked in a cage on this farm. My family rescued me."

"In the future, you should not communicate with foreign governments on your own," Mr. Umar said. "You should have given me this information before talking to the British. We have a state department that conducts foreign affairs."

"I'm sorry, sir," Andy said. "I don't believe the Iranians know anything about the loss of their martyrs and warheads, except the *Spirit of Long Beach*."

"Why?"

"We captured a couple of cell phones that the Iranian martyrs had. Nobody has called them in several days. I still have those phones, and I'm monitoring them. The fact that the *Spirit of Long Beach* had seven more days of transit time to London probably means that we have at least seven more days before Israel's neighbors descend on them."

The president hesitated. "The British and the Israelis are rightfully nervous about the sinking of the *Spirit of Long Beach*, as well as Ras

Tanura," he said. "Neither has implicated the Iranians publicly. They're waiting for documentation, *just like I am*."

Andy did not respond.

"I've not shown anyone the email you sent me concerning the warhead at Long Beach," the president said. "I can't sit on all these warheads you've found much longer. I need to get my hands on everything you've got, Carlson. I'm meeting with my national security advisors in a couple of hours."

"Mr. President, do you remember when President Bush went to war in Iraq without clear evidence of WMDs?"

"I certainly do," the president said.

"If the United States and Britain are no longer in any danger of nuclear attack," Andy said, "then there's no reason why your national security advisors can't wait until I have clear documentation regarding what the Islamic Jihad is and who supports them. Wouldn't you like to clarify the role of the Russians?"

"Of course."

"That's what I'm working on, sir. I should be able to provide your team with complete information within a week. Please advise the British and the Israelis not to take independent action."

"Dr. Carlson, you are conducting foreign policy again," Mr. Umar said. "I only asked for your help finding warheads and defusing them. You should have handed the Iranian cell phones over to me or the CIA. I'm the Commander-in-Chief."

"I've been on this mission night and day since you called me, Mr. Umar. I'm exhausted and injured. I must react immediately to threats in the field. I must follow up on leads that I find. With all due respect, your CIA can't move as quickly or as quietly as I can, and they don't know what I know. As long as you control the stream of information I provide, no one can challenge you. I will try to keep you better informed as I proceed."

"See that you do that."

"One more thing," Andy said. "There's no reason why you shouldn't inform the Israelis that an attack is probably seven days away."

"I'll take care of that," said the president. "Keep out of foreign policy. You talk to me only."

The president ended the call.

"I think you pissed him off, Dad," said Jack. "Let's roll."

"Not yet," Andy said. "Call Bernard Pollard."

Jack made the call and put Andy back on the speaker phone.

"Hi Dr. Carlson."

"How's the leg?" Andy asked.

"Most people can't even tell I have a prosthetic leg, except Charlotte, of course."

"How's the trip going?"

"Great. What can I do for you?"

"I need you to find me a safecracker."

"What kind of safe?"

"It's a Diamond, Model 1947."

"Want it drilled or picked?"

"Picked if possible, drill if necessary. The most important thing is not to damage anything inside. I don't know what's inside, so I don't want heat or explosives involved."

"When do you need this?"

"The safe will be at my farm in the barn next to my shed on Wednesday morning at nine o'clock. This safecracker needs to have a poor memory in order to get top dollar. Bring him with a bag over his head. Don't bring anybody to the farm that you can't vouch for. I want you to stand there and watch him work. Leave the combination on top of the safe. Don't allow your safecracker to look inside. You won't see me. Your money will be on top the safe. How much for the whole job?"

"I can do it for twenty thousand dollars, in cash, of course."

"That's acceptable."

"I'd like to do this for nothing, Dr. Carlson, but like my daddy says, business is business."

"Thanks, Bernard."

"I'm going to bring your satellite phone back."

Andy restarted the diesel and pulled out on the road.

In the Oval Office, President Umar put his encrypted cell phone back in his pocket and circled his desk. "He thinks he's Douglas MacArthur and George Patton reincarnated."

48.

L indsey and Ava scurried to get ready for the arrival of King Fahd. Clean the blood stains in the great room. Order the black bras for the king's wives. Prepare the remote timer for the fifty kiloton warhead. Make sure the new tritium reservoir from Long Beach fits the threads in the core of the warhead. Do the shopping. Study the suitcase full of records and the laptop from the Ivanov farm.

Andy and Jack required two and a half days to make their way back to Farmville with the big rig. They arrived on Tuesday evening. The five warheads were unloaded down the ramp in the garage to Lindsey's lab in the Confederate cave. The new tritium reservoirs were stored in their lead-lined footlocker in the Gold Room. The safe was unloaded in the barn.

On Wednesday morning at 10:00 the Carlson family walked outside the farmhouse toward the barn. Bernard Pollard had left in his truck a few minutes before, leading a scrawny man with a black pillow case over his head.

On top of the safe was an empty envelope and President Umar's satellite phone. The safe had four shelves. The top shelf held a box with the passports of every member of the Ivanov family. Andy flipped through Aleksi's passport. He was, indeed, a world traveler.

"Aleksi has been in both Russia and Iran within the last year," Andy said.

"No doubt selling bull semen," Lindsey said.

"Dad, you never explained to me how they collected that stuff," Jack said.

"Maybe you'll time to explain it while we're on the plane," Ava said.

On the second shelf was Aleksi's laptop. A small blue book was next to it. Andy flipped through the pages and handed it to Lindsey.

"Is this what it looks like?" he asked.

Lindsey examined the blue book.

"Yes, it is," she said. "Kids, listen up. Let me tell you about computer security. The more complex the security system, the more impossible for anybody other than brainiacs like you to remember everything. A Swiss bank isn't going to let you pick any user name or password that the average person can remember. They give you a numbered account and a password. The password requires so many uppercase letters, so many lower case letters, so many numbers, one or two gang signs, a hieroglyph, and at least one drop of blood from a virgin from Jerusalem. The passwords are delivered separately and securely, not by email. Thus, the information needed to access a person's most secure accounts must be kept within arm's length of his computer."

Jack and Ava pondered this information.

"You'll need to take this laptop and the blue book back to the cave," Andy said. "Concentrate on bank accounts. Your goal is to transfer any money in these accounts into our own foreign accounts without leaving a trail. We need to take the money before anyone realizes that the Ivanovs are no longer with us. It's possible that some of the accounts will only respond to Aleksi's laptop."

Lindsey took the blue book and laptop.

"What's on the third shelf?" Ava asked.

The third shelf held a box of manila files with numbers on each file. Andy looked at one of the files. Some of the pages were in Russian and some in English. He handed the first file to Lindsey. She studied the pages in the file.

"This is an individual file for a warhead," she said, "with manufacturing date, modifications, information about the tritium reservoir, the buyer, the price, and the date of the sale. These numbers and letters on the tab of the file are the serial numbers of the weapon. This file is the warhead used at Ras Tanura."

"How do you know?" Andy asked.

"Ras Tanura is scribbled in the margin of the second page in Russian," she said. "We should be able to match the dates of sale to the Iranians with deposits in one of the accounts in Aleksi's blue book."

"So take the warhead files back to the cave as well," Andy said.

The bottom shelf held a box of cash—$100 bills in wrappers—and two pistols.

"Maybe a million here," Andy said. "We can put it to some good use."

"Is there enough there for a new bicycle?" Ava asked.

"You know that superheroes don't use dirty money on themselves," Lindsey said, picking up an empty envelope on top of the safe.

"The safecracker was kind enough to leave the combination of the safe on this envelope," Lindsey said. "I need somewhere to put personal things where the prying eyes of certain short people can't see them."

"Mom," Ava said, "I already saw the numbers."

Lindsey held the blue book and Aleksi's laptop in her left hand while she drove the Kubota Diesel RTV back to the cave entrance in the garage. The box of files and the money were in the bed of the RTV.

"This would be a lot easier without this shoulder immobilizer," Andy said, as he opened up the president's satellite phone on the workbench in the barn. He removed the GPS chip and the recording device.

Back in Lindsey's lab in the Confederate cave, Andy and Jack went to work loading the fifty kiloton nuclear warhead onto a pallet and lashing it down. Most of the work was done with the forklift. Andy estimated the warhead's weight at less than 200 pounds, something he could have easily picked up before his shoulder injury. They lashed down the lead box with the new tritium reservoir, Lindsey's toolbox, the remote timer, and President Umar's satellite phone to the same pallet. The pallet was covered with a lead apron. Jack placed a wooden crate over the lead apron and nailed it to the pallet. An opaque shipping box covered the crate. The box was held to the pallet by metal strapping. The warhead was ready to travel.

One of the most valuable vehicles on the farm was the flatbed truck with the forklift slots and eight wheels in the back. After using the forklift to load a pallet onto the flatbed, the forks were elevated and inserted into the slots in the rear of the flatbed. By lowering the forks, the forklift itself was raised to ride on the back of the flatbed with the load. This made it possible to unload the cargo at its destination and transfer it to another vehicle. In this case, the unloading would be onto the ramp in the rear of the king's private jet.

"Andy, when you finish loading the truck, go to the hospital and get an X-ray of your shoulder," Lindsey said.

"From the tone of her voice," Ava said, "I don't think that's negotiable."

"Yes, ma'am."

Lindsey attacked the bank accounts in the blue book. Jack and Ava watched over her shoulder. Within forty-five minutes, the accounts were cleaned out.

A tone announced movement somewhere on the farm. Lindsey looked up at the row of video monitors in the Grand Chamber of the Confederate cave. Andy had returned from the hospital.

"How's the shoulder?" she asked.

"Nothing I didn't expect," he said. "The left clavicle and scapula are broken, but neither one needs any surgery. I had the orthopedist look at the X-rays. He agreed. Gives me a good excuse to take another week off. What's your news?"

"What makes you think I have news?"

"You're smiling too much," Andy said. "We already know you're pregnant, so it must be something new. Was Aleksi rich?"

"I don't think most of these accounts belong to Aleksi."

"Go ahead."

"Too much money and too many transactions that don't match the warheads."

"Methamphetamine chemicals?"

"I don't think so," Lindsey said. "Most transactions involve other numbered accounts. There's no way to know who the account belongs to without the blue book. The blue book matches account numbers to individuals, businesses, organizations, and countries."

"Like who?"

"Five deposits from an Iranian bank totaled 1.5 billion dollars."

"That would buy a lot of Girl Scout cookies," Ava said.

"That's not all," Lindsey said. "There are payments to a Russian bank account owned by an individual in the blue book. Aleksi transferred 500 million dollars to this man in the past year."

"Who?"

"I have a Russian government official's name," she said, "but I can't identify what he does for a living yet."

"Maybe he delivers new tritium reservoirs," Andy said. "Russian government officials are more likely to get bribes than bonuses."

Lindsey kept smiling.

"Okay," Andy said. "How much money did you steal from the KGB?"

"Six billion, give or take a few hundred thousand."

"Six billion?"

"I spread it out over four accounts. All of the transfers are confirmed."

"Can the money be traced?"

"Not to us," she said. "The United States has worked out a deal with the Swiss whereby the IRS can access American accounts. King Fahd opened our accounts. The Swiss are only too happy to have the king as a customer. It would not be unusual for the largest exporter of oil in the world to have huge amounts of money in four accounts."

"So what happens when the KGB looks in their piggy bank?" Andy asked.

"The money will be gone," Lindsey said. "Since few people would have access to KGB accounts, they will conclude that Aleksi took it. I have given them a little help coming up with this conclusion. They have no idea what happened to the Ivanovs. The Swiss will be reluctant to identify the owner of the numbered account to which the money was transferred."

"You transferred all that money to Aleksi's personal account first?"

"His personal account has never been accessed by anyone else," Lindsey said. "If the KGB somehow managed to access Aleksi's account, they would have to identify the owners of the four accounts to which he transferred money today. The Swiss won't give them this information either, but the KGB could bribe someone inside the Swiss banking community. They will be confronted with a big problem. All four accounts are owned by the king of Saudi Arabia."

"I don't think the KGB would accuse the king of stealing their money," Andy said. "I do think we should offer this money to the king. He would enjoy the fact that it came from the KGB. He can pretend that he doesn't know anything about the Russian contribution to bombing Ras Tanura, while using their money to build a new pipeline to the Red Sea, bypassing the Strait of Hormuz."

"That brings up a troubling question," Lindsey said.

"Like what?"

"Where did all this money come from?" she asked. "So far as I can tell, Iran's purchases only account for 1.5 billion dollars. Is someone else buying nuclear weapons from the KGB, or is this just a slush fund for covert operations?"

"You should have a chance to study all of the files on Aleksi's warheads on the way to Saudi Arabia," Andy said.

Boxes of black bras arrived by Federal Express the next day. Andy loaded everything onto the flatbed and used his own tractor rig to pull it to the airport next door. The rig and the flatbed had been left at the airport many times.

The single employee at Farmville Municipal Airport was accustomed to the Carlson family coming and going on private jets, never supporting his restaurant. There was nothing unusual about Dr. Carlson transporting crates.

Andy called Charlie Dodd and Ben Carlson. He asked them to keep an eye on the farm while the family was visiting the king of Saudi Arabia.

"Tell him how sorry I am about his oil terminal," Charlie said.

"He'll appreciate that."

49.

On the trip from Dulles to Riyadh, Andy made a deal with Lindsey. She would stay in the forward cabin of the king's plane and explain to Jack and Ava exactly how bull semen was collected, frozen, and subsequently used to fertilize cows, while he would go to the rear cabin and talk strategy with the king.

"Your scowl wounds me," Andy said. "Be sure that Ava knows that bull semen has nothing to do with disasters in Guatemala."

"Payback is hell," Lindsey said. "I'm going to work up a deal for you. But first, there's something you need to know before you talk to the king."

"He's waiting on me."

"You've miscounted the warheads Iran bought," she said.

"Give it to me straight."

"I've been studying the records that came from the Ivanovs' safe," Lindsey said. "There were two warheads in the container that arrived in Bushehr, Iran, before Ras Tanura was destroyed. The only way to know this was to examine the individual warhead files and crosscheck them with Aleksi's list of buyers and deposits from Iranian banks. The Iranians paid an additional 500 million dollars for this warhead."

"You do very good work, Mrs. Carlson," Andy said. "You don't deserve to be burdened with a wretch like me."

"That's more like it," she said. "So where do you think this warhead will turn up?"

"I think I know," he said, hurrying toward the rear cabin.

"We have a contact in Pakistan who is in the import-export business," the king said. "He has been interested in getting out of Pakistan, but he's been such a good source of information and hard-to-find items that I have been reluctant to move him. He was so happy that I invited him to work for me in Saudi Arabia in exchange for sending one container to Natanz."

"When does this ship arrive at Ali Jabayl?" Andy asked.

The king looked at his watch. "Fifty-two hours," he said. "As you know, Al Jabayl is well north of Ras Tanura, but directly across the Persian Gulf from Bushehr, Iran."

"How can you be sure that Iran will take this container to Natanz?" Andy asked.

"I learned from you, Dr. Carlson," said the king. "When I visited your caves I noticed that you bought things that would someday be in high demand by your enemies, even though you didn't intend to use them yourself."

"It's a good business plan for us," Andy said, "because we have so much storage room underground."

"Several years ago I was contacted by a man named A. Q. Khan," the king said.

Andy nodded his head. "I've heard of him. He's responsible for Pakistan's nuclear weapons."

"Mr. Khan was desperate for money at the time," said the king. "He offered me 100 centrifuges for enriching uranium. Saudi Arabia has no nuclear weapons program, but I thought that such a hard-to-find item would make a good bargaining chip someday."

"That does sound like something I would do," Andy said.

"The Iranians already have over 3000 centrifuges at Natanz," the king said, "but it's taken them ten years to collect these. Ahmadinejad was in love with his centrifuges. There are many pictures on the Internet and even in newspapers of the president of Iran proudly standing next to his centrifuges."

"And you're willing to give the new Iranian president your centrifuges?" asked Andy.

"It's the least I can do for the Iranians, after all they've done for me," the king said. "Of course, the Iranians believe they are coming from Mr. Khan."

"How can we get this container off the ship and load it with the centrifuges and the warhead?" Andy asked.

"I think it would be best to substitute another container, already loaded in my palace, rather than risk someone seeing the centrifuges or the warhead."

"I like it. And you have the same GTIN number, container number and lock as the container from Pakistan?"

The king nodded.

"Your wife will be able to take her time and prepare your warhead in the very back of this forty foot container," the king said. "The centrifuges are taller than your warhead. I have seen you work with a MIG welder. What if you built a metal table over the warhead and then cut off the tops of several centrifuges?"

"I could weld them to the top of the table," Andy said. "Anyone who opens the container to inspect it in Natanz would see only centrifuges."

"Are you sure you can do this with your shoulder injury?" the king asked.

"I'm sure."

"These centrifuges are much too heavy to unload without special equipment," the king said. "Eighty centrifuges would have to be removed before the warhead could be seen."

"Such equipment is unlikely to be outside the bunker," Andy said. "After they see all the centrifuges, they will likely close the container and the same truck will drive into the tunnel entrance of the bunker. During this stop for inspection the warhead could be armed by satellite phone. I would suggest a sixty minute delay before the timer explodes the warhead."

"Even if they were in a hurry to unload inside the bunker," the king said, "they could never unload enough centrifuges in sixty minutes to get to the warhead."

"We must watch this container carefully on a GPS monitor," Andy said. "It's possible that the Iranians won't want any inspection outside. Once the container enters the bunker, we won't be able to arm the warhead."

"I understand," the king said. "You will have plenty of time to install satellite phone antennas and GPS transmitters and receivers."

"Have you arranged a paper trail back to Pakistan?"

"The truck and the container will be gone forever, but the paperwork will say that a shipment went from Pakistan to Natanz. Who can say if this shipment had anything to do with the destruction of Natanz?"

"Can you guarantee that no one on the dock in Ali Jabayl will remember switching the containers?"

"Yes," the king said. "Container ships come and go every day at Al Jabayl. The dock workers are paid handsomely to load and unload. They only care about the weight of the container and its identification numbers. They don't speculate why a container is removed or why one is added. They know it's not their job to wonder what's inside a container. They know that anyone who talks about shipments loses his tongue, or worse."

"If Natanz is destroyed," Andy said, "the president of Iran will be distraught and confused. Some experts will say that the explosion was an accident."

"The Iranians may scream at Pakistan," the king said, "but no one in Pakistan will know anything about my centrifuges. My contact in Pakistan will disappear. His company books will disappear. Mr. Khan knows nothing. The Pakistan government will back up his innocence."

"What could Iran do even if they thought that Pakistan was responsible?" Andy asked. "Pakistan already has nuclear weapons, thanks to Mr. Khan. Saudi Arabia doesn't have any nuclear weapons program.

The president of Iran will try to blame the Israelis, the British, or the United States. They will all be indignant, don't you think?"

"Very indignant," the king said. "Especially since there will be no radar or satellite identifying any bombers, or missiles, or drones from these countries. Everyone will know that the explosion came from inside the bunker. How could other countries possibly be responsible?"

"The less they know, the more convincing their indignation will be," Andy said.

Upon their arrival in Saudi Arabia, Lindsey and Andy set to work preparing the substitute container. The container ship from Pakistan was approaching Al Jabayl. Before attaching the timer to the warhead, Andy and Jack tested President Umar's satellite phone.

Andy smiled when the timer activated from Jack's call on the satellite phone. The minutes and seconds began to count down. Lindsey reset the clock and mounted the timer to the metal table Andy had welded over the warhead. The timer was connected to the satellite phone antenna on top of the trailer. Andy and Lindsey's work was complete when the tops of four centrifuges were welded onto the table.

On Monday morning, just as the sun came up, they stood on a hill overlooking the Saudi port of Al Jabayl. Andy handed the binoculars to Lindsey. "Take a look at that orange container ship leaving the harbor. In less than twenty-four hours it will be in Bushehr, Iran. By tomorrow morning our favorite container should be at the bunker in Natanz."

Lindsey pulled back her veil and found the container ship. "Godspeed."

"I wish I believed that God had something to do with it," Andy said. "Then if something went wrong, I could blame it on Him."

"A point well taken."

"Can you spare me for a few hours while I make a quick trip to Israel?" he asked.

"Why would you want to do that?" she asked. "I thought you wanted them to be innocent."

"They will be," he said. "This trip is about President Umar."

"We'll be under the protection of the king here," Lindsey said. "I do think the king's staff is fearful of Jack and Ava's knowledge base."

"I completely understand," Andy said. "I'll be back before the king makes his call to Natanz."

Andy met with the king in his private chamber.

"King Fahd, I need to go to Israel for a few hours, long enough to speak with the Prime Minister confidentially. Can you arrange this?"

"What's the purpose of your visit?"

"We must be sure the Israelis are not planning independent action against Iran within the next twenty-four hours. It would be a shame for them to take blame when they don't have to."

"That is a good precaution," King Fahd said. "Does your government know about this visit?"

"Certainly not," Andy said. "I would like to travel in secret."

"We have back channels to the Israelis," the king said. "The Prime Minister knows that I do not support attacks on Israel. We must act like we are enemies to please our constituents, some of whom are rabid hawks on both sides. If I tell him that you have information about an Iranian plan to attack them, how can he refuse you?"

"It would be nice not to be seen in Israel," Andy said. "I'm sure our president would not be happy seeing me in a newspaper, strolling the streets of Tel Aviv with the PM."

"I'll arrange a meeting with the Prime Minister aboard my personal jet in Tel Aviv. You will not need to get off of the plane. Only the PM will know that you are in Israel. I will make your introduction as Mr. James Lee."

"Thank you, King Fahd. I should be back long before tomorrow morning."

"That's good to hear," the king said. "I'd like for you to enjoy the moment with me, the moment when the world no longer has to worry about Natanz."

50.

Andy sat in the king's jet inside a hanger at the Tel Aviv airport, waiting for the Prime Minister of Israel. He didn't have to wait long. The Prime Minister entered the luxurious cabin and approached Andy with his hand extended. "I've heard good things about you, Mr. Lee."

"Exaggerations."

"I'm sorry to see that you have an injury."

"It's nothing. A broken shoulder will heal in time."

The Prime Minister smiled and sat down. He had gained weight since Andy last saw him on TV. Probably stress. Andy guessed that the PM was sixty years old. His smile faded. "The king indicated that you had important information about Iran."

"Sir, I would like to share information with you, but I must have your word that you will never mention my visit to anyone."

"Are you a messenger from Mr. Umar?"

"No sir. He doesn't know that I'm here."

"You have my word that your visit to Israel will remain a secret."

"It's important that you be candid with me about all of your communications with the United States," Andy said. "Can you tell me if you have seen this letter before?"

Andy handed the PM a copy of the letter sent by the Islamic Jihad to President Umar. He studied the PM's face as he read. The PM's eyes widened until they appeared to bulge. Tiny droplets filled the furrows of his brow. He raised his left hand to his chin and then wiped his face on the sleeve of his suit.

"This is dated eleven days ago," the PM said. "We suspected Iran was behind the bombing of Ras Tanura, but we have no evidence for this. The IAEA is dragging its feet over the details of the soil samples.

The warhead was built in the old Soviet Union. They can't agree on the age of its tritium reservoir. We couldn't tie Iran to the loss of the American container ship."

"Has Mr. Umar talked to you since Ras Tanura?"

"No. You must know that Mr. Umar and his Secretary of Defense are not sympathetic toward Israel," the PM said. "Umar has only been here once, briefly, in two terms. Your secretary of state drops by to let us know that there will be grave consequences if we unilaterally bomb Iran's nuclear facilities, especially Natanz. The last time I went to the United States, Umar refused to meet with me."

The PM studied Andy's game face.

"Go on," Andy said.

"After Ras Tanura, I sent our foreign minister to see Umar. He was referred to the secretary of state. We told your secretary of state that we intended to strike Natanz with or without support from the United States."

"How did he respond?" Andy asked.

"He said that the U.S. would cut off all aid to Israel, including military aid, if we proceeded with our plan. Umar has tried to do this before, but our friends in Congress have blocked his attempts to reduce aid. The secretary gave us no information about Ras Tanura. Now that I have read this letter, I have some understanding of his reluctance to tell us that Israel is the ultimate target. Do you know the status of the nuclear threats to the U.S. and Britain?"

"I do."

"What can you tell me?"

"There were two Iranians in a refrigerated container on the *Spirit of Long Beach*. They had an armed nuclear warhead. London was the target. I uncovered their plan as the ship was passing through the Panama Canal. The captain was able to steer the vessel out of the shipping lane before the Iranians panicked and detonated the warhead. This is the only threat to Britain that I know of."

"What about the American cities mentioned in the letter?" asked the PM.

"With the king's help, I was able to find the source of these warheads and defuse them. The details are not important. I don't think there are any other Iranian warheads in the United States."

"I'm glad for the United States," the PM said. "I'm curious. Do you work for the CIA?"

"I work for peace. I despise the CIA. I am neither Republican nor Democrat. I have worked for four presidents. They were all liars."

The PM smiled and crossed his legs. "You're not Jewish, are you?"

"No sir. I'm an American citizen who doesn't turn his back on his allies."

"We appreciate your support," the PM said. "I'm always curious about what Americans think of Israel. Do you mind if I ask you a question?"

"Shoot."

"Do you think that the Jewish people stole the land we live in?"

"I know the history of the state of Israel," Andy said. "You have far more claim to your land than the United States had to Texas. We expanded our western and southwestern borders by driving out the Indians and the Mexicans. God never promised us this land. We killed its rightful owners and took it. Even if you did *not* have a biblical claim to your land, I would say that you earned it."

The PM smiled. "Why do you say that?"

"My enthusiasm for religion waxes and wanes as I watch so many people kill in the name of God. I believe that any God who slept through the Holocaust should cut Israel some slack about the Promised Land."

"An interesting opinion," the PM said.

"Five days ago I told the president that all the warheads in the United States were accounted for. I told him that there was no reason not to notify Israel that Iran intended to initiate a war with them in about seven days."

"You mean the day after tomorrow?"

"Yes, sir."

"Why this date?"

"The day after tomorrow is when that ship should have arrived in London," Andy said. "Incinerating London would certainly blunt any British response to a Middle East war."

"If there is no longer a warhead headed to London, how would such a war begin?"

"The Iranians do not know that *all* British and American warheads are neutralized," Andy said. "I suspect that Iran intends to deliver Israel a crushing blow the day after tomorrow. They must gain the advantage quickly, while the U.S. and Britain debate whether to risk coming to your aid. After your Islamic neighbors attack you, Iran plans to detonate all the warheads in the U.S. and Britain."

"The real battleground would be Israel," the PM said. "The Jihad soldiers would be from many Islamic countries and they would fight a guerilla war within our borders."

"You have received no warning from Umar?"

"None."

"That's what I expected," Andy said. "That's why I'm here. I needed to hear this from you."

"I'm not surprised," the PM said. "I don't think that many Americans understand Umar. He is a member of an oppressed minority. He views himself as a victim of his own country. So few Americans understand his policy toward Mexican immigrants."

"How do you see U.S. immigration policy?" Andy asked.

"Umar identifies with the Mexicans, whose land was stolen by the Americans. These Mexicans are victims of the United States, just like him. In his mind, Israel stole Islamic land with the help of the United States and Britain. His father was a victim of British colonialism. Umar is even today contemptuous toward Britain."

"What are you referring to?" Andy asked.

"The first thing Umar did when he moved into the Oval Office was to send the bust of Winston Churchill back to the British."

"I remember that," Andy said. "But I didn't know what to think of it at the time."

"Your press gives Umar a pass for insulting your allies," the PM said. "The rest of the world was shocked when Umar didn't even send the vice-president to Margaret Thatcher's funeral. Your president doesn't hide his hatred for Britain or for Israel. What did you think of his failure to renew the Cooperative Threat Reduction program with Russia in 2013?"

"It didn't make much sense to me. My wife worked in that program when she was in the CIA. By her account the U.S. helped deactivate over 7,600 warheads from the old Soviet Union."

"Umar knew that there were thousands of these warheads left," said the PM. "He made no attempt to renew a treaty that was considered by every other president before him to be the most important result of America's victory in the Cold War. At the same time he unilaterally cut America's warheads in half."

Andy asked, "Why should the Russians continue to disarm if Umar is disarming America far beyond the guidelines of the treaty?"

The PM said, "When Umar broke America's promise to maintain missile interceptors and radar in Eastern European countries, he strengthened Russia. Russia is watching America cast off its allies and weaken itself. Britain needs to wake up before they are stabbed in the back."

Andy started to stand up, but sat back down. "This shoulder immobilizer throws me off balance."

"What startled you?" the PM asked.

Andy stared past the PM.

"Your face," the PM said. "You appear to be in pain. Are you sick?"

"I am," Andy said. "When I discovered that a warhead was traveling toward Britain on a ship, I notified the British myself. I didn't notify the president."

"Interesting," the PM said.

"When I later spoke to Umar, he scolded me for not informing him first. I never considered that he might want that warhead to explode in London."

"I'm glad you trusted your instincts," the PM said. "There would have been no one left in London to confirm or deny a warning."

"I see that now. Umar would only have to kill me and my family to cripple a country he despises. I wonder..."

"You probably saved your own life by warning the British," the PM said. "To many, Umar is a symbol of America's triumph over racism. Hardly anyone stands back and looks at all of the things he is doing, and draws reasonable conclusions about his ideology. In full view of the eyes of the world, Umar is loading the U.S. up with unskilled immigrants, who will be an economic drag on your country for decades. In twenty years there will be forty or fifty million new Democratic voters."

"I worry about these things," Andy said, "although I have no problem with legal immigration."

"Umar is a master of cloaking his intentions with slogans like 'America is a nation of immigrants.' Even if all of these immigrants do not become citizens, Umar will enroll them in your welfare state. He is already doing this. The huddled masses of your past were yearning for freedom, not a welfare state."

"What do you think about green energy and climate change?" Andy asked.

"Umar appears to care about the environment," the PM said. "In fact, he is doing everything he can to delay America's energy independence at a critical time in your nation's history. I am no scientist, but real climatologists have found no global warming for the last eighteen years. There is no clear relationship between human activity and climate change or global warming at this time. Some day this might change. These long-term issues allow Mr. Umar to divert attention from what he is doing now--trashing your currency with deficits and debt, while blocking as much domestic oil and gas production as possible. He denies that America has a spending problem. All of these things easily fit together and complete the puzzle of Umar."

"You're not painting a very attractive picture of our president," Andy said. "I'm also suspicious of Umar. However, our two-party system in the U.S. creates only the illusion of choice. The Republicans are no better than the Democrats. Each party seeks to grow the power and size of government in different ways. Few honest men get elected to Washington. It costs so much money to get elected that by the time a person reaches Washington, he's already sold his soul to the devil several times over. Name one president who didn't face the cameras and lie through his teeth."

"Think about this," the PM said, placing his hand on Andy's right forearm. "Umar is always talking about leveling the playing field. Are Americans blind to the fact that the only way to level the world playing field is to weaken America? Not even China's economy can grow in this economic environment. Thanks to Umar, the United States military is no longer a feared presence in the Middle East. The Islamic countries have learned to fight wars that don't favor technology. If they need technology, Umar will give it to them, sell it to them, or let them steal it."

"I wish I could refute you," Andy said, "but the Republicans did just as much damage by sacrificing liberty and individual freedoms in the name of fighting terrorism."

"Umar encourages Muslim immigration and mosque building in the U.S.," the PM said, "citing peaceful Islam. Those countries in Europe who opened up their borders to 'peaceful Islam' now deeply regret it. Sometimes I wonder if Americans read newspapers. Your NSA can spy on ordinary Americans, but they cannot spy on mosques, where their enemies congregate. Your economy stagnates as your government policies punish success and subsidize failure. I have a question for you." He paused.

Andy raised his eyebrows.

"Umar supports everything that weakens America," the PM said. "Can this be an accident?"

Andy said, "I cannot answer that question. Perhaps Umar is misguided. Maybe America is naïve. I have been called paranoid by my own family. I think America is headed for disaster, no matter who is sitting in the White House."

"Tell me what you meant by a crushing blow to Israel," the PM said.

"Your Islamic neighbors don't want to destroy Jerusalem because it's also sacred to them," Andy said. "I suspect that the Iranians want to launch this war with the destruction of Tel Aviv. They have the means to deliver a warhead here."

"You're referring to the stealth drone that Iran captured two years ago?"

"Yes," Andy said. "This drone can carry a 250 pound payload. It's nearly impossible to shoot down unless you see it with the naked eye. Patriot missiles can't target it. The Iranians detected the video feed from this drone and hacked into its guidance system. They published pictures of the drone on the Internet after landing it in Iran."

"I sent Umar a message that Israel could destroy this stealth drone on the ground," the PM said. "He insisted the pictures were faked. We had our own pictures."

"So far, all the warheads I found were updated versions of old Soviet Cold War tactical nukes. As you know, many of these are unaccounted for. Someone in the KGB is helping the Iranians, but the extent of the Kremlin's knowledge of this is uncertain. I just learned that Iran bought one more warhead than I thought. I suspect it's for Tel Aviv."

The PM said, "We will not wait for this drone to arrive."

"The good news is that the stealth drone is likely in the bunker in Natanz, being armed."

"How do you know this?"

"About two weeks ago, Iran received two warheads in a container at their port of Bushehr, in the Persian Gulf. One of these was used at Ras Tanura. Natanz is only a short distance from Bushehr. It's the perfect place to arm the stealth drone with a nuclear warhead and make its guidance system impervious to United States control."

"Then time is not on our side," the PM said. "We must act immediately."

"Sir, I'm here to tell you that by this time tomorrow, Natanz will no longer exist."

"That's quite a prediction."

"I can't tell you how this will happen, Mr. Prime Minister, but you have my word that it will. Prepare your bombing missions for noon tomorrow. If Natanz does not explode from the inside by then, it will be up to you to do the job."

"Any wait is risky," the PM said, "but this is a small wait. We need some time to arm our bombers anyway."

"When Natanz explodes, you should have no aircraft anywhere near the Persian Gulf. You will be overjoyed, but you will have no idea who destroyed Natanz. You will point out that the explosion came from inside the bunker, and that your air force was grounded. When Umar's representative calls you, you will deny any involvement."

"President Umar doesn't know who is going to destroy Natanz?"

"Like you said, he has his own agenda. Not even his own cabinet seems to understand it. America doesn't understand it. I don't understand it. Let's just say—if he cared anything about Israel, he would have warned you once the threats to the U.S. were dealt with."

"Mr. Lee, you must come back to Israel soon, so that we can get to know you better."

"I would like to do that," Andy said. "In the meanwhile you must show no sign of alarm unless nothing happens by noon tomorrow. Arm your bombers in hangars. If Natanz is not destroyed from within by noon tomorrow, I recommend you bomb it and mobilize your entire military."

"I will pray for the destruction of Natanz tonight," the PM said.

Andy handed the PM a card. "Should you need to contact me at some time in the future, use this number or email address. There are powerful and wealthy men in Saudi Arabia who would like to destroy Israel. King Fahd is not one of them, but he can't afford to say so. He knows that if Israel is destroyed, a Sunni and Shiite war would follow."

"I will not forget either of you," the PM said.

They shook hands. The PM left the plane.

51.

Andy returned to the king's palace from Israel. He found Lindsey inspecting the contents of the original container from Pakistan. This container held 3,000 Uzi submachine guns, packed in grease, in boxes.

"These guns were part of the inventory of our contact in Pakistan," the king said. "They fire the 9 mm cartridge available around the world. This collection includes the original Uzi SMG, the Mini UZI SMG, and the Micro UZI SMG. Consider them a gift, Dr. Carlson. I will ship this container to your farm."

"That's very gracious of you."

"It's my pleasure," the king said. "The world is full of irony. Who would believe that the king of Saudi Arabia would give Israeli guns to an American? My contact in Pakistan needed something to add weight to the container."

"King Fahd, I have just the right place to store these."

"I know that you do."

Tuesday morning, May 22, 2015, was a sunny, clear day, like most every day in Saudi Arabia. Over breakfast on the palace veranda near Ali Jabayl, all eyes were on the final journey of a container. The container moved steadily on a huge GPS monitor mounted on the veranda. Andy zoomed the map with a remote to show the road from Bushehr to Natanz in greater detail.

They watched the container enter the compound at Natanz and stop.

"This must be the inspection," the king said.

Andy punched the correct number into Umar's satellite phone and handed it to the king. "As soon as that truck begins to move, press 'Call.'"

Lindsey snapped, "It's moving again."

The king pressed the button.

Andy and Lindsey looked over the king's shoulder at the satellite phone. The digital screen read, "Connected." After five minutes the GPS signal disappeared from the monitor screen.

"They're in the bunker," Jack said.

Andy looked at his watch. 8:04 AM. "King Fahd, once the electromagnetic pulse passes, my family and I must begin our own journey home."

"I understand," said the king. "It has been my pleasure to work with all of you. I would like to spend the next hour praying for peace."

Jack and Ava ran to say goodbye to the king.

The underground facility for the production of WMDs at Natanz exploded at 9:04 AM. The detonation was felt and heard throughout the Persian Gulf, but no mushroom cloud marred the sky. The EMP was weak. Andy and his family took off for the United States. From the king's private jet, the Carlson family listened as world-wide news organizations tried to come to grips with the event.

"The Iranian government has confirmed a powerful explosion at its peaceful uranium enrichment compound at Natanz this morning," the anchor on a French morning news show said.

Lindsey translated for the kids, "No foreign reporters are allowed in Iran. The explosion was felt in Paris. No pictures have been released. Governments around the world are scrambling for accurate information. The Iranian government had no further comment besides confirming the explosion."

"Let's turn that thing off," Ava said. "I'm tired of nuclear warheads."

The Carlson family slept for twelve hours.

As the king's jet neared American airspace, Andy called Mr. Umar.

"I hope you're not calling me about another warhead you blew up," the president said.

"No sir. I think we got them all. Aren't you thrilled about the accident at Natanz?"

"You think it was an accident?"

"No country could bomb Iran without the whole world seeing it," Andy said. "You've got satellites and AWACS. Did you see anything?"

"Just the explosion."

"Then what else could it be but the Iranians playing with fire and getting burned?"

"I'm just glad you didn't have anything to do with it," Umar said. "Covering your tracks is a full-time job."

"What about the Israelis?"

"I warned the Israelis after my last conversation with you," Umar said. "Iran appears to be shell-shocked. I don't think there will be a Middle East war."

"And the Russians?"

"The CIA says that those two warheads in the barn in Wisconsin had forty year old tritium reservoirs," the president said. "The two other warheads you found had forty year old tritium reservoirs. It's their opinion that this was a black market deal. If the Russian government wanted to hurt us, they would have supplied new reservoirs."

"My wife's analysis of the soil at Ras Tanura confirms a forty year old reservoir," Andy said.

"Glad to hear that. The International Atomic Energy Agency had no trouble identifying the origin of that warhead," Umar said. "But their final report said the age of the tritium reservoir was indeterminate by their tests."

"My wife would be glad to share her findings with you," Andy said. "I need to bring you my documentation anyway."

"Your paperwork is no longer critical," Umar said. "All the threats have been dealt with. My national security advisors are satisfied with the outcome. I'll send someone to your farm to pick up what you have."

"So you don't need me to come to Washington?"

"I was thinking about your family's safety," Umar said. "I've kept your name confidential, but I had to tell my national security advisors something about you. Otherwise, they would get the impression you were freelancing, instead of working for me. If you come to Washington, somebody might take your picture. Somebody might want to ask you questions. I wouldn't want anybody to follow you back home."

"I appreciate your concern, Mr. Umar," Andy said. "Tell the CIA to call first. The last time they came to my farm uninvited, things didn't work out well. I don't want anybody to get hurt."

"Carlson," Umar said, "you don't know how glad I am to see you stand down."

The president hung up.

"You're welcome," Andy said.

The twins were walking down the aisle of the king's plane toward Andy.

"Dad," Jack said, "Mom said you could explain to us how Ben and you had a common ancestor."

"She also said that you would explain why a drop of blood from a virgin in Jerusalem was required to open safes," Ava said. "What's a virgin?"

ALSO BY CHARLES A. ANDERSON

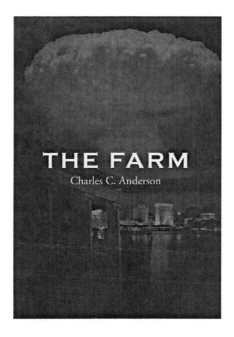

THE FARM

When Navy SEAL Andy Carlson uncovers evidence that the U.S. government is secretly buying old Soviet tactical nuclear weapons for purposes other than disarmament, he responds by throwing a monkey wrench into the deal and resigning from the Navy. Hoping to settle down on his family's Virginia farm and resume his career as an emergency physician, Andy instead finds himself and those he loves the targets of his own government and a Russian arms dealer.

The Farm—Andy's antebellum plantation—is a major player in the action, with its network of limestone caves, family treasures, historical surprises, and natural defenses, and Andy enlists three unlikely allies to help him defend it: a pregnant CIA agent, a male descendant of a slave who shares a common ancestor with Andy, and a teenage Saudi girl. Andy is a capable warrior and field surgeon, but he is also disillusioned and scarred by personal loss. And what he and his ragtag band are up against may be more than this former Navy SEAL can handle.

Learn more at: www.outskirtspress.com/thefarm

ALSO BY CHARLES A. ANDERSON

THE FIRST TO SAY NO

The female doctors in the Parkview Hospital emergency department are tired of dealing with thugs and gang members who attack healthcare workers in their community—and they're going to do something about it.

This inner city Virginia neighborhood is being terrorized by the Plagues, a gang of violent criminals and drug dealers, and the local police are taking payoffs to ignore their criminal activity. After one of the ED doctors, Elita Romanov, is kidnapped and raped, she and her best friend, Dr. Kate Taylor, decide to take definitive action against the Plagues. These unlikely heroines systematically recruit coworkers, friends, and family members who are willing to break the law to restore the rule of law.

The First To Say No is the story of Kate's quest to make peace with her past and eliminate those who threaten her future—and the future of her hospital. This landmark novel illustrates many of the failings of today's healthcare system, and chronicles Kate and Elita's unique prescription for the problem in Parkview.

Learn more at: www.outskirtspress.com/thefirsttosayno

ALSO BY CHARLES A. ANDERSON

BLUE FARM

Dive into the continuing saga of the Carlsons—the uniquely talented family who makes preparedness a way of life—in the third installment of The Farm series. Those who are visiting the Carlson's 4,000-acre plantation for the first time will quickly be drawn to their anything but routine lifestyle.

On a pre-enrollment visit to the University of Virginia, twin teenage prodigies Ava and Jack Carlson are devastated when their physically handicapped five-year-old brother Peewee is kidnapped in the Rotunda in Charlottesville. Days later, after paying a ransom, the family finds Peewee's body buried on their own farm. Adding to the family's grief and anger, the murderers leave a message indicating that Peewee is only the first of the Carlson clan to be targeted. The twins' parents, emergency physician and former Navy SEAL Andy Carlson, and his wife, former CIA operative Lindsey Carlson, join forces with their precocious twins to bring the murderers to justice. As the family fights to defend their lives Jack and Ava stumble into their first loves, their first broken hearts...and the horror of who killed Peewee.

Learn more at: www.outskirtspress.com/bluefarm

CPSIA information can be obtained at www.ICGtesting.com
Printed in the USA
LVOW11*0014050214

372377LV00003B/94/P